PERFECT
GIRLS

ALSO BY ALISON JAMES

Lola is Missing
Now She's Gone

PERFECT GIRLS

Alison James

Bookouture

PART ONE

'A man's face is his autobiography. A woman's face is her work of fiction.'

Oscar Wilde

ONE

It's all so easy. The website had promised 'a super-slick check-in process', and it is.

A message with the address and directions arrives twenty-four hours in advance, and another suggests an arrival time, stressing that this is negotiable. On the day, there's a quick hello, a mention of a couple of important things to remember, handover of a printed list of instructions and a set of keys, rounded off with wishes for a pleasant stay and the promise of help being at the end of the phone.

It really is that simple.

The next part is just as simple too. The blow from behind is quick and clean; its deadly trajectory neither seen nor heard. A reverberating aftershock follows, the temporal lag of realisation that this has actually just happened. That this is all it takes; the work of less than three seconds. Grab. Swing. Strike.

Dead.

TWO

Strike One.

DI Rachel Prince clipped the edge of a concrete column with the front offside wing of her car as she negotiated the overflowing underground car park. She was driving carelessly because she was late, and she was late because despite the rain she had hit a perfect stride and ended up running for forty minutes instead of twenty.

Strike Two.

Her kitbag caught in the lift doors as they were closing, requiring such force to free it that she crashed against the far wall. And then, since she was still in her running gear and trainers, her blonde hair scraped back in a high ponytail, she entered the fifth-floor office at a jog and attempted to vault straight into her desk chair. But her bag clipped the chair arm and sent it skittering to the right. Her backside caught the edge of the moving seat, then slid off. She tumbled inelegantly to the floor.

'Morning,' said DS Mark Brickall. 'Strike Three, by any chance?'

He was making a calculated guess, since Rachel was usually punctual. The office rule was that if you screwed up three times on your commute to work and were more than ten minutes late, it was your turn to buy the drinks at their local pub, the Pin and Needle, that evening.

'Strike Three,' admitted Rachel, booting up her terminal. 'It's definitely that kind of day.'

'Fucking weather,' Brickall flicked a rubber band across his desk for emphasis. Raindrops were streaming steadily down the outside of the windows of the National Crime Agency and condensation was misting the inside. The NCA had been set up to tackle serious and organised crime, and its staff included police officers and ex-servicemen, but also civilian analysts and intelligence personnel. They were a cutting-edge team, and the atmosphere was usually lively, but with the backdrop of gunmetal February sky above an olive-drab river Thames, the effect today was of being trapped in a giant grey box.

Brickall's phone rang.

'International Liaison, DS Brickall speaking... you'll want my colleague.' Brickall gestured to the receiver in his hand and mouthed '*For you*'.

Rachel straightened her chair and picked up. 'DI Prince.'

She listened for a few moments, scribbling notes on a pad. When the call was over, she leaned back in her chair with her arms behind her head, her eyebrows raised.

'Nothing like being given a bit of a wake-up on a Friday morning.'

'Bit of a weird one, was it? Bloke sounded like a Yank.'

'Correct. It was the Alien and Fugitive division at US Interpol HQ, no less. A Mis-Per found dead in unusual circumstances. A twenty-something female and – guess what – she's a UK national. Looks like blunt force trauma, but apparently the body's a bit too far gone to be sure. So they want someone from this end to go out and liaise with the local police department.'

'And where would that be then?'

'Los Angeles. Hollywood, to be exact.'

Brickall laughed. 'Unbelievable. That'll be one for Patten. He's not going to pass up a chance like that: a jolly in Tinseltown.'

'Except...' Rachel said with a grin, standing up and collecting a pen and her notes, 'I happen to know that his new baby is due next week.'

*

Commander Nigel Patten, Deputy Director of International Crime, glanced quickly away from his computer screen and started shuffling files in a transparent attempt at looking busy. Although he'd recently celebrated his fiftieth birthday, he had a much younger second wife who was about to give birth to baby number two.

He waved at the chair opposite his desk, and Rachel sat down and filled him in on the little she knew of the case that had come in.

'So they need someone from Investigation Support out there?'

'I know that would normally be your call, but with the pregnancy…' She summoned what she hoped was a caring facial expression.

Patten frowned. 'Not great timing; you're spot on about that. Danielle would have kittens if I left the country at this point.'

'Or possibly a baby,' suggested Rachel.

Patten sighed. 'I suppose your firearms training might be useful. And if I remember rightly, you've done a stint in Crime Analysis?'

Rachel nodded. 'I did a placement there soon after I came to NCA.' She had started out as a regular beat officer before joining the Metropolitan Police's CID and then Interpol, before it had been absorbed by the National Crime Agency. That had been nearly five years ago, when she was still in her mid-thirties.

Patten considered this.

'Apparently, whoever goes out there needs to start out at Interpol in DC for a briefing,' Rachel explained, 'then fly to LA to help them fill in the gaps and liaise with the family.'

'And you're happy to go, Rachel? What about your promotion board?'

Following her investigation into a child grooming ring in Edinburgh, Rachel had been invited to apply to become a Detective Chief Inspector.

'I'm still waiting for the date of the assessments to be confirmed, sir, but they won't be for at least a month. I'll be back by then.'

'Okay, go and hand over your existing files and I'll get Janette to book your travel.'

'For today would be great, if she can swing it.' Rachel looked over her shoulder as she left the office, 'Oh and good luck, sir. With the new sprog.'

'Jammy cow' Brickall took some files from her and placed them at the bottom of the heap already on his desk. 'You'd do anything to get out of buying a round. And if you think I'm actually going to do any work on these, you're dreaming.'

'No change there. You always were a lazy tosser.' Rachel grinned.

'And I hope the jet lag's horrific.'

'Sod off.'

She blew a kiss at Brickall over her shoulder as she hefted her bag and headed for the door. She knew the jealousy on his part wasn't entirely faked. Rachel and Brickall both worked in the team that covered international coordination. They occasionally travelled to Interpol headquarters in Lyon, Rachel had been to Spain, Portugal and the Netherlands the previous year, and Brickall had recently attended a security briefing in Brussels. But this was the first time in their three years at the NCA there had been a long-distance case. The excitement gave Rachel an added bounce in her step as she ran down to the underground car park.

She honked and swerved her way through the three miles to her flat, and wasted no time once she was there; hurling her carry-on suitcase onto the bed and reaching into drawers and cupboards to fill it. No frivolous holiday brights or heels; just plain-clothes policewoman garb. Well-cut black trousers that flattered her athletic shape, plain white cotton shirts and T-shirts, her trainers and running gear and – her sole concession to California warmth – a bikini and flip-flops. Toothbrush, hair products and face wash, a minimal stash of make-up.

The kitchen, with its exposed brick walls and open shelves, was rarely used. The fridge was more or less empty already apart from the beer she stocked for her son Joe: no need to deal with leftover salad and half-used milk cartons. Rachel didn't cook often. She didn't know when she was going to be at home, so she'd got into the habit of surviving on takeaways and the work canteen. No young children, no pets, no spouse: leaving was gratifyingly easy.

Her phone buzzed as she was closing her case.

Okay if I crash tonight? Got Friday night drinks and it could get messy. J xx

Her son Joe was working as an intern at a management consultancy in Canary Wharf. He had been adopted as a newborn – when she was estranged from her ex-husband and Joe's birth father, Stuart Ritchie – and had only made contact with Rachel the previous summer, when he turned eighteen. After navigating painful guilt on her part and bitter recrimination on his, their relationship had thrived, and he now occasionally spent the night in Rachel's spare room when it was too late to catch the train back to his adoptive parents' house in Sussex.

Packing ready to head to Heathrow early doors on a last-minute job – but use your key and help yourself to anything. xx

Once she'd sent the reply, she opened her taxi app, booking a car for the morning.

The next morning, as she was heading to the lift, she got another text. It was from Brickall.

I'll miss you, you flaky tart.

Rachel smiled at the closing lift doors. She was sorry she wouldn't be working with her right-hand man on this case, but that didn't prevent her from being excited about escaping wintry London and getting her teeth into an intriguing international job. She typed a reply.

Get a grip, loser ☺

THREE

Disposing of a corpse in an unfamiliar location is a lot less simple. It takes some thinking about, and some planning. In the meantime, it lies in the hallway covered with a sheet. With the air conditioning temperature dial set as low as it will go, the body will be all right there for a while. But the clock is ticking.

There's a trip to obtain equipment. The local Target has everything that's needed. It's important to maintain an anonymous appearance, for the inevitable CCTV. So: unisex jeans and work boots, a nondescript sweat top, beanie hat. Glasses with tinted lenses. A quick in and out, not behaving strangely but avoiding unnecessary eye contact or glances in the direction of the cameras. Plastic sheeting, duct tape. Bleach, hydrochloric acid and floor polish. Latex gloves. Spray paint. A couple of power tools and other items to make the trip seem part of a home renovation project. They can be ditched later.

The body has not yet started to bloat, but it's discolouring rapidly. Putty grey in places, peony purple in others. Fingernails white, ringed with pale ochre. Leaking and oozing a little, but fortunately the wood floors are varnished and will clean up okay. Wrapping and taping requires a little patience, but the resulting package is surprisingly neat, if heavier than expected. It can now be moved, but this shouldn't happen until the plan is fully worked out. And that will take a little more time.

Which isn't a problem. It will all come together in the end. You have to be patient, and wait for the opportunities to present themselves. Because they will.

FOUR

Rachel woke from a thick, dreamless sleep. The hotel window was screened with fiercely efficient blackout blinds, so it was impossible to discern time of day. Her watch said 10 a.m., but after a few seconds of muzziness she remembered it was still set to UK time. The clock radio by her bed told her it was five in Washington DC.

She opened the blinds and looked out. It was dark, and very quiet. To her left was the empty splendour of Pennsylvania Avenue, and the mysterious blank space to her right was the Ellipse. She ordered coffee and juice from room service and switched on the TV. Only local news was available until 6 a.m., when national network coverage kicked in, so she watched the WLJA anchors expressing concern about a collision on the I295, and horror at a house fire in Clarksburg. The repetitive bulletins were punctuated with weather forecasts from the toothy weatherman, Brad, who told her it was going to be thirty-nine degrees Fahrenheit and sunny.

She had emailed her contact at Interpol as soon as she landed at Dulles the previous evening, and at seven thirty there was a reply from him.

From: Robert J. McConnell
To: Rachel Prince
Apologies for the early shout, but assuming you'll be on London time. Let's meet for coffee – 8.30 too soon? Suggest Slipstream on 14th.

From: Rachel Prince
To: Robert J. McConnell
Your assumption was correct. See you at 8.30.

Rachel showered and dressed, and went down to the lobby carrying her sweater, jacket and scarf. The central heating in the building was set to sub-tropical, so within its confines it was impossible to wear anything warmer than shirtsleeves. The reception area was already teeming with people on weekend trips swigging the complimentary drip coffee, and busboys moving luggage on tall gilt trolleys. Rachel registered the doorman's dismay with a smile as she stepped out onto the street in her T-shirt, then bundled herself into her warm layers on the pavement.

The air was sharply cold, but in contrast to London's late-February drabness it felt powder-dry and bracing, the bare trees dark shadow puppets against a gleaming duck-egg sky. She enjoyed the brisk mile walk north along 14th Street, the pavements filling with runners wearing headphones and clutching take-out coffee cups. Arriving at Slipstream early, she ordered an espresso and sat in a corner with a copy of the *Washington Post*.

'Rachel?'

She looked up to see a tall, tanned man extending a hand with a broad smile. 'Robert McConnell. Rob.'

'Thanks for meeting me at the weekend, Robert *J* McConnell,' Rachel said, shaking the hand. 'What's the J for?'

'Justin.'

She had a sudden, wrenching flashback to sitting in a bar in Edinburgh and asking Giles Denton the exact same question when they were embarking on a case together. It made her shiver, but she suppressed the thought instantly. She didn't want to think about her brief liaison with child protection specialist Giles the previous summer, one that had hit major trouble almost as soon as it began. Not now; not ever. She wouldn't be making a mistake like that again.

Rob sat down opposite her, tugging off a padded MA-1 bomber jacket with an Interpol logo on the left sleeve. Underneath he wore a fitted grey T-shirt which betrayed a gym addiction. *Sod's law that he's really attractive*, Rachel thought. *A complication I really don't need.* He had grey eyes, slightly creased with tan lines in the corners, thick light-brown hair that sprung from his forehead with a life of its own. And, naturally, the standard issue good American teeth. He could have been a model for yachting apparel, Rachel decided. Despite herself, she shot a quick glance at the bare ring finger of his left hand.

He ordered filter coffee for himself and toast and jam for them both.

'You need to eat at US mealtimes,' he told her when she attempted a refusal, 'Only way you'll power through the jet lag.'

As they ate, he told her 'I've got a written briefing note, but if it's okay with you, I'll just give you a quick summary so you can ask questions while we're face to face.'

'Go ahead,' Rachel spoke through a mouthful of toast. Annoyingly Rob was right: she was feeling better now her blood sugar levels were heading up. 'This jam is bloody delicious. Or jelly, I suppose you call it.'

He did not attempt to hide his pleasure at the way she was demolishing the food. 'Glad I got that right. They make it in-house... Okay, so our victim is called Phoebe Stiles. Twenty-five years old, born in Weoley Castle, England.'

Rob pronounced it *Wee-olly*, making Rachel smile. He caught her smirk and paused. 'Sorry. Go on.'

'She was here on a temporary work visa. From what we know, trying to find film or TV work in Los Angeles. The LAPD will give you more detail on that. Her remains were found in a dumpster behind a Macy's, very badly decomposed. The Medical Examiner estimated she had been dead between four and six weeks at that point.'

He paused again to let Rachel digest this. She put down her piece of toast.

'There was no ID on or near the body, and the police had to rely on dental records. Fortunately, Ms Stiles had been seeing an LA dentist quite recently to get a set of veneers fitted, so a positive identification was possible.'

'And the family have been informed?'

He nodded. 'They're on their way to Los Angeles now. The troubling aspect of this is that they claim to have had very recent contact with Phoebe, up to a few days ago. But from the condition of her remains, the Medical Examiner is one hundred per cent positive that this is an impossibility. But, again, they'll be able to tell you more when you meet them.'

Rachel grimaced. 'Family liaison work is really *not* my forte. But I'm definitely going to need to speak to them about the alleged recent contact with their daughter. It could generate a lead.'

Rob grimaced too, in sympathy. 'There are a whole bunch of questions you need to ask. We were contacted because Phoebe was a non-US citizen, but another female victim around the same age showed up in San Diego a few months earlier – an American – and there are some striking similarities with the Stiles case.'

Rachel rested her chin on her hands, her interest piqued. 'Really? That's interesting.'

He drained his coffee and pushed a manila envelope across the table to Rachel. 'There's more detail in there. When do you fly out to LA?'

'This afternoon.'

'You'll have a little time to read through this then.'

Rachel wiped the sticky crumbs from her lip with a napkin and their eyes met for an intense second.

'Rob…' Rachel interrupted her own train of thought. 'Listen, thanks for this.'

'Sure, no problem. Anything I can do; you have my email address, and my cell number should be on the email too.'

Rachel smiled weakly. 'Great.'

For an insane split second she had been about to ask him if he fancied a drink later. But it really wasn't relevant either way. Not only did she not have enough time in DC, but after Giles Denton she had vowed never again to become involved with someone working on the same case. That was her new, absolute rule.

He stood and held out his hand. Their eyes met again. 'Good luck, Rachel.'

The three hours before check-out were spent sitting at the desk in her hotel room and reading through Interpol's briefing note.

Phoebe Stiles. The name was familiar for some reason. Rachel took her laptop from her case and googled it. A huge hit of results, and a whole portfolio of images. A pretty, Cuprinol-tanned, fake-lashed blonde girl captured by paparazzi at D-list events, or as part of tabloid and gossip mag features. Of course. She was *that* Phoebe Stiles. A soap actress who had been sacked and then set off down the reality TV road, involving herself in more and more desperate attempts to take up column inches: drunken nights out, Instagram nudity, social media fights with rivals, on again-off again relationships with fellow reality show victims, plastic surgery and pregnancy scares. A career of sorts.

Rachel clicked on a tabloid headline: *Why I'll take LA by storm, by Phoebe Stiles*. There was a photo of Phoebe, all duck lips, fierce brows and custard-blonde angel waves. She was, she said, fed up with the negative attention and lies of the UK press and was going to Los Angeles 'to further my acting career.' She had an agent there, and several projects were in the pipeline. She was excited about her future.

Rachel set up an alert for updates on her search, closed her laptop and zipped it into her case with a deep sigh. Phoebe's future. Rotting in a dumpster at the back of Macy's department store.

FIVE

Transport is the next step. A rental car, picked up and returned in the least conspicuous way possible.

The airport is the obvious choice of location. Hundreds of cars are collected there daily, usually for short periods, and no one is likely to pay much attention. The trunk needs to be big enough to house a human-sized package, but in every other respect should be as bland as possible.

So the free upgrade to a flashy sports car has to be refused, and a plain blue mid-size, mid-range family compact taken instead. Dragging the package to the car without being seen involves disabling the cameras in the building with the spray paint, and using the elevator at a time when partygoers have returned to bed but any workers on an early shift are not yet about. 4.45 a.m.: this works out to be the optimum time slot.

Then a drive of around a mile and a half, headlights off, licence plates obscured, to the final location. The car is parked away from the building for the rest of the night, and the next day will be returned to the rental zone in the airport car park. Keys in a deposit box. A shuttle to the nearest public transit bus stop, baseball cap pulled down, shades on.

Done.

SIX

The bikini may have been a little optimistic, Rachel reflected, as she woke the next morning. The California sunshine was there on cue, but the air was cold enough for her to see her breath. She abandoned the planned dip in the hotel pool in favour of a run.

This was not the Hollywood she had pictured. She had envisioned gracious homes bordered by lush landscaping, sweeping boulevards fringed with towering fan palms and the pale Pacific beaches. It turned out those were all in Beverley Hills, Santa Monica and Bel Air. The LA police district dealing with Phoebe Stiles's death was North Hollywood, a dusty, flat valley suburb of sprawling strip malls on the far side of the Hollywood hills. The ocean might as well not have existed, and there was only a distant glimpse of the San Gabriel mountains. Rachel ran past endless fast food and auto part outlets on Lakershim Boulevard before finally finding a small park, full of early Sunday runners like herself. She paused long enough to have a breakfast burrito and coffee, then went straight to the North Hollywood PD building on Burbank Avenue, pulling her Interpol warrant card from her fanny pack and showing it to a poker-faced desk sergeant.

'Wait here ma'am: you need to speak to Lieutenant Gonzales.'

Frank Gonzales was a box of a man, as broad as he was tall. Sweat glistened on his round cheeks and on the edges of his black moustache, despite the morning chill and the air conditioning. He continued sweating once they were in his office and seated on either side of his desk. A lemon air freshener gave off an overpowering scent that filled the small room. Next to it were several framed family portraits with the awkward poses, forced grins and matching sweaters mocked in online memes.

'Glad to have you here, Detective Prince.' He was sombre as he shook her hand. 'This is a difficult case. Sensitive, you know?'

'Have Phoebe's parents arrived?'

'Yes, they flew in yesterday. They're very distressed, very confused. As you would expect. One of my officers will take you to meet with them.'

'Thanks,' Rachel paused. 'I'm here to do what I can for them.'

'Appreciated,' Gonzales pulled a handkerchief from his pocket and mopped his face with it. 'I think it will help them to speak to a law enforcement agent from their own country.'

Rachel nodded.

'For now, there isn't a whole lot we can tell them. The autopsy report hasn't been super-helpful, I've got to tell you.' He dabbed his top lip. 'The remains were skeletal only, but skull injuries suggest cause of death was a blunt force trauma to the back of the head. As for what else she might have suffered – sexual abuse or torture – that's impossible to tell.'

'No third-party DNA?'

Gonzales shook his head. 'No discernible traces. We tested the plastic sheeting and tape she was wrapped in but they were clean. I'll let you see a copy of the report.'

'And the photos, please.'

'Sure. Give me the details of where you're staying and I'll have them sent over.'

'And she was found behind a department store?'

'Macy's, just up toward Valley Glen.'

'Anything on their CCTV?'

Gonzales shook his head regretfully. 'Their recordings are kept for four weeks. We've checked everything they have. Nothing.'

'How about where she was living?'

'Same situation at the apartment block. We're in the process of speaking to the other residents: that might give us something, but there were no reports of suspicious behaviour.'

'I'd like to take a look at Phoebe's apartment.'

He shook his head. 'There's really nothing to see. The CSI guys have taken as many samples as they can, which are still undergoing analysis. The place looks like it's been cleaned though. Her laptop and cell have gone to the tech people for data analysis, and whatever they find looks like our best hope of moving this forward.'

'I'd still like to take a look.'

Gonzales shrugged. 'All righty then. I'll have someone arrange it.'

'And in my Interpol briefing, I was told there could be similarities between this and another case?'

Gonzales patted his armpits with his handkerchief. Rachel had never seen anyone sweat so much. 'A body that was found in San Diego a few months ago. Database flagged up some similarities.'

'Could you get me some more information?'

'I'll do what I can, but you gotta understand, it's outside of LAPD jurisdiction. Crossing county borders… that's a decision for the FBI to make.'

'Anything you can get would be helpful.' Rachel stood up. 'I should go and change before I talk to the family.'

The first thing she was going to do was have a long shower. The blend of the drying perspiration from her run, Lieutenant Gonzales' sweat sheen and the sickly sherbet-lemon aroma was making her skin crawl.

Gonzales heaved himself up and lumbered to the door to open it. 'I'll have an officer to you in an hour.'

Officer Dean Brading was already waiting for her in the motel reception after Rachel had washed and dried her hair and dressed in her preferred uniform of black trousers and white shirt. Clean shaven, with a mousey buzz cut and big, soulful brown eyes, he looked barely old enough to handle the 9mm Smith & Wesson on his belt. He addressed her as 'Ma'am', and only spoke when spoken to on their ten-minute journey.

Derek and Pamela Stiles were staying in a budget hotel on the outskirts of Studio City. Rachel had offered to go up to their room, but they insisted they would come down to the coffee area (it didn't warrant the word shop) in the lobby. They appeared looking red-eyed, dazed and pale; the stupor of grief written all over their faces. Derek Stiles hadn't shaved; Pamela had made an attempt at make-up, which only accentuated her puffy pallor. Apart from that, Rachel reflected, they couldn't have looked more ordinary. Just a regular middle-aged, middle-class couple, thrust into an unimaginable nightmare. Rachel stood up, wondering if she should embrace them, but the presence of the silent Officer Brading held her back. She extended a hand.

'Rachel Prince. I'm an international division investigator from the National Crime Agency.'

Hearing an English accent was too much for Pamela, who crumpled, weeping. The weeping continued for some time. Rachel guided her into a chair, pulling out one of the tissues she had put in her shirt pocket especially for this eventuality. 'I'm sorry. I'm so sorry.'

'You've got to find out who did this to our Phoebe,' Pamela sobbed. 'Tell me you're going to find them.'

'We're going to do all we can, Mrs Stiles.'

While she waited for the sobbing to subside she addressed Derek. 'Mr Stiles, can you tell me when you last had contact with Phoebe?'

'That's the dreadful thing about this: we don't even know.' He had a thick West Midlands accent. 'We thought we'd heard from her just last week, but the police here are telling us she must have already been dead then.'

'When you say you'd heard from her?'

'Messages, you know… on the WhatsApp. She was on that thing all the time. Chatting away, almost every day she'd do the little picture things, or send us a photo of something. But it's got to have been someone else, someone who'd got hold of her mobile.' He looked up at the ceiling for a second, then shook his head repeatedly. 'It makes me sick just thinking about it. Why would someone do that?' Rachel rested her hand on his arm as he struggled to breathe away the tears. 'Sorry. I'll be all right, just give me a second.'

She waited while he took out a handkerchief and blew his nose. 'Okay? So thinking back, when did you hear from her and know for sure it must have been her? Talking on the phone.'

'It was on Skype,' Pamela said thickly. 'The fifteenth of January.'

'The fifteenth? You're quite sure of the date?'

Pamela nodded. 'Yes because it was my mother's birthday the next day, and I distinctly remember her blowing a kiss and saying "Give that to Nana".' She turned to her husband. 'She did, didn't she.'

Derek nodded slowly. 'That's right. After that, she kept saying she'd phone or Skype, but she was always too busy. But we heard from her regularly, so we weren't worried…' He drew in his breath heavily, as though even speaking was distressing him. 'We've told the police all of this already, and they took our phones from us to check.'

'Well that's good,' said Rachel, 'It gives us a definite timeline to work on.'

'She was all excited too, because she'd got some work,' said Pamela. 'Wasn't she, Derek?'

'She was. She said her agent had got her a shampoo commercial, to go on the television, and it would be very decently paid. She was worried about running out of money, you see, what with the car, and rent, and agent's fees.'

'And getting her teeth done,' said Pamela. 'That cost something ridiculous. Twenty-five thousand dollars, I think she said.' She shook her head sadly.

'So she had financial problems?'

Pamela's head-shaking became more vigorous. 'I wouldn't exactly put it like that. But being here was a lot more expensive than she thought it was going to be, and she didn't have her press and appearances and stuff she normally relied on. She's not a celebrity here.'

Becoming a 'celebrity', the unfortunate career choice of so many girls with more ambition than talent, thought Rachel.

'I think she definitely found it harder with nobody knowing who she was over here,' reflected Derek. 'But she was determined she was going to make it.'

This brought on a bout of fresh weeping from Pamela. Rachel fetched them cups of stale overheated coffee from the drip machine in the corner.

'Not like a proper English cup of tea, eh?' Pamela managed a weak smile as she sipped the weak coffee.

'I'll need the details for her agent if you have them.'

'She's called Marion. Marion Miller. That's all we know. She hasn't been in touch.' Pamela looked up at Rachel. 'Can we see her, do you think?'

'The agent?'

'No. Phoebe. We just want to, you know… say goodbye.'

Rachel felt Brading stiffen beside her. She hesitated.

'I'll certainly talk to Lieutenant Gonzales about that. Leave it with me.' Rachel despised herself for not having the guts to tell these people that little remained of their daughter beyond bones and liquid putrefaction. And the pricey veneers.

'Thank you.'

Pamela reached for Rachel's hand and gave it a little squeeze, intensifying her guilt. But she had to trust her gut when it came to judging how much these grieving parents could bear. Dealing with a victim's relatives was certainly not her favourite part of the job, but she considered it the most important. And their distress drove her to do her best.

'Why don't you two go and have a rest, and we'll speak later. And don't worry: I'm going to do everything I can to find the person who did this to Phoebe. I promise you that.'

SEVEN

After the car has been returned, it's back to the apartment, to finally enjoy it, properly alone.

'What's mine is yours…'

But first, the cleaning has to be done. Gloves on, the floor where the body has lain disinfected and re-polished. Then every surface bleached and scrubbed. Every item of clothing and linen is boil-washed and handled with gloves. There will be no tie-in, no connection possible: the only person who lived here is Phoebe Stiles.

Then, eventually, it's time to move on to the next one. There are plenty more of them online, waiting to play host. You just need to get your research right.

To find the perfect girl.

EIGHT

Rachel and Brading headed back to the patrol car in silence.

'I need to go to Phoebe's apartment,' Rachel told him as she opened the door. 'Can you take me there?'

He hesitated.

'It's all right Officer, I okayed it with Lieutenant Gonzales.'

He held open the car door for her. 'Yes ma'am.'

The apartment was only a few blocks away, but the landscape changed as they drove, becoming greener and more undulating than the dusty valley floor. Phoebe's rented apartment was in an attractive development built into a slope just off Ventura Boulevard. It was compact and anonymous, comfortable and functional. And cordoned off with crime scene tape.

Brading had pulled latex gloves and shoe covers from the glove box when they parked, and they both put them on without speaking: a solemn little ritual. He knew to double glove, Rachel noted. A single pair would start transmitting the wearer's sweat after twenty minutes, causing DNA cross-contamination.

The apartment's spacious hallway was lined on one wall with louvered storage cupboards. In the bedroom, the mattress had been stripped and the all bedclothes and any clothes from the wardrobes and drawers bagged and removed. The marble bathroom contained only cleaning materials in the vanity; the laundry area only detergents and a gallon bottle of bleach. The kitchen cupboards were bare of food, the inside of the fridge and oven like surfaces in an operating theatre. Everywhere was spotless; any discernible traces of Phoebe gone.

Rachel looked over the sofa in the living area; a large L-shaped unit made from pale grey tweedy fabric and dotted with grey and white scatter cushions.

'Did they test the sofa?'

'I believe the forensic people removed fibre samples, ma'am.'

'They need to take these cushions. And –' Rachel opened the doors of the hall cupboards to reveal a vacuum cleaner – 'the contents of the vacuum bag should be analysed too. And the washing machine and dryer.'

'Yes ma'am. I'll get on it.'

Rachel looked at the young man's face. 'What do you think, Brading?'

'Ma'am?'

'About this case. About Phoebe, and how she died.'

'To clean up like this… it seems cold.' He hesitated. 'And it makes me think she died here.'

'Go on.'

He gestured around the apartment. 'It's as if the victim didn't exist. Like she's been made to disappear. But I think the perp must have known her. It wasn't just a random killing, or opportunistic. That's what my gut tells me.'

'You know what, Officer Brading: I agree.'

'And they didn't do this on impulse. They thought about it.'

'Planned it, too.' Rachel took one more look round. 'But why? Why could they possibly want Phoebe gone. What had she done?'

'She definitely pissed someone off.' Brading tugged off his shoe covers once they were on the communal landing.

Rachel nodded, bending to pull off her own. 'Even if she didn't mean to.'

*

Back in her room in the Ventana Vista Suites, Rachel sat down with her laptop and searched for Marion Miller. It didn't take her long to find the website for MM Creative Management. A heavily filtered head shot showed an angular woman with big hair and professional make-up. It was hard to guess the age of the face, which had been lifted, injected and plumped. She could have been anywhere between forty and sixty-five.

She dialled the contact number on the web page.

'*You've reached MMCM. I'm afraid we can't take your call right now, but please leave your message after the tone.*'

Rachel left a voicemail explaining who she was, and asked for her call to be returned as a matter of urgency. It was Sunday, so she wasn't optimistic that she'd hear back before tomorrow. She changed into her bikini, put on the bathrobe provided by the motel and headed out to the pool area. Although the sun was setting, ten hours of its rays had left a pleasant lingering warmth, and the cloudless sky was streaked with apricot and rose. No one else was brave enough to take on the unheated water in February, so she could breast-stroke her way to twenty lengths in solitude.

As she ploughed through the chilly water, her mind ran over and over what Phoebe's parents had said, and what she and Brading had seen – or not seen – at the apartment. If the forensic analysis threw up nothing at all, then it was difficult to see how the investigation could move beyond ground zero. But her experience told her there would have to be something, however fragmentary, however apparently insignificant. If you looked hard enough there was always something.

After her swim, Rachel looked through the papers Gonzales had given her. The photos of Phoebe's remains were not an ideal accompaniment to a meal, but it was the series taken at the deposition site that interested her. The plastic-wrapped corpse had been left in a warehousing area at the rear of the store, where the discarded shop mannequins were put to be recycled. Propped in a large dumpster amongst rows of rejected blank-faced dummies, their limbs contorted in a bizarre approximation of human life. This could not have been accidental. In placing Phoebe here, the killer was making a statement. Throwing her away. Cutting her down to size. Rendering her merely one of many.

She put the photos down and picked up her phone, noticing an earlier text from Brickall.

Enjoying your holiday, Prince?

She messaged him back.

Walk in the park compared to sitting next to you all day.

He replied immediately, despite the fact it was after midnight at home.

Seriously you idle cow: when are you coming back? Work's piling up here,

Rachel looked at her phone for a few seconds, trying to decide how to answer. Even at this early stage, it was obvious there was more to this case than a random homicide. She was supposed to be preparing for her promotion board back in London, and then there was Joe. Like most teenagers he was engrossed in his own life, but he would still notice her absence. Sighing, she started to type.

Seriously: it's going to be a while. Longer than we thought.

'Hello.' Rachel spoke into the intercom. Silence ensued, accompanied by a faint buzzing.

She raised her voice. 'Hello?'

Marion Miller's offices were on the second floor of a building on Santa Monica Boulevard in West Hollywood. She had waited all morning for a response to her voicemail of the evening before, and when, past midday, there was still nothing, she had availed herself of Officer Brading and his patrol car and paid an impromptu visit, warrant card in her back pocket, notebook in her shoulder bag and irritation in her demeanour.

The intercom crackled, making her jump. *'Do you have an appointment?'*

'Police.' The lock clicked.

She was met by a fresh-faced girl who introduced herself as Marion's assistant and told her Marion preferred people to make an appointment.

'This is a murder investigation, I don't need an appointment,' Rachel told her briskly, refusing a seat in the plush dove-grey reception area and holding up her warrant card.

'May I tell Marion what this is regarding?'

'Phoebe Stiles.'

'One moment please.'

The girl returned after a few seconds and ushered Rachel into a gaudily decorated corner office, all gilt and glass and faux leopard skin cushions. Like a throwback to the TV show *Dynasty*, Rachel thought. Portrait photos of the talent lined the wall. She scanned them for Phoebe's image, but couldn't find her.

'Marion Miller.' The woman behind the desk extended her hand. She was dressed in a blonde cashmere sweater and her hair was freshly blown out. In the flesh she was a lot older than her flattering online picture, the face unlined but so waxy, so stretched and pillowed with collagen that it had an oddly cat-like appearance. And the hands gave her away – there was no hiding the veins and the liver spots, no matter how much gold jewellery she wore. Rachel's age estimate rose to somewhere nearer seventy.

'I'm so devastated about Phoebe,' Marion told Rachel, her rigid features unable to mirror the emotion she was laying claim to. 'Anything I can do to help, of course I'm happy to.'

'You could have returned my phone call first thing this morning, then I wouldn't have had to turn up unannounced like this.'

Marion pushed out her lips in a pout: the only part of her face that could move. 'My assistant – she's new. What can you do?'

Rachel ignored this. 'I understand you'd recently found Phoebe some work?'

Marion waggled her wrists, making her bracelets jangle. 'You know, what she really wanted was an acting job, on a daytime drama or a comedy. I sent her out to some casting calls, but...' She appeared to be trying for a more-in-sorrow-than-in-anger face, 'let's just say the feedback wasn't the best. Sweet girl, pretty girl, but she couldn't master a believable Stateside accent.'

Rachel thought back to Phoebe's parents' broad West Midlands inflection.

'But she was photogenic and had a great body, and I got her a TV commercial with Lovely Locks. I don't think you have it in the UK, but it's a big hair brand out here. It was a one-day shoot and they used someone else for the voiceover, but it was great money for her. She was really lucky to get it. And the client was pleased,' she added, as if this mattered now.

'And the date of that shoot?'

'It was around three weeks ago.' Marion checked a spreadsheet of bookings on her desk. 'February 2nd.'

Rachel stared at her.

'Are you sure?'

Marion rummaged in the client file in front of her. 'I'm one hundred per cent sure. I have a copy of the call sheet here, and the invoice for her fee, which has the date of the shoot.'

Rachel checked the date on the paperwork. It would give them a timeline that established the date of Phoebe's death as

2nd February or later. That was less than three weeks ago. Which could only mean the medical examiner must have estimated the date of death wrongly. The remains must have been stored in a way that accelerated decomposition. It would also explain why Mr and Mrs Stiles had still been receiving messages.

'The investigating officer at North Hollywood PD will need to take a formal statement from you, and to see the records that you have. For now, I'll need a copy of these job details. And we'll need to see the commercial footage, if you could organise for that to be sent to where I'm staying.'

'Of course. I'll get the production company to bike over what they have on a disc right away.' Marion barked at her assistant to make photocopies, then sat down heavily at her desk, pressing her hands to her forehead. 'Honest to God, I don't know why anyone would want to hurt the girl. Could it not have been a burglary that went wrong?'

'We don't think so. We think the killer must have known her.'

'But that's insane.'

'Tell me about it,' said Rachel drily.

Brading was waiting outside, eyes front, one hand on the steering wheel, the other on his holster.

'Where to, Ma'am?'

'Back to my motel, please.'

Rachel had decided she would use what was left of the afternoon to write up her notes and answer some of the emails that Brickall was forwarding to her.

Brading nodded and pulled out of the parking lot. 'Ma'am, while you were in there I had a call from Lieutenant Gonzales. Preliminary forensics are back. Trace samples from the luminol used on the floor suggest that Ms Stiles was killed there in the apartment.'

'You called it right, Officer,' Rachel said, as he started the ignition. 'We'll make a detective of you yet.'

NINE

The temperature had shot up to the mid-seventies, causing Frank Gonzales to sweat even more profusely. He had called Rachel into his office the following morning to discuss the forensics results from Phoebe's apartment.

'Checking the vacuum cleaner was a smart idea,' he conceded. 'Someone emptied it, but there were a few long blonde hairs still in there. Preliminary results show some were Phoebe's; some were not. We've requested further analysis on those.'

'Any other results back?'

Gonzales shook his head. 'Everywhere had been scrubbed down with bleach and ammonia. Same with the linens and Phoebe's clothes: every single item had been washed at high temperatures and steam pressed. Every dish, plate and fork had been put through the dishwasher; the garbage pail was empty, and bleached. Never seen a crime scene like it; not in thirty years.'

'Wow.' Rachel leaned back in her chair.

'So I talked with Mr and Mrs Stiles and they said this wasn't like Phoebe at all. She was messy, kind of sloppy. Left dirty clothes where they fell, never cleaned the kitchen.'

'Could a maid have cleaned it?'

Gonzales shook his head, which made the beads of sweat on his forehead trickle towards his nose. 'I don't think so. The real estate company that Phoebe rented the place from didn't provide any sort of maid service, nor did the building's management.

And it's unlikely that Phoebe could afford that kind of additional service.'

'Officer Brading said forensics found something on the floor?'

'That's the good news. In the hallway there were traces of materials associated with body decomposition. They contain Phoebe's DNA.'

'So… it's likely she died there and was kept there for a while.'

'It looks that way.'

Rachel fixed her gaze on Gonzales' face. 'The person who cleaned up is our killer.'

He shrugged. 'Or an accomplice to the killer. There were some skin cells that weren't Phoebe's found on the cushions: another good call. I'll update you when we have those results.'

'Lieutenant, I think we may have to review the timeline; specifically, time of death. Phoebe shot a commercial on the second of February.' Rachel pulled a package out of her bag. 'This was delivered to my motel, just as I was leaving. It's a disc of the footage, but I haven't had a chance to look at it yet. Can we do it now? We probably ought to view it together.'

Gonzales looked uncomfortable. 'Mr and Mrs Stiles are on their way here to sign the paperwork for the release of their daughter's remains. They viewed them yesterday, against my advice. It was pretty rough on them.'

'They might like the chance to watch this,' suggested Rachel. 'In fact, seeing her alive might be helpful.'

Rachel fought back a vivid mental image of Trevor and Pamela looking down at their daughter's skeletal remains, sodden, half-dissolved shards of flesh still clinging to the bones. She cleared her throat, 'Listen, I'm sorry I didn't tell them how badly… how far gone she was. I should have done. I wimped out.'

Gonzales gave her a steady look. 'I appreciate your honesty, Detective. There's just no kind way to tell relatives something like that. I prepared them as best I could. Even so,' he exhaled hard, 'they still insisted on seeing her. I only hope it gave them some closure.'

'Believing in closure's a bit like believing in unicorns,' observed Rachel, 'It's a nice idea, but that's about all.'

The Stiles' arrived ten minutes later, and the four of them went to a meeting room where there was a large computer monitor and space for four chairs. After a certain amount of wrestling with the technology, and calling for assistance, Gonzales played the CD.

'*Lovely Locks…*' breathed the voiceover.

The opening shot was of a girl running along a rain-streaked street. She was dressed in a flimsy red silk dress, stark against grey sky, dark brick and slick cobblestones. Within the five seconds or so of the shot's duration she was drenched: her hair slicked around her face and neck. Cut to the head and naked shoulders of the girl, shampooing her hair with improbably lush suds (*Nobody uses that much shampoo in real life*, thought Rachel). Then a hairdryer was blowing through her gleaming blonde locks, fanning them. The final shot was the girl, impeccably coiffed with bouncing waves, looking back over her shoulder with a smug smile.

'*… makes long hair lovely again.*'

There was the obligatory pack shot, then the footage came to an abrupt end.

Absolute silence.

'She looks very pretty,' Pamela Stiles said tentatively, clutching her handkerchief to her mouth. 'Could we see it again – d'you mind?'

They watched it again. And again. Rachel had looked through many images and video clips of Phoebe, but never seen her as close up as this. Conventionally pretty, heart-shaped face with regular features and the dazzling blue-white, people-pleaser smile.

'She looks different somehow,' Pamela observed after the disc was finally ejected. 'There's something… I can't put my finger on it. I suppose it's her hair being wet. And all that make-up they use.'

'Well, we know she'd changed her appearance,' Rachel reminded her, putting the disc back in her bag. 'Her hair colour, and getting her teeth done. And then there's the professional lighting, and the footage may have been digitally altered in post-production. It's quite common practice.'

Pamela put both hands to her cheeks. 'I don't know, it's just… there's something… *off…* about her.'

'It's just strange, seeing her like that.' Derek put his arm round his wife. 'It's the shock.'

Gonzales leaned forward in his chair. 'I told you guys over the phone that the County Medical Examiner has agreed to release the body. So you just need to sign some papers, then you can go ahead and make arrangements for repatriation.'

Pamela's face crumpled again at this word.

'I'm sure Detective Prince will be happy to give you any pro-cedural assistance you need.' He shot a forced smile in Rachel's direction. 'For as long as she's still here.'

Early evening found Rachel back at the Ventana Vista, swimming in water that was now warm enough to be soothing rather than bracing, trying to get her thoughts in order. She was missing being able to talk through the case with her colleagues, especially Brickall. He had a sharp, logical brain and was good at sifting the pieces of the jigsaw puzzle to create a picture. *This is what we know,* he would say, listing the relevant facts in order, *and this is what we need to find out.*

She showered and sat at the small desk in her room with her notebook. She preferred to do this with pen and paper rather than a tablet or laptop; the process tuned in the analytical hemisphere of her brain.

— *Apartment block – someone must have seen something*
— *Phoebe's phone – she probably communicated with her killer – where is it now?*
— *Commercial producers – what did they notice/discover about Phoebe?*
— *Check timeline with Medical Examiner*
— *Friends P's made in LA?*

Her phone pinged with a message from Joe.

Tried to leave everything tidy on Saturday morning. He added a goggle-eyed emoticon. *Where are you and when are you back?*

Rachel started typing – *The States, and I have no idea* – when the phone rang in her hand.

'Frank Gonzales. You'll probably want to get over here. We've made an arrest.'

TEN

Rachel arrived at Burbank Avenue just in time to see two armed officers hauling a good-looking young man from the back of a patrol car. He wore a ripped T-shirt and Havaïanas, and had a road map of tattoos on his arms. She followed as he was taken into the building, then stood waiting as he was searched, photographed and fingerprinted, then led away to an interview room.

Rachel turned to Brading, who had just appeared at her elbow. 'What's going on?'

'Suspect is named Matt Wyburgh. Phone records show he was in a relationship with Ms Stiles, but she ended it, and he wasn't too happy about it. Short time later, she's dead.'

'Beware of the post hoc fallacy, Officer.'

Brading frowned. 'Ma'am?'

'*Post hoc ergo propter hoc* – it's Latin. Means that just because one event follows another, it's not necessarily caused by that first event.'

'Whatever. We'll be running his DNA.'

Gonzales waddled back into the lobby, his face shining, his shirt stained with dark patches.

'Wyburgh's exercising his constitutional right to have a lawyer present, so we now have to wait a while I'm afraid, Detective Prince.'

'What do we know about him?'

'Not much. Grew up in Sherman Oaks, Dad has a successful import business. Works part-time in a coffee shop and lives off his old man the rest of the time. Smokes pot, likes to party. Typical middle-class LA kid.'

'Previous?'

'A DUI; nothing else on his sheet.'

Before Rachel could ask more, he cut in. 'Maybe go grab a coffee, Detective Prince – shouldn't be too long.'

She shook her head. 'I'm good thanks. I'd like to see the phone records while we're waiting though.'

Gonzales jerked his head in the direction of the stairwell. 'Tech guys will talk you through it.'

Mike Perez, North Hollywood PD's chief technology officer, was not what Rachel had imagined. He had beautiful olive skin, aquiline features and biceps that strained against his shirt sleeves. She had, however, needed to go down to the basement to find him. That part of the IT guy cliché held up.

'So you're the British detective?' His tone implied that she was not what he had imagined either.

'I think so. Last time I checked, anyway.' In the split second it took him to realise she was being ironic, she cut to the point: 'Phoebe Stiles?'

'What can I do for you ma'am?' Mike had the grace to colour slightly.

'Can I take a look at what you found on her phone?'

'No handset was picked up at her property, but we subpoenaed her cell phone records.' Mike swung his chair briskly to the left so that he was facing his computer and pulled up a document on screen.

'Okay, so firstly what we have here are a bunch of WhatsApp messages from the victim's phone to the suspect, Matt Wyburgh.'

'And he was definitely her boyfriend?'

'Looks that way. We've got messages going back a couple of months, and they seem to be pretty into each other.'

He clicked the screen to enlarge part of the text. 'See here…' Rachel read Phoebe's message.

Hey babes! Missing my boo so much today. Can't wait to see you tonight!!

There followed a series of heart, smiley and kissing emoticons. Wyburgh's reply was along the same lines.

Hey Sweetie… how's my bae? Can't wait to kiss you and love on that gorgeous ass of yours…

There were many more messages in a similar vein, interspersed with cutesy selfies and soft-porn sex chat.

Rachel pulled a nauseated face.

'I know, right?' Perez mirrored her facial expression. 'The unusual thing is, these continue all day, every day until January nineteenth.'

'So… that's four days after her parents last spoke to her on the phone.'

'Oh really? Well anyhow, there's silence for twelve hours, then she starts messaging him again, but much less frequently, and cuts down on the schmaltz.' He pointed to the timeline on his screen. 'On twenty-first January he asks her what's wrong. Silence for forty-eight hours, then she dumps him.'

Sorry, but this just isn't working for me right now. I need to concentrate on my career ☹

'He tries messaging her back, and then when she ignores him, he tries calling her number multiple times, but she's blocked him.'

Rachel looked at the date on the screen: 23rd January. Phoebe didn't film the commercial until 2nd February, which implied she was very much alive on the twenty-third and that the dumping text must have come from her. But why the sudden change of heart? Then again, it seemed plausible that she might cool like this: perhaps she'd just tired of Wyburgh. The press coverage of Phoebe's love life suggested that steadiness and fidelity were not part of her approach to romance.

'I'd like a hard copy so I can go through the messages in detail. If that's okay?' Rachel asked.

'Sure.' Mike tapped a key, and the whirr and slap of a printer started up. 'There was another thing; something that turned up on her tablet.' Mike clicked to another file. 'Back in December, Phoebe opened an account with CasaMia.'

Rachel knew about the online home-sharing phenomenon; everybody did. Most of her friends and acquaintances used it when they travelled and had the CasaMia app on their phones; a distinctive duck-egg blue icon with two hands shaking below a sloping roof.

She frowned. 'But she wasn't renting her apartment through CasaMia. She had a long lease through a realtor.'

'She was illegally subletting. CasaMia have her listed as a host. She could get four hundred bucks a night for that apartment in Studio City, so she was renting it out every now and then. I'm guessing to supplement her income.'

'So where did she go when she had guests?'

'From the earlier messages exchanged with Matt, it looks like she originally planned to crash at his place. He mentions here –' he flipped back to the original document – 'that he's already given her a key. From what I can pull off her tablet she'd agreed a rental for the period January 18th through 22nd. Then she doesn't show up at Matt's after all, and he starts asking her why the change of plan.'

'And that's when she dumps him.' Rachel was thoughtful. 'Do we know who the sub-letter was?'

Perez shook his head. 'No, or even whether they went ahead with the rental. But whoever it is, you'll probably want to talk to them. I'm afraid I can't access CasaMia accounts from here: their firewall is pretty tight. I know their head of online security is called Paulie Greenaway, if you need a contact.'

Mike closed down the screen, retrieved the stack of printed sheets and swung back to face Rachel, holding them out to her.

Rachel took the printout and stuffed it in her bag. As she did so, her fingers grazed the Lovely Locks disc. She pulled it out. 'Can I ask you another favour?'

'Shoot.'

'Can you do some analysis on this footage?'

'What kind of analysis?'

'Facial recognition.'

Mike stared at her a beat, then held his hand out for the disc. 'May I?'

He played the commercial, frowning slightly at the screen. 'We don't really have the right software for this.'

'Know anyone who does?'

'We sometimes use a place called PsyLab in Pittsburgh. They're the leaders in 3D analysis. They can do biometric authentication up to a hundred frames per second.'

Rachel grinned. 'Wow.'

'Hey, you know we geeks love our geek speak, right? Want me to send it to them?'

'Yes please.' Rachel handed him her business card, and stood up. 'And now if you'll excuse me, I'd better go and see what our suspect has to say.'

By the time she returned to Gonzales's office he had gone, his interrogation of Wyburgh already underway.

'You're welcome to watch through the one-way glass,' Brading told her.

'Of course,' Rachel gave a brief smile. Starting the interview without her was a way for Gonzales to mark his law enforcement territory, underlining her status as visiting officer. As she turned to go, she caught sight of the file on Gonzales's desk. *Tiffany Kovak*, it said on the front. It also bore the official stamp of the San Diego Police Department.

'Is that the other case Lieutenant Gonzales told me about? The one that may be linked?'

Brading gave the briefest of nods then, as Rachel tried to pick up the file and look at it, added a firm 'Let's go, ma'am', reflexively touching his holster.

Matt Wyburgh was seated on one side of a small table, his lawyer to his left. Opposite him were Gonzales and his superior officer Captain Steve Dench, a balding fifty-something wearing button-down shirt and khakis.

'I'd like you to account for your movements between January 21st and February 3rd.' Gonzales was nervous, his fingers straying frequently to his black slug of a moustache.

Wyburgh leaned back in his chair, looking straight at the police officers while keeping both hands in the front pockets of his jeans. He seemed tense, but not afraid, Rachel thought.

'The weekend of twenty-fourth to twenty-sixth I was in Reno at my friend's bachelor party.'

'We can corroborate that,' his lawyer interjected.

'And after that?'

Wyburgh shrugged. 'I was at work, or at my apartment.'

'But you must have left the apartment some time.'

Wyburgh's lawyer objected. 'Of course he did, to run his regular errands, but my client can't be expected to have total recall of such a wide time period.'

'Did you make contact with Phoebe Stiles? After she'd broken off the relationship?'

'I already told you guys: when she didn't answer my messages I tried calling her. I don't see why that's such a big deal. Anyone would do that, right?' He glanced sideways at his lawyer, who nodded affirmation.

'How many times?'

'I don't know – a few, I guess.'

'So you were mad at her?' asked Dench.

'No. I was surprised, for sure. A little pissed off maybe. But this wasn't, like, this big serious relationship. We'd hang out, we'd have sex. It wasn't a massive deal, you know?'

'Did you go round to her apartment after she'd ended it?'

Wyburgh glanced sharply at his lawyer, who gave the slightest nod. 'Yes. I did go. Once, just before I left for Reno. But there was no one home. Or if there was, she didn't answer.'

Gonzales dabbed his face triumphantly.

Brading, who had left Rachel watching alone, reappeared.

'Lab results are back,' he whispered. 'DNA found on the couch cushions is definitely Wyburgh's.'

Rachel was itching to get inside the interview room, convinced that she would make a much better job of getting through to the impassive young man. Thus far, she found his account of events perfectly credible. She resisted the temptation to voice her doubts out loud.

Instead she said: 'Look, the tech guys have thrown up some interesting stuff, so there are some new avenues it could be helpful to go down with Wyburgh, if I—'

Brading held up a hand, his chocolate-drop eyes doleful. 'Only officers who have Los Angeles operational jurisdiction can question a suspect I'm afraid, ma'am.'

*

After a couple of days staying at the Ventana Vista, Rachel had developed a routine. She would walk down the street to the nearest drugstore and buy something for her evening meal. Avoiding the aisles of massed salted snacks and neon-bright sugary drinks, she would head to the chiller cabinet for a pre-prepared salad and some fresh fruit. Back at the motel, she would swim as the sun sank in the sky, then shower and eat in her bathrobe, watching one of the news channels until she fell asleep. Which was early, the jet lag having not quite worn off. It wasn't that different from her usual evening routine in London, now that she was single. Except there she had regular visits from Joe. She already missed him.

This evening she turned the volume low on the TV, opened up her laptop and started searching travel websites. Her phone buzzed. The message was from Brickall, even though it was around 3 a.m. in London.

Patten's had the sprog. Another boy, called Algernon.

She typed a reply: *Algernon. Jesus.*

Kidding, Prince. They're calling it Max or Oscar or something equally middle-class. P.S. Still pissing with rain here.

All the more reason to do some work, you lazy git. Get to sleep.

Smiling, she tossed her phone back onto the bed and went back to looking at available flights to San Francisco. It was odd working a case without Brickall. She relied on him, not just as a colleague, but as a friend and confidant.

Her phone rang.

There was a brief silence on the other end, then a flat voice said, 'DI Prince, it's Derek Stiles.'

'Call me Rachel, please. What can I do for you?'

'It's about the arrangements for Phoebe. We've decided not to fly her – the body – back home to the UK. There's… there's a lot of rules and regulations. It's difficult and expensive, with the zinc-lined coffins and suchlike.' There was a little muffled gasp. 'Sorry.'

Rachel leaned back with her left hand on her forehead, staring up at the ceiling through her fingers, 'It's okay. Take your time.'

'Because of what happened to her… the state of, you know… we thought it would be best to have her cremated here and just take the ashes back with us. We'll have a proper memorial service for her in our local church when we're home again.'

'I'm sure that's sensible. I think I'd do the same, if I were in your position.' Was that reassuring? She hoped so.

'The service is going to be tomorrow, at Valhalla Memorial Park. We'd like you to be there.'

Tomorrow. Rachel's heart sank slightly. 'Of course. What time?'

'Three o'clock.'

Rachel opened a fresh page on her laptop and consulted an online map. The Valhalla cemetery was less than two miles from Bob Hope airport in Burbank. If she booked a return seat around lunchtime, she would just about make it. Just.

'Of course. I'll be there.'

'Thank you, DI… Rachel.'

Rachel completed her reservation, making sure her return flight landed at Bob Hope, then started to read through the very humdrum exchanges between Phoebe and Matt. *'Renting out my place for few days next week,'* she had written on 12 January, *'Will be crashing at yours every night.'*

Matt responded with an icon of an aubergine followed by an ogling face with tongue hanging out, presumably in anticipation of a greater intercourse quotient.

Rachel sighed and carried on scanning down the pages, eventually falling asleep with a blur of emoticons dancing in front of her eyes.

ELEVEN

San Francisco Bay was there somewhere, Rachel's taxi driver assured her, but it was masked by the drifts of fluffy white Pacific fog that softened the morning light. From the plane, the city had looked as if it was enrobed in a cloud, like a magical kingdom. And down on the ground it was chilly, at least twenty Fahrenheit colder in the San Fernando valley.

After a forty-five-minute journey from San Jose airport, during which she could see very little, Rachel was dropped on Brannan Street, outside the renovated art deco building that housed CasaMia's San Francisco headquarters.

The immense atrium featured circular windows and extruded glass meeting rooms that appeared to be suspended in space, and an interior pitched roof structure that mimicked the brand's roof icon. On the wall above the reception desk was the brand's strapline in three-feet-high letters: *MY HOME IS YOUR HOME.*

The space had been designed to within an inch of its life; a company recently valued at $25 billion was not afraid to make a statement. Rachel reclined on one of three crocus-yellow sofas at the atrium's centre and gratefully accepted the espresso the receptionist brought her.

'Paulie will be with you presently.'

Rachel had wrongly pictured Paulie Greenaway as a young male, but a woman bounded up a few minutes later, and rather than extending a hand, lunged in for a hug. Aged somewhere between thirty and forty, her light red hair was scraped up into a messy bun. She wore cargo pants and trainers and sported multiple piercings.

She led Rachel through thousands of feet of open desk space, breakout areas, circular meeting rooms ('less hierarchical') and a games room ('We have an ethic of randomness, spontaneity and play'). Rachel wondered how an ethic of randomness would go down at the NCA. Some of her more cynical colleagues might say it was already in operation. She wished Brickall could see this place. He'd find it hilarious.

Everywhere you looked there was wall art featuring the light blue app logo, and either the words '*Mi Casa e su casa*', or the translation, '*My home is your home*'. What's mine is yours.

They settled opposite each other on non-hierarchical foam pouffes, and Paulie logged herself into one of the tablets that seemed to be lying around everywhere. She listened intently as Rachel told her about Phoebe's death.

'So you haven't spoken to the press or made this public via an appeal?'

'Not yet, no.'

Paulie grimaced as though someone was suggesting root canal work with no anaesthesia. 'I have to tell you; this would be disastrous for perception of the brand. Totally disastrous. We're synonymous with security; it's one of our key values.'

'With respect, Ms Greenaway, this is a criminal investigation. Your brand's profile is not our paramount concern. '

'Paulie. Please. We think use of surnames is patriarchal.'

Rachel pulled herself up as tall as she was able to on her ridiculous foam toadstool. 'Paulie – a young woman has been murdered around the time her home was rented to a customer from your site. It's possible that she was killed within that same home. We need to know everything you can tell us about the identity of the person who rented it.'

'The privacy of our users—'

Rachel glared. 'Everything you can tell us.' she repeated, folding her arms across her chest. 'We wouldn't want to go down the route of getting a warrant to seize all your systems hardware. Though of course we could.'

Paulie glanced at Rachel's face, then started tapping furiously on her tablet. 'Okay, I have the listing right here. The account is in the name of Heather Kennedy.'

'What information do you have on her?'

'When members register we ask for a face photo, a home address, email address, phone number and a social security number. And a credit card number, the one that any rentals are charged to. They can write a short bio, but it's optional.'

'But you don't run police checks?'

Paulie shook her head. 'That would take way too long and be far too expensive. It's free to register as a guest. We just run a basic address validation. Heather Kennedy gave an address in Colorado Springs.'

'You have a photo of her?'

Paulie passed her the tablet.

Rachel stared, feeling a chill stab of shock. A heavily filtered selfie of a young, blonde girl with generically pretty features and a vermilion-lipsticked pout. She could have been the girl next door. She could have been Phoebe.

'No bio?'

Paulie shook her head.

'What about her account history? Has she stayed anywhere else?'

'This was a new account, opened January 12th this year. The booking at Canton Place in Studio City was the first and only reservation "she" made.'

She made quotation marks in the air, to indicate that the account holder could be any gender.

'Give me a second.' Taking out her phone, Rachel called the number on the account.

'*This number is no longer in service.*'

She tried sending an email from her own account to 'heather. kennedy91'. It bounced straight back with an 'Undeliverable' system message.

She handed the tablet back to Paulie. 'Try putting a charge on that credit card number.'

Paulie tapped some buttons. 'Card declined.' She shrugged. 'The reservation was paid for using that card, but it looks like it's now been cancelled. I don't know what else I can do. We don't have any further information on this person. The email service provider might be able to supply an IP address, I guess.'

'Send all the details you do have to my email,' Rachel handed her a card. 'And I'd be grateful if you could organise a cab back to Mineta San Jose. I have to attend the victim's funeral this afternoon.'

'Of course. I'll organise it right away.' Paulie looked suitably chastened.

As they headed back towards the door, Rachel paused. 'Actually, there is one other thing, if you wouldn't mind?'

'Sure.'

'Do you have an account in the name of Tiffany Kovak?'

Paulie sat down and started tapping at the tablet again. 'Tiffany Kovak… yes, we have a host called Tiffany Kovak – she has a property in downtown San Diego, the Gaslamp district.'

'Had. I'm afraid she's dead too.'

Paulie's eyes widened. She set the tablet down slowly on the table in front of her.

'Oh my God. Are you telling me these two deaths are related? That would be very bad news.'

'For the brand?' Rachel couldn't resist.

'Just bad news. Awful.'

'It's far too soon to reach that conclusion, but I'll need you to send me Tiffany's account details too.'

'Sure, anything. I'll need to discuss all of this with our CEO, and obviously we'd appreciate—'

'We won't be going public with this. Not at this stage, anyway.'

Paulie looked so terrified that Rachel couldn't help feeling a little sorry for her. 'But I have a feeling you and I are going to need to speak again.'

The flight to Bop Hope Airport was delayed by twenty minutes, landing at three fifteen. As the plane taxied, Rachel switched on her phone to look at a map and work out the quickest way of getting to Valhalla Memorial Park. Her email alert sounded.

From: Robert J. McConnell
To: Rachel Prince
Subject: How's it going?
Hi Rachel, just thought I'd check in with you and find out how things are going. Our liaison officer here said the LAPD now has a suspect? Regards, Rob.

There was no time to reply properly, so she simply wrote '*Will call with an update. R.*' as she made her way through the arrivals hall, searching for a cab.

The service had just begun as she crept into the crematorium chapel and sat in one of the rear pews. The white coffin, heaped with pink and white roses, was at the head of the aisle on its catafalque, and Snow Patrol's 'Run' was playing on a hidden sound system.

I'll sing it one last time for you, then we really have to go…

The stress from rushing to get there, the bleakness of the occasion, the bittersweet message of the chosen song all collided in a rush. They brought tightness to Rachel's throat, and the sudden sting of tears. She looked down at her hands while she steadied herself, listening to Pamela's animal cry of pain and Derek's dry cough. There were only a handful of guests: a couple who looked as though they could be relatives from the UK, Gonzales and Brading, Marion Miller and two representatives from the British Consulate, one of whom stood to read a prayer.

The memorial park official gave a brief cookie-cutter eulogy that must have been from the 'Taken Too Soon' chapter of the funeral officiants' handbook, slotting in Phoebe's name where applicable. Then the coffin, barely visible beneath its heavy mantle of flowers, trundled on invisible rollers through a red velvet curtain, to the strains of 'All Things Bright and Beautiful'. And that was it. Phoebe Stiles's existence was officially over.

The paltry cohort of mourners emerged blinking from the gloom of the chapel to a cerulean sky above sweeping sunlit lawns, crimson and violet azaleas and murmuring fountains. It was a surreal ending for the girl from Birmingham's Weoley Castle.

'Thank you so much for coming. It means ever such a lot to us, doesn't it Derek?' Pamela enveloped Rachel in a hug and Derek nodded stiffly, putting a hand on his wife's back.

Rachel disentangled herself and pulled Frank Gonzales to one side.

'I'm just back from San Francisco, following up a lead that the IT guys found on Phoebe's tablet.'

'I'm afraid you've had a wasted trip, Detective Prince.'

'That remains to be seen,' Rachel said pleasantly. 'Can I brief you on it later?'

'Let's leave it until we see how Wyburgh checks out. We're still following up his alibis.' Gonzales pulled out his pocket square and wiped the back of his neck.

'And?'

'He was in Reno for approximately forty-eight hours at the bachelor party, and he showed up for work every day as usual, but he can't account for all his movements the rest of the time. That still gives him plenty of opportunity to go to Phoebe's apartment, have a fight with her, kill her.'

Rachel shook her head firmly. 'With respect, Lieutenant, that's exactly the problem: the time frame is too wide. Which of us can remember exactly which stores we visited, who we spoke to, everything we did a month ago? If we have evidence she was still alive to film the commercial on the second of February and her parents spoke to her on the fifteenth January, then that gives us almost three weeks. And what about witnesses?'

'Witnesses?'

Rachel bit back her first response. 'Anyone who can place Wyburgh at the scene? Anyone who heard a fight?'

'Not yet. But he has a cast-iron motive,' said Gonzales stubbornly. 'She dumped him, and he couldn't take it. Crime of passion; story as old as time.'

Rachel was still shaking her head. 'I read all the messages between them, and I just don't buy it. It doesn't feel like that kind of relationship. Did you speak to his previous girlfriends?'

'So far we've only identified one.'

'And?'

Gonzales mopped his brow vigorously. 'She denies there was any violent behaviour.'

Rachel inclined her head slightly.

'But that doesn't mean he didn't just snap. And his DNA is the only sample found in that apartment.'

Rachel struggled to maintain a professional demeanour in the face of rising exasperation. 'He was her boyfriend. He visited. The presence of his DNA links him to the apartment, not to the crime. And what about the other hair in the vacuum cleaner?'

Gonzales looked smug. 'Purchased non-native hair. Matched the profile of imported Russian hair used by the salon where Phoebe had extensions put in.'

The cemetery staff were politely ushering the guest towards their cars, but Rachel stayed doggedly with Gonzales. 'Have you bailed Wyburgh?'

'For now. We don't have enough to charge him yet,' he conceded.

'Then the case remains open.' Again, Rachel kept her tone as pleasant and non-confrontational as she could manage. 'So, I'd like to come by Burbank Avenue and brief you on my trip. Also, I need to look at Tiffany Kovak's file, if that's okay.'

Gonzales glanced sharply at Brading, then back to Rachel. 'I'm afraid that's not going to be possible.'

'But I saw it in your office.'

'Sorry; it's now been returned to San Diego PD.'

Marion Miller marched past in an ostentatiously large hat and designer black cashmere, using her sunglasses to avoid eye contact.

Rachel abandoned Gonzales and went after her. 'Ms Miller?'

'I'm so sorry, I have another client appointment. Call my office.'

'Could I hitch a ride?' Rachel called after her retreating back, but Miller pretended not to hear, climbing into her waiting town car and disappearing down the long drive. One dead client buried, another living one to represent.

Rachel turned back to see that Derek and Pam were also watching the car, their expressions bleak.

'Don't worry,' she said, squeezing Pam's shoulder. 'We will find whoever's responsible.'

Back at the Ventana Vista, Rachel changed into her bikini, grabbed her phone and laptop and went out to the pool, flopping onto a lounger. For a few minutes she closed her eyes and didn't move a muscle, soaking up the warmth from the last rays of early evening sun. She ached all over, with a bone-deep weariness.

Her phone bleeped. Reluctantly she sat up and looked at it. The text message was from her new pet IT guy, Mike Perez.

Have had facial recognition results in from Pittsburgh. 99.9% certainty woman in the shampoo commercial NOT Phoebe Stiles. Have emailed their report.

She stared at the text for a few seconds, then opened her laptop and checked her emails. Before she got to PsyLab's report, she saw another unopened email in her inbox, marked with a red '*Urgent*' flag. It was from Paulie Greenaway, with the subject line '*Thought you should see this ASAP*'.

Rachel opened it and scrolled through the booking history on Tiffany Kovak's CasaMia account. There had been eight reservations in the last nine months. Rachel clicked through them all in turn, finding nothing unusual. Then she reached the last one. The guest account was in the name of Stacey Gunnarson. And the profile photo was a familiar blonde twenty-something. Blandly pretty with artful make-up and a bright red pout.

Heather Kennedy.

Sitting bolt upright, she grabbed her phone again and tried phoning the number filled in under the account details. Out of service. She tried emailing the contact address: message undeliverable, just as before. She made a note of the property address, closed her laptop and dived into the pool, crawling several lengths until her heart had stopped thumping and her pulse slowed. She flipped onto her back and floated, staring up at a deepening indigo sky, car headlights twinkling and dipping on the horizon as they wove through the Hollywood hills. This had to be the connection between the deaths of Phoebe Stiles and Tiffany Kovak. It couldn't simply be a coincidence...

'Ma'am?'

The voice startled her, deflating her buoyancy. She flapped her arms to stop herself from sinking, then rolled over onto her front, her right foot just making contact with the bottom of the pool. Dean Brading stood a few feet away from her, his holster at eye level.

Rachel pushed her hair back from her forehead, water streaming over her face and down her neck, snot smeared over her top lip and chin.

'Sorry to disturb you, ma'am. There's been a development.'

Turning his gaze from her cleavage, Brading waited a few seconds, as though expecting her to emerge. She hopped through the water to the side of the pool and grabbed her towel, wiping down her face.

'Officer?'

He spoke as though reading aloud from a crime report.

'During the search of suspect Matt Wyburgh's home residence, officers found a blunt instrument with the victim's blood on it. He has consequently been charged with her murder.'

TWELVE

'Phoebe Stones?'

'Phoebe Stiles.'

'I'm sorry ma'am, I don't know anything about that.'

'The client was Lovely Locks, and the date of the shoot was February second.'

'Mmmm hmmm…' There were background sounds of rustling paper and scribbling. 'You know what – I'll speak to my manager and get someone to call you right back. Where did you say you were calling from?'

'I'm from the National Crime Agency in the UK, international division.'

'Sorry, what?'

'I'm an Interpol officer. And I don't have time to wait for a call back. Tell your manager that I'll be coming to your offices tomorrow, and I expect to get access to all information regarding that shoot. Is that clear?'

There was silence for a beat. 'Yes ma'am.'

Rachel hung up and planted her forehead on her hand for a few seconds. Then she checked the time on her watch. Eight fifty. Her rental car was due to be dropped off in a few minutes.

She opened her laptop and checked Rob McConnell's details. A phone call would be most efficient, given the time restraint. His mobile went straight to voicemail. She hesitated, then decided she was at risk of waffling and hung up. She composed a text instead.

On my way to check out the case that was similar to Phoebe's. IP = Tiffany Kovak, I think. LAPD not exactly being cooperative, plus it's out of their jurisdiction, so I'm out on a limb here. Anything you can get me about the case and contacts who might be willing to speak to me would be fantastic. Status urgent – only have a few hours. Rachel.

She added a kiss then deleted it. *No more work-centred flirtation: that was the new rule*, she reminded herself. Grabbing her bag, she went outside to wait for her hire car.

It was now Thursday morning, and she was flying back to London on Sunday. Three days left, and so much still to do. Nigel Patten had phoned the previous evening and demanded an update. It was the middle of the night in London, and in the background Rachel could just hear the faint sound of a mewling newborn.

'Night feed?' she enquired.

'Something like that,' sighed Patten. 'If you're wide awake at four in the morning, you may as well make use of the time difference. That's what I'm telling myself.'

Rachel had kept the debrief as vague as possible, but he had pressed her. 'So the local police have made an arrest in the case?'

'Yes,' admitted Rachel. 'The victim's ex-boyfriend.'

'And charged him?'

'Yes. First degree murder.'

Patten took this in. The baby made a series of rhythmic squawks, as though being jiggled over his shoulder. 'Well, that's a good result, I suppose. And the victim's family?'

'They held a cremation here today and they're returning to the UK with the ashes. I attended the service.'

'Well… good. Excellent. I'll ask Janette to find you a flight back, and you can debrief me in the office on Friday.' The baby let out a high-pitched wail. 'I'm going to have to go—'

'No, wait, sir… one second.'

'Make it quick. Shhhh, Max, there's a good boy.'

'There are a few loose ends I need to tie up, some people I need to talk to. Can the flight be pushed back until next week?'

'I want you in the office on Monday morning. Janette will book you a seat for Saturday.'

'Sunday.' pleaded Rachel. 'The overnight flight from LA will land at stupid o'clock on Monday, and I'll come straight to work from Heathrow.'

Patten's response had been drowned out by infant mewling and Rachel had hung up before he had chance to change his mind.

Rachel's phone rang as she was easing the car into fast-moving traffic on the I405. She let it go to voicemail and checked her messages as she was held at a red light.

'Rachel – hi. Rob here. I guess you're en route… I've emailed you a copy of the crime report and contact details for next of kin. Speak soon… Hope you're good, by the way?'

She parked and retrieved the email once she had entered the San Diego city limits. It contained an address for Tiffany's mother, Letizia Kovak. *'Hope you get a chance to talk to her,'* Rob wrote, *'Although from the enquiries I made, it sounded like the Stiles case is being wound up?'*

As she drove to Mission Hills, Rachel decided that this, here, was the Southern California of her imagination. She left behind the sweeping blue bay dotted with sailing boats, and drove through steep streets of handsome Spanish-style homes dripping with bougainvillea and palms swaying in the warm breeze. Letizia

Kovak's house was a stucco-splattered, terracotta-roofed villa in a garish shade that reminded Rachel of school custard. Through the metal gates, she glimpsed a pool and a couple of Mexican gardeners raking leaves off a pristine lawn.

A maid let her in and told her sorry, Madam was out at the mall, and would she please call later. Rachel explained that today – now – was all she had. She showed her warrant card and was permitted to wait, seated under a pergola with a glass of iced tea.

Letizia Kovak appeared fifteen minutes later; a petite pretty woman of Latino origin with prematurely grey hair.

'Hi!' she said, grasping both Rachel's hands. Her own were shaking. It was clear from her combined agitation and excitement that she thought Rachel had come to tell her that her daughter's killer had been found. Disabused of this idea, her mood visibly deflated.

'I'm here because I have some new information that could potentially take the case forward.' Rachel told her.

'What information is that?' asked Letizia flatly, pouring herself iced tea. She wore immaculately tailored trousers, a chiffon blouse and a lot of silver and turquoise jewellery.

'I can't disclose details at the moment, but if I could find out a bit more about Tiffany, it would be extremely helpful.'

Once Letizia had recovered from her disappointment, she seemed eager to talk about her daughter, as the recently bereaved often are.

'Was she an only child?'

'Kind of. I have a son, eight years older, from my previous marriage, but they didn't exactly grow up together.'

'My family's the same,' interjected Rachel. 'I've just got one much older sibling. I always felt a bit like an only.'

Letizia nodded in sympathy. 'Gerry – Tiffany's father – and I are now divorced. He doted on her, spoilt her. Bought her anything she wanted. Fancy sports car when she turned sixteen, her own apartment when she turned twenty-one. Any problem she had, she'd just call her dad and he'd fix it for her. I'm not sure that was so good for her. But –' she sighed heavily – 'sure, she could be a handful, but she was a good kid at heart.'

'Could I see a picture of Tiffany?'

Letizia went into the living room and came out with a fabric-covered photo album. Inside was the story of a life, from naked chubby babyhood to high-school graduation. Tiffany was olive-skinned, but had the grey eyes of her father's Polish ancestry, with mid-brown hair that she started to bleach blonde when she reached her teens. Bikini-clad beach shots showed that she had a perfect figure, and the broad white smile confirmed she had been on the receiving end of top-quality dentistry all her life. Pretty, but not memorably so. An archetypal Californian blonde.

'So when Tiffany disappeared…'

'I'll be honest; I didn't think anything of it at the time. I mean, I hadn't seen her for a couple of weeks, but – it sounds awful now – that was kind of normal. And she'd messaged me from her cell phone, so I had no reason to be worried.' Letizia looked down at her fingernails. 'Then, when they found her, the police said she must have been dead for weeks. Someone else must have been using her phone.'

'Someone was pretending to be her?'

She nodded. 'Exactly.'

'So when did you know something was really wrong?'

'Christmas,' said Letizia with a grimace. 'This all happened in December. And you know, everyone's busy then, with holiday season events and shopping. But then when she didn't show up on Christmas Day, and wasn't answering her cell, that's when Michael – my son – called the police. They found Tiffany ten days later, but she'd been dead for weeks by then. They said they couldn't be sure exactly how long.' Her eyes swam with tears.

Rachel paused a few seconds before asking, 'And where was it, where she was found?'

'At her high school.'

'But –' Rachel wished she'd had time to read though the crime report – 'she was no longer a pupil?'

'No, no, she graduated four years ago. She was studying fashion at Mesa College. But they found her on the Mission Hills high school campus, just near here. Where she used to go to school. And there were pictures of her car on the school CCTV.'

'And what have the police come up with in terms of a theory? About who could have done this.'

Letizia sighed heavily. 'They think it could be someone who was at school with her. They've questioned all her classmates, but… nothing.'

'And did they talk to you about the fact she had her apartment listed on CasaMia?'

Letizia looked blank. 'I don't know anything about that. She only had the place on 9th Avenue – downtown – that Gerry bought for her, but she was living there herself.'

Rachel surreptitiously checked her watch. She had planned to drive back to Los Angeles by that evening, and she needed to use the time as efficiently as she could.

'Mrs Kovak, is there anyone else I could talk to while I'm here; someone who could help me build a picture of Tiffany's last days?'

Letizia thought for a few seconds. 'I guess the obvious one is her best friend. Paige Chen. They were always as thick as thieves, ever since middle school.'

'Do you have an address for her?'

'I have no idea where's she living now, but I know she works at Lucky's Tattoo Parlor on Broadway.'

Lucky's didn't open til midday, so Rachel went into a coffee shop on the next block, ordered espresso and scrambled eggs and acquainted herself with the contents of the crime report from Tiffany's case.

The photos were disturbing, so disturbing that she had to abandon the scrambled eggs. The corpse – or what was left of it – was in the school's gym; the face and torso wrapped in plastic but the arms freed and wrists hooked through the rope cuffs on the wall bars. The whole scene was reminiscent of a crucifixion. But in a high school gym. Very *Bye Bye Miss American Pie*.

Just as with Phoebe's crime scene photos, it seemed the killer was trying to say something with the choice of disposal site. But what? Rachel ran through the rest of the report. Tiffany's car was caught on CCTV entering the school grounds on the night of 12th December. The significance of the date was that it was the day the school closed for the Christmas holidays. And the body was found on January 4th, when the janitor went to unlock and clean the gym in preparation for the new term, which started the next day. The alarm had been disabled and the padlock on the gym door forced with bolt cutters. Because there was no heating on in the building and there had been an unusually cold spell for Southern California, the body was not as badly decomposed as Phoebe's had been, but there had been no signs of sexual assault, no third-party DNA.

There was another anomaly. The medical examiner thought she must have died on or around December 12th, but her expensive sports car was seen several times on CCTV footage at her apartment building over the subsequent three weeks, leaving or entering the parking garage.

Rachel flicked to the forensic report on Tiffany's apartment. It had been scrupulously cleaned, and no touch samples were found bearing traces of DNA other than Tiffany's. It was the same story with the car – the analysts crawled over it, but every inch had been cleaned with an acid-based cleaning solution. The report writer noted that this was probably Citranox, a solution used in laboratories to remove DNA residue.

Rachel leaned back in her chair as she took this in. The killer really knew their stuff. The combination of audacity and attention to detail was something that she had never encountered in her police career; not at this level of psychopathy anyway. This was what Brickall would call hardcore.

Paige Chen was a chubby Chinese-American with waist-length dip-dyed hair and a nose ring. When Rachel returned to the tattoo parlour, Paige was busy with a client, so she sat on a stool and waited, watching as the girl expertly wielded the buzzing needle in her black-gloved right hand, dabbing the spots of oozing blood with her left.

'Decided what you want?' she asked when she was finished. 'We've got books of sample pictures if you're not sure.'

'Oh no, I'm not getting a tattoo,' Rachel told her, though now she thought about it, the idea quite appealed. She'd always wanted something discreet but distinctive on her wrist or ankle, or shoulder blade. One day. 'I'm a police officer. Here to talk about Tiffany Kovak.'

'You're from here?' Paige was clearly thrown by her accent.

'From Interpol, in London.'

'Why the hell would London be interested in Tiffany's death? She never even went to England.'

'I'm not able to tell you that.' In fact, Rachel could have tried explaining, but she was aware that time was a scarce resource and wanted to cut straight to the chase. 'Would you mind telling me what you remember about the time period around your friend's death?'

Paige hesitated, frowning. Rachel showed her warrant card.

'Okay, what do you need to know?'

'Did you know about her listing her apartment on CasaMia? The home-sharing site?'

'Yeah, she did mention that. It was a good way of paying for her studies. It's a nice apartment, you know?'

'And she was renting it out when she went missing?'

'Um, not totally sure. I think she said she was going to stay with her dad for a bit while she had a sub-let, yeah. Think so. I didn't hear from her for a few days, but I kind of figured it was because she was hanging at her dad's place in La Jolla.'

'Do you remember the date you last saw her?'

'Few weeks before Christmas I think. I've deleted the messages now, so I can't be more specific.' Paige looked down at her fingernails. 'Christ, I feel so bad about not paying more attention now.'

Rachel smiled sympathetically. 'We can check with your phone service provider… You went to high school with her?'

'Mission Hills, yeah. That's where they found her body. Still really creeps me out thinking about it.'

'Can you think of anyone who was at school with her who might want to do this?'

Paige shook her head slowly. 'Not really. I mean she was definitely one of the popular kids. Prom Queen, head of Student Council.'

'Or why they would choose to leave her in the gym?'

'She was super good at gymnastics. And other sports. I always used to tease her about being a jock.'

Rachel remembered the photos of sports teams in Letizia's album.

'How did she get on with your other classmates?'

'Like I said, she was popular.'

'With everyone?' Rachel pressed.

Paige frowned. 'There were people who were jealous of her, I guess. You know, because she was really pretty, and good at most things.'

'How about boyfriends? Was there anyone special?'

'She never said so, but I doubt it. She was the total player. Screw 'em and dump 'em; that was her style.'

'So someone she dated could have had a grudge?'

Paige put her head on one side, considering this. 'I guess so.'
She did not sound convinced.

The bell on the door rang and another potential client walked
in. 'Sorry, I have to get back to work.'

'Just one more thing: what happened to her apartment?'

'It's listed for sale with a realtor, I think.'

Rachel handed over one of her cards. 'If you or any of Tiffany's
other friends think of anything else that might be relevant, please
get in touch.'

The address of Tiffany's apartment was on the copy of the CasaMia
rental record that Paulie had emailed to her. The period 12–15th
December inclusive; for the use of the mysterious Stacey Gunnarson.
A quick check on her phone map showed it was only a few blocks
away from the tattoo parlour, so she left the car where she had
parked it and walked. There was still time, if she didn't hang around.

A real estate agent's board outside the slick, modern tower
advertised a one-bedroom apartment for sale on the eighth floor.
The apartment number on the CasaMia property was 803, so this
was almost certainly Tiffany's former home. Rachel phoned the
agent, who – when she had mastered her disappointment that
this was not a potential buyer – reluctantly confirmed that the
concierge kept spare keys at the front desk.

Rachel went into the slick marble and glass lobby and produced
her warrant card for the doorman, and after a certain amount of
discussion and a further phone call to the realtor, was handed
the keys. Walking into apartment 803, she couldn't help but be
reminded of Phoebe's apartment in Valley Village. It was smart,
forgettably bland; a paean to beige and brown. Floor-to-ceiling
windows gave onto a small balcony with chocolate-brown wicker
furniture and a spectacular view over the city skyline to the San
Jacinto mountains in the far distance.

A minimal furniture package remained: two sofas and a glass coffee table, a small dining table and four chairs in the living room; a double bed, a tallboy and two bedside tables in the bedroom. A few lamps and some generic framed prints on the walls. It was, as she had anticipated, very clean, apart from traces of the titanium oxide powder that had been used to dust for fingerprints. Rachel worked her way through the kitchen cupboards one by one, standing on tiptoe to reach to the back of the highest shelves. She found a pack of coffee filter papers, but they were otherwise empty. It was the same in the drawers in the bedroom and the built-in shelving in the walk-in closet, where there were just a few clothes hangers on the rails.

The beige marble bathroom had a full width vanity unit with inset double sinks and a fitted cupboard underneath. Rachel opened the doors and squatted down to look in the cupboard, even feeling in the space behind the downpipe, but apart from a packet of toilet rolls it was empty. The glass-fronted medicine cabinet above the sink was empty too. She grabbed the edge of the vanity unit and stretched her right arm as far as it would go, so that she could just – only just – reach the back of the cabinet. Her fingers brushed against a smooth, tubular object. A lipstick case.

Rachel pulled a glove from her pocket and put it on before removing the lid and twisting up the bright orange-red lipstick. Close examination of the label on the bottom of the rose-gold tube revealed that the shade was 'Tangier Nights'. She carried the lipstick over to the living room window and examined it in daylight. Then checked the email from Paulie Greenaway. Checked the lipstick again.

Her hunch was right. It was the exact shade of lipstick worn by Stacey Gunnarson. Also known as Heather Kennedy.

THIRTEEN

If I use a stolen credit card to book a flight, it's going to reveal my destination to anyone who's able to access those account details. But it can still be used to withdraw cash, and in turn that will purchase a seat at the airport ticket desk. And of course it can only be the real deal when it comes to showing a passport; flying on a dead person's passport will be an immediate red flag.

It's good to get home and rest for a while in familiar surroundings. Unpack, arrange the souvenirs, go through the photos. Just like after any regular trip or vacation. The place needs to be cleaned, too, after sitting empty awhile. Then back to research.

There are over 1,500,000 listings to search through, but only a tiny fraction of that total have potential. It's frustrating being told 'Over 300 homes fit your requirements' after the initial search, when this is absolutely not the case. Each profile photo has to be examined in detail then – for the right matches – the secondary research has to be done. This is not just about what people look like. It's so much more than that.

FOURTEEN

Friday morning found Rachel driving on the LA freeway, badly. She still hadn't mastered the skill of changing lanes without risking death, and exits seemed to come and go without warning. Since Officer Brading's squad car was no longer at her disposal, she had decided to extend the rental period when she returned from San Diego the previous evening.

She missed the turn-off for Cypress Park and was forced to do a circuitous backtrack, arriving in the studio parking lot of Baker Boys Productions with clammy hands and jarred nerves. After composing herself for a few seconds, she headed into reception and flashed her warrant card. The receptionist – who Rachel decided was probably a Film Studies student doing an internship – was eager to please, and set about fetching coffee and finding someone who had worked on the Lovely Locks shoot.

'Our in-house staff work on a rotating shift system,' she explained apologetically. 'And directors and producers are on freelance contracts. So the only employee currently here who was working on that day is Tamara. She takes care of wardrobe and make-up.'

If she did 'Phoebe's' make-up, so much the better. 'Perfect,' Rachel smiled.

Tamara was a tall willowy girl with raven-black hair, wearing an embroidered red kimono and Doc Martens. 'I don't really remember it,' she said unhelpfully. 'Like, I've worked on tons of shoots since then. Like, literally hundreds.'

Rachel doubted this, but she had come prepared with stills from the shoot as an aide memoire.

'Oh, right, okay,' Tamara said when she saw them. 'Yeah, I do remember her.'

'What was she like?'

'Quiet. Polite, but, like, very quiet. Didn't say a whole lot.'

'Accent?'

Tamara looked confused.

'Did she speak with a British accent.'

'Hmmm. Not really. Her accent sounded phoney.'

'Phoney how?'

'I dunno, just phoney. But tons of people in this town have phoney accents; I mean it's hardly unusual. It's pretty much, like, normal.'

'Anything else you can remember?'

'Um…' Tamara reached in her pocket for an e-cigarette and started puffing clouds of cinnamon-scented vapour. 'Helps me concentrate…' She screwed up her face. 'I remember her getting freaked out when I did her eye make-up because she was, like, wearing contact lenses and she said the eyeshadow was getting in her eyes. And she didn't want to have extensions put in. But that wasn't a problem, because she had really good hair.' More cinnamon smog. 'Oh yeah, and there was the thing with the shoes.'

'The shoes she wore in the commercial?'

'Yeah, the call details supplied by her agent said she was a shoe size seven and a half, so we ordered them in that size, but they didn't fit her. She needed, like, a nine? She said something about mixing up British sizes and American sizes. We had to phone a freelance stylist to find us another pair.'

'Right…' Rachel absorbed this. Marion Miller would surely have supplied Phoebe's correct size details. 'And where are the shoes now?'

Tamara shrugged, emitting a stream of vapour through her pursed lips like a boiling kettle. 'Gone back to the stylist, I guess.'

'And the dress?'

'Hold on.' Tamara went to fetch a file and checked the contents. 'That was one of ours. It would have gone for dry cleaning. Could still be there?'

Rachel handed over a card through force of habit, even though this was now to all intents and purposes an exhausted lead. 'Well thanks, Tamara. You've been very helpful.'

Tamara waved her spice-scented wand. 'Hey, no problem.'

Visiting Phoebe's former residence in the middle of the day would be unlikely to yield much, given that the apartments were designed for young professionals who would be at work. Rachel returned reluctantly to the Ventana Vista for a few hours.

She couldn't settle. Any time spent doing nothing felt like wasted time now that she had a deadline for her return. She went for a short run in Valley Plaza Park then sat by the pool with her laptop, logged onto Facebook and started searching. There were over 500 Heather Kennedys, and after scanning through dozens of profile photos, her vision was starting to blur. She could find no Stacey Gunnarsons and only one Stacy Gunnarson, who looked as though she was aged twelve or thirteen.

She phoned Mike Perez, the IT guy, who picked up on the first ring. There was a roaring noise in the background.

'Where the hell are you?'

'At the race track in Long Beach. It's my day off. You should come join me.'

Rachel adopted her most professional tone of voice. 'Thanks Officer Perez, but I'm afraid that's not possible. Are you back in Burbank Avenue tomorrow?'

'Um… tomorrow's Saturday. I'm not rostered on this weekend.'

'Any chance you could meet me there, really quickly? I fly back to London on Sunday.'

Perez hesitated a second. 'Sure. I have a bunch of stuff to do, but I could swing by there first thing. Nine o'clock?'

Vowing eternal gratitude, Rachel went out to her tank of a rental car and drove to Canton Place. There were forty apartments in the building, and her first round of knocking on doors led to only five being opened, two of whom were abusive and none of whom remembered Phoebe. Rachel waited in the driver's seat of the tank for another forty minutes, listening to a Christian rock station on the radio, until at least ten cars had driven into the parking garage. Then she started again, excluding the doors that had been opened to her in her first round of knocking. It was pretty hopeless. Only a handful of residents knew who Phoebe was, and none of them could remember noticing anything over a month ago, despite the subsequent police presence.

Finally, she knocked on 509, the door opposite Phoebe's own apartment, and a young bearded man answered. A dog yapped sharply in the background.

'Yeah, I remember her,' he said. 'She was real friendly to start with, would say hi, you know? Nice smile.'

'To start with?'

'You know what; it's weird that you mentioned it, but around the time you're talking about, she kind of changed. In her attitude, you know? She kept her shades on, usually a baseball cap too, and she didn't want to talk. Just kept her head down and hurried past. It only happened once.'

'But it was the same woman?'

'Yeah, it must have been. Long blonde hair. She was wearing the same T-shirt she always wore to the gym. It had "Karma" written on the front. It was round the same time someone sprayed paint over the camera in the garage.'

Rachel showed him Heather/Stacey's selfie. 'Well, yeah. That could be her. Hard to tell when she's smiling and not wearing shades.'

'Do you remember the last time you saw her?'

'Maybe… ten days ago, couple of weeks… Jesus Christ, Van Damme!' He turned to silence the yapping dog. 'Will you cut it out!'

'Did you see anyone else coming and going? Hear anything unusual?'

Beardy Guy shrugged. 'Nope, don't think so. There was a dude I think she was dating, but he always came off like an okay kind of guy.'

'Ever hear them arguing?'

'No, never. But mostly I have my headphones on. And then I guess there's the dog. He's kinda noisy.'

Van Damme let off another volley of yaps to reinforce the point.

'Thanks, you've been very helpful. I'll leave you to enjoy your evening.'

Beardy held up his hand for a fist bump or some other kind of hipster leave-taking, but Rachel was saved from getting it wrong by her mobile ringing in her pocket. She mouthed a goodbye as she answered it, heading back towards the elevator.

'Hi, it's Tamara.'

Rachel's mind was a blank.

'Tamara from Baker Boys. We spoke this morning, about Lovely Locks?'

Ah yes. The cinnamon-breathing dragon.

'Only I went and, like, checked and the red dress used in the shoot didn't go to the dry cleaners yet. I have it here.'

'Fantastic.' Rachel pressed her hand to her forehead, thinking fast. 'Okay, first – do you know if anyone has worn it since Phoebe Stiles did her shoot? Second, do you think you can get it to me?'

'Like, it's possible, but I don't think so. That it was used again. And yes, I can have it biked over.'

Rachel gave her the address of Ventana Vista Suites. God bless America and its twenty-four-hour service culture.

'Also, I talked to the stylist, and she has the shoes. The larger ones that we had to borrow, when the first pair was too small. She works from her home in Topanga, but she says she's happy for you to have them if someone can go pick them up.'

Rachel fumbled in her bag, found a biro and scribbled down the address. Back in the car, her GPS confirmed it was only about five miles away, so she drove to the stylist's pretty whitewashed bungalow and collected the shoes. Beige suede: Prada. And only half a size smaller than Rachel's own size. She resisted the temptation to try them on, placing the bag carefully on the clean rear seat of her car.

She sat in traffic for what seemed like hours, stopped to buy food, and finally reached the motel long after it had gone dark. Her phone rang again as she parked, and her heart sank when she saw the name on the call display. Her sister.

'Have you forgotten what day it was yesterday?'

Skip the niceties and go straight into attack mode: that was Lindsay.

'Of course I haven't,' Rachel said. This was true, sort of. She had remembered the second she saw her older sister's name light up on her phone. 'Mum's birthday.'

'She's ever so upset not to have heard from you.'

'Christ Lindsay, it must be –' she checked her watch – 'five in the morning in the UK.' Only Lindsay, high priestess of passive aggression, would phone at such a ridiculous time.

'I'm aware of the time difference, that's why I'm ringing now. Mum told me you were in States.'

'Exactly. I'm working.'

'You could still have phoned Mum,' said Lindsay sourly.

'Look, things are… I will, okay, I'll phone her. And I'm about to fly back, so I can see her soon.'

'It's not me you need to convince.'

'Bye, Lindsay.' Rachel hung up abruptly, annoyed at her sister for being right. She should have remembered her own mother's birthday. There were amends to be made. As ever she'd been so taken up by her latest case that normal family stuff had taken a back seat.

'Detective Prince.' The receptionist stopped her on her way through the lobby. 'This came for you.' She held up a plastic garment bag.

Back in her room, Rachel found it strange looking at the poppy-red dress she had scrutinised on the screen so many times. The dress worn by Phoebe, or as it turned out, not-Phoebe. Without the ambient wind machines and lighting it seemed two-dimensional. Mundane. She didn't want to contaminate it by touching the delicate silk charmeuse, but it was on a hanger which she removed carefully from the bag, having first slipped on some latex gloves. The label said it was Alexander Wang, US size 6.

Rachel hung it on the back of her wardrobe door, switched off her phone and sat back on her bed. She ate her solitary salad and then leaned back on the pillows, staring at the patch of scarlet silk until her eyes closed and she fell asleep.

FIFTEEN

At nine o'clock on Saturday morning the Burbank Avenue police station was quieter than usual, but there were still a few cars in the parking lot. Rachel recognised the number plate belonging to Officer Brading.

Mike Perez was waiting in his subterranean lair. He was wearing workout gear, and he had brought coffee and iced doughnuts. Rachel looked askance at the pastries.

'Doughnuts, Perez; seriously?'

'I'm pretty sure they're organic.' He grinned.

'Gluten-free too, no doubt.'

Rachel accepted the coffee gratefully and sat down next to him at the computer monitor. 'Officer Perez, now that I'm officially off the Stiles case, and returning to London, I'd like to take this opportunity to thank you for all your technical help and support.'

Perez cocked an eyebrow as he munched on the doughnut. 'But?'

'I'd like your help with one last thing. One second –' she took out her phone, pulled up the selfie of Heather/Stacey and emailed it to Perez – 'check your email.'

He opened the photo on his monitor.

'That's the profile picture from the CasaMia account that was used to book the rental of Phoebe Stiles's apartment around the time she died. The same photo was used on a separate CasaMia account to rent the apartment of a girl called Tiffany Kovak last

December.' She gave Perez a second to catch up. 'She went missing around the same time, and was later found murdered.'

Perez stared at the screen. 'Wow.'

'If it's a coincidence, it's an extremely striking one.' Rachel said blandly.

'But you don't think it is.'

'Of course I don't. There are just too many similarities between Phoebe and Tiffany. And I've only scraped the surface: if I had time and resources I'm sure I could prove the link.'

'And there could be more. More victims targeted via the app.' Perez swung back from the screen to look at her.

'Exactly.'

'So how can I help?'

'I'd like your friends at the biometric lab to compare this face with the face of the girl in the shampoo commercial. The one they've already proved is not Phoebe Stiles.' She took a swig of her coffee, thinking for a few seconds. 'Did you pass that result on to Gonzales?'

'I did, but he said it proved nothing, except that Phoebe died before the date of the shoot. Before February second.'

Rachel screwed up her face in exasperation. 'But doesn't he want to know who that girl in the video is?'

'Not relevant, according to him, since the boyfriend did it.'

'What do you think?'

Perez swung his chair slowly to and fro, as if to calibrate his thoughts. 'What I think and what I can do are two different things. Privately, I think you may be on to something. Officially, the investigation is closed pending Wyburgh's trial, so I can't devote any of my time to it. *Officially.*' He stressed the last word.

'But this is evidence in the case,' Rachel said, stubbornly.

'Trouble is: if it's evidence, then it's effectively evidence for the defence. I'm not in a position to pursue it.'

Rachel gulped down the dregs of her coffee and stood up. 'Okay, I understand. I just had to ask.'

'But…' Perez went on, 'There's nothing to stop me sending this to the lab off the record, as it were. In my own time.'

'Would you do that?'

Perez winked at her. 'Sure. I can call in a favour or two.'

Rachel sighed. 'There's a deadline. I only have till tomorrow.'

'Leave it with me.'

The evidence room and supplies storeroom were at the back of the building on the ground floor; Rachel remembered seeing officers go in there to fetch latex gloves. She found it, and knocked on the door. Nothing.

Cautiously, glancing over her shoulder to see if she was being observed, she opened the door and went in. Rows of open metal shelving lined the room, filled with labelled boxes. The older ones were cardboard, the newer ones clear plastic. The forensics supply cupboard was definitely in here somewhere. She worked her way methodically around the edge of the room.

'Can I help you, ma'am?'

Officer Brading stood in the doorway.

'I need gloves, Officer, and evidence bags.'

He gave Rachel a long look with his sad brown eyes but did not demur, reaching onto a high shelf and handing her boxes of both. She helped herself, stuffing them into her own bag.

'So,' she said to him, 'case solved. I guess I should be congratulating you.'

His face was sombre. 'Wyburgh's definitely putting in a not-guilty plea, so a jury will get to decide.'

'Will he be remanded until then?'

Brading shrugged. 'Probably not. Bail hearing's on Monday morning.'

'So where is he now?'

Brading hesitated. She knew he didn't want to answer her, and she knew exactly why he didn't want to. The time they had spent together had made it easy for her to read him. After a few seconds he relented.

'He's right here in the cells, ma'am.'

'May I speak to him?'

Brading kept his eyes fixed on a point slightly above her head, his right hand resting reflexively on his pistol. 'I'm afraid that won't be possible.'

'Officer.'

'Ma'am?'

She forced eye contact and held it. 'There's a whole lot more to this case than a slighted boyfriend and a crime of passion. I know it, and I know you know it. So let's cut the crap.'

He shifted his weight fractionally, hand still on his holster, but said nothing.

'Look, I'm about to go back to the NCA in London. My part in this is over. So, off the record, tell me what you really think. I know you have good instincts, and that they're speaking to you, even if you're keeping a lid on them.'

Brading sighed, looking like a fifteen year old being taken to task by his mother for leaving dirty socks under the bed. 'I don't know who killed Ms Stiles, but I don't think it was Wyburgh.'

'Despite the forensic evidence found at his home?'

'Despite the forensic evidence, yes ma'am.'

'So,' She reinstated the uncomfortable eye contact. 'Why do we find ourselves here?'

'Because Captain Dench is retiring at the end of the summer and he just wants a quiet life. Wants the case tied up before he goes. So he leaned on Gonzales to charge the suspect.'

This was the frankest thing that Brading had ever said, as well as his longest utterance. Rachel stared down at the empty evidence bags while she adjusted her expectations. 'I need to talk to Wyburgh,' she said finally. 'It's not going to change anything at this stage – I'm getting out of here – but for my own satisfaction I just need to eyeball him. I can always tell.'

'Your instincts, ma'am.'

'Precisely.'

Brading scrunched up his eyes. 'Okay,' he said, exhaling hard. 'Just five minutes. But I know nothing about it. And I didn't give you the key.'

He handed her the key, and for the first time ever she saw him smile.

Matt Wyburgh was sitting on the edge of the bench that also served as a bed, dressed in prison sweats and shoes with the laces removed. He hadn't shaved in days, and there were magenta circles underneath his eyes. He raised his head when Rachel came into the cell, but his expression remained blank. He was clearly too exhausted to experience an emotion as piquant as curiosity.

Rachel sat down next to him on the vinyl mattress and extended a hand, which he did not shake. 'Hi, Matt. I'm Detective Inspector Prince.'

The meaning of his look was clear: *I don't care if you're Santa Claus.*

She knew she had to employ extreme caution in what she said now. If she told him that she believed he was innocent, and that she might have evidence that someone else killed Phoebe Stiles – if she even implied it – the ramifications would be huge, catastrophic even. His lawyers could claim the LAPD had at best been incompetent and, at worst, framed Wyburgh. And the fact that she was a British police officer who currently had no jurisdiction carried international implications. So she had to be very, very careful.

He wouldn't make eye contact, but she plunged on regardless. 'I'm from the police in London, here to help the LAPD because Phoebe Stiles was a UK citizen.'

He did not look up, or react to the sound of Phoebe's name.

'I'd like you to tell me what you know, or remember, about what happened around the twentieth of January.'

'I've been through it over and over. I've made a statement.'

'Please, Matt. What do you think happened?'

The use of his first name caught his attention.

'Is this some kind of trick? Because I'm pleading not guilty? You guys hoping I'm going to say something to incriminate myself?'

There was a glimpse of anger amid the outright weariness.

'Look, I'm not writing this down, and I'm not recording it.'

'You could be wearing a wire.'

Rachel smiled slightly, stood up and lifted her T-shirt, high enough to reveal all of her bra. She turned slightly so he could see the back view. Wyburgh flushed slightly, but did not avert his gaze.

'Could be in your pants.'

She unzipped her trousers and lowered them as far as decency would permit, then pulled up the legs to show there was nothing attached to her calves. 'Feel free to pat me down if you like.'

'No, it's okay.'

He relaxed fractionally. Rachel sat down again and they faced each other.

'Just tell me anything that comes to mind, in your own words. That's all I want.'

'I didn't kill her.'

I know, she wanted to say, *I know you didn't.*

'How did you and Phoebe meet?'

'In the Furnace. It's a club in West Hollywood.'

'And how did you feel about her?'

'I really liked her, you know, she was great. She had that weird British accent; I thought it was cute.' He shrugged. 'She was fun to be around.'

'Did you love her?'

'Man…' Wyburgh leaned back against the wall and ran his hands over his face. 'Not really. I mean, I loved hanging out with her and stuff, but not like, *love* love.'

'You weren't *in* love with her?'

'No. Fuck's sake, we'd only known each other a few weeks. That's why this is all so fucked up.'

'So you weren't heartbroken when she ended it?'

'No, man! I mean, sure, it seemed kind of odd the way she went dark on me like that. I wanted to talk to her, but it was really just to check she was okay. She was supposed to be staying with me when she rented out her apartment, and as far as I knew she didn't have any place else to go. She didn't really know anyone in LA. That's why I went over there when she wasn't answering the phone.'

'And the weapon they found in your apartment?'

'They're saying it was a marble doorstop from the hallway of her apartment. I'd never seen the fucking thing before, but they said it was in the corner of my garage, propped against the wall.'

'You didn't see it there?'

'I only know last time I went in the garage it wasn't there. I know that for a fact.'

'And when was that?'

'Just before I went to Reno. I was putting my surfboard away.'

'So how could it have got there? Did anyone else have keys?'

'My folks. And I had a set cut for Phoebe because she was staying over quite a lot and it just made things easier, you know?' There was the ghost of a smile. 'Put them on a funky little keyring with a P on it. I told the cops that, but they said the keys weren't found at her apartment. They disappeared.'

'So the doorstop definitely wasn't there before your Reno trip?'

'For one thousand per cent sure. Whoever put it there must have known I'd be away.'

'You're saying it was planted?'

Wyburgh rolled his eyes wearily. 'Come on, Detective, do I really seem that dumb? I go to my girlfriend's place, hit her over the head with something from her own apartment, then I take it back to my place, covered in her blood, and leave it against the wall of the garage in full view, blood and all? Nobody would do that unless they were completely stupid, or completely insane.'

His look challenged her. She couldn't fault his logic. She had known criminals rely on logic to stand up their stories many times, but this was different. She believed him; it was as simple as that. The casual sexual attraction he described did not fit with a calculated brutal slaughter, and he was right: the weapon would either have been left at the scene or tossed.

'Indeed,' she said, trying to keep her tone neutral. *Fingerprints*, she was thinking. *Tell me about fingerprints.* She didn't dare ask, because he would be assuming she knew about that detail already.

'They didn't find a single fingerprint, but the cops just said I must have wiped them. Like I'd wipe off every single print but somehow leave all the blood right there. Makes no fucking sense.'

I know, Rachel wanted to say. *I agree.* Mustering her neutrality, instead she said calmly. 'Your defence lawyers will no doubt be looking into all of that.' She stood up and extended her hand. 'Good luck. I mean it.'

SIXTEEN

Rachel put on a single pair of gloves. There was little point in double-gloving at this stage: the items had all been handled by multiple un-gloved hands. She dropped the Tangier Nights lipstick, the red dress and the shoes into separate evidence bags, sealed them and labelled them with Phoebe's full name, date of birth and the linked LAPD case number. Then she dialled Rob McConnell's cell phone number.

He picked up straight away. There were voices in the background which became fainter as he adjusted his position.

'Two minutes.' He hung up.

When he called back, the background noise was gone. 'Hi,' he said. 'Nice surprise on a Saturday.'

'Sorry to call at the weekend… I have some stuff to courier to you. Real stuff, not digital stuff. Okay to send it to you at National Central Bureau?'

'Are you still in Los Angeles?'

'Yes, but not for long. Leaving tomorrow morning.'

'One second, let me just check something.'

The line was muted for a couple of minutes. When Rob came back he asked, 'What's the address where you're staying?'

She gave him the street address of the Ventana Vista.

'Cool. Someone will be there to collect the items in a few hours.'

'Okay.' Rachel was thrown by this. 'Well, I guess I can put everything else in an email.'

'Great. Listen, I have to run.'

And he was gone.

This was probably her last chance to use the motel pool, and she was going to make it count. For the first time since she arrived, she was not a solitary user. There were a couple of people swimming, and several more on loungers. Rachel swam forty lengths and lay in the sun for half an hour, topping up what was now quite a respectable tan.

She would miss this: but she needed to get back. There was Joe, for a start. And Brickall had been less communicative than usual. Her sixth sense and years of experience of his moods told her something was troubling him. It was time to get back to her real life.

As she unlocked the door to her room, heading to take a shower, her phone rang.

'Hi, is that Detective Prince?' It was an unfamiliar voice; female, middle-aged bordering on elderly.

'It is. Who am I speaking to?'

'Renée Foster. Blair Lundgren gave me your number.'

'Blair Lundgren? I'm sorry—'

'He lives here. At Canton Place apartments. We both do.'

Ah, Phoebe's neighbour. Mr Beardy.

'We were chatting by the garbage chute, and when I told him I'd seen her, he gave me your card.'

'You saw her?'

'The girl from apartment 510. The English girl.'

Rachel dropped her towel and grabbed her notebook and pen. 'When was this?'

'About a week ago, I believe. I was at Valley Plaza with my daughter and I saw her outside the pharmacy. I recognised her from her baseball cap, and the blonde hair. It was the Padres one she always wore around the building. You noticed it because everyone wears Dodgers caps here. The Padres are San Diego. I said to my daughter, "That's the English girl who's living in Canton Place."'

San Diego. Rachel's stomach did a little flip.

'And you're sure this was around a week ago?'

'Yes, certain, because we were shopping for my grandson's birthday party, and his birthday's February 23rd.'

It was now February 28th. Ten days since Phoebe's body was found, many weeks since she was killed.

'I phoned my daughter just now, and told her I was going to speak to the police. She said she thought it was February 21st, but that the CCTV at the mall would be able to confirm it right away. They have cameras everywhere.'

'I'll phone the shopping mall and ask them if they can assist. Thank you Renée, that's very helpful.'

'They're saying she died, but that can't be right, can it? She's not dead. We definitely saw her.'

'I'll look into it.'

Still in her damp bikini, Rachel googled the office number for the Valley Plaza Shopping Centre. There was no reply. After five minutes more of online searching and clicking, she found a customer service number, which was answered on the third attempt by a bored sounding clerk.

'Office opening hours are Monday to Friday, nine thirty to five thirty.'

'It's Saturday: the stores are still open. There must be security guards there right now?'

'Mmmm hmmm.'

'Well I need to speak to their supervisor.'

She was given an alternative phone number, which went straight to voicemail. 'You're through to Secure Group at the Valley Plaza. There's nobody here to take your call, but please leave your message after the tone.'

Rachel hung up, exasperated. The chances of anyone calling back seemed slight, and even if they did, unless she could view in person whatever footage they still had, this would not progress the lead. She considered driving to the mall. It was only four o'clock; there was still time. But the chances of finding someone authorised to identify the correct CCTV footage and show it to her seemed vanishingly small. They would almost certainly tell her to come back on Monday. She picked up her laptop and started trying to compile everything she knew into an email to Rob, but her brain felt as though it was about to explode.

Stop. You need to stop, she told herself. *It's time to take a step back.*

After a shower, and with the warmth of the day receding, she drove to the drugstore to pick up some supper, treating herself to a bottle of chardonnay to mark the fact that this was her last night in North Hollywood. She would have preferred to walk there and back to help unscramble her thoughts, but the courier still had not arrived to collect the evidence bags, and she didn't want to increase the odds of the service arriving while she was out. At six o'clock there was still no courier. Rachel checked with reception, but was assured nobody had asked for her. Seven o'clock: still nothing. She tried to phone Rob, but her call went straight to voicemail. At seven forty-five there was a knock at her door. She grabbed the evidence bags and opened it.

Rob McConnell was standing there, a flight bag slung over his shoulder.

Rachel looked him up and down. 'What the fuck?'

He grinned. 'Thought I'd pick up those exhibits in person.'

'From Washington DC?! That's on the other side of the country. Are you insane?'

'You going to ask me in?'

She let him pass her. Instantly the room felt too small, too shabby for his large, glowing presence. She was hyper-aware of the gleam of the golden hairs on his tanned forearms, the chrome of his expensive pilot's watch, the flash of his even white teeth. She also felt acutely conscious of her make-up-free face and sloppy jogging bottoms, the half-eaten salad on the desk, the open suitcase she was in the process of packing. She made a token attempt at tidying away the clothes on the bed, but Rob held up a hand.

'Hey, don't worry, I booked a room down the hall. I have my own space to mess up.'

'You're staying here?'

'I was actually at Dulles when you phoned. I'm on my way to Seattle to meet with the FBI office there and talk about drug trafficking. Heroin from Mexico: the usual. So I was flying west anyway.'

'This is the scenic route, is it?'

'Kind of. I managed to change my flight last minute, and book one from here to Seattle in the morning.'

He turned his light blue-grey eyes to meet Rachel's. She flushed slightly. *Stop acting like a clueless schoolgirl.*

'I see.' She could sense his need for her to say more. 'Sorry, I'm just trying to take this all in. It's a bit like walking into a darkened room and all your friends leaping out and shouting "Surprise!"'

Rob laughed. 'I get it. Why don't I go and dump my stuff and we can catch up later?'

'Meet me by the pool,' Rachel told him. 'I have wine.' She brandished the half empty bottle of Chardonnay.

Twenty minutes later, Rob was waiting for her on the pool terrace. She was carrying the wine and two plastic cups and had exchanged her sweats for jeans. She was also wearing the minimum amount of make-up that could be applied without looking as though you had applied make-up. A complex balancing act that a man would fail to recognise. This thought was making her smile as she sat down beside him.

'So – am I forgiven for the surprise party?' he asked, pouring them both wine.

'Absolutely. I'm actually very glad to have you here,' she confided. 'To have someone to discuss the case with,' she added quickly.

They moved to the edge of the pool and sat with their feet dangling in the cooling water, while Rachel worked her way through every angle of her investigation. The list was a long one: the trip to San Francisco and the discovery that the renter of both dead girls' properties used the same profile picture, the fact that both profiles were fake, her interviews with Phoebe's agent, neighbours and accused boyfriend, the forensic reports on both apartments, the visit to the production crew, the analysis that proved the girl in the shoot was not actually Phoebe, her visit to San Diego to find out more about Tiffany Kovak. Then she voiced her doubts about the evidence the LAPD had on Matt Wyburgh.

'You've done all of this in a week, alone? For real?' Rob stood up and refilled their plastic cups, then sat down beside her again.

'I have.'

'That's seriously impressive: you're like some kind of machine. Little Miss Tenacity.'

'Think how much I could have achieved if there were a whole team on this, and not just me. God!' She slapped her hands down on the pool edge to emphasise her frustration. 'I've got to walk away now and there are so many more questions.'

'What can I do to help?'

'For starters, can you see if the dress, the shoes and the lipstick give us anything?'

'Of course. I'll send them off to CODIS. That will tell us if any DNA matches samples on existing crime databases… their reach is nationwide. And we'll cross-check the items with each other.'

'Can you get someone to check footage from the shopping mall where Phoebe was seen? Except obviously it can't have been Phoebe.'

'Sure. Don't know how long it will take, but I'll try."

'And maybe the CCTV images of Tiffany Kovak's car…'

'Yes ma'am.' He put down his cup of wine and made a mock salute.

'It's okay, I'm going to email everything I have to you, you don't have to try and memorise it.'

'You really care about what you do, don't you?' Rob turned to face her, placing his hand lightly on her arm. Rachel nodded.

'Yep. It's pretty much all I do care about.'

He did a double take. 'Really? No significant other, no kids?'

Rachel hesitated. 'I have an eighteen-year-old son. I care about him, obviously. But he doesn't live with me.'

'Oh, I'm sorry.'

'Don't be: we still have a great relationship, and he's going to university soon anyway. Actually, he's never lived with me: I gave him up for adoption.'

Rob could not quite hide his shocked reaction. 'Jesus, Rachel, that's—'

She put her fingers on his lips to stop him. 'If you're about to say it's awful then think again. You wouldn't want to patronise me, would you?'

He held her wrist, her fingers still against his lips, holding them there for a few seconds. His breath on her fingertips set off a familiar tingle in her core.

'Patronise you?' he spoke very quietly. 'That's not what I want to do.'

They finished the wine, and Rachel stood up and collected up the empty bottle and cups. Rob followed her into her room, as she had known he would. *You shouldn't do this*, the voice in her head said sternly. *You've only just made the new rule and you're already breaking it. Rob's an important professional ally, and if you're ever to have any hope of resolving this case you're really going to need him. Romping around with him in a motel room is potentially risking that goodwill.*

'We shouldn't do this.' She voiced her thoughts out loud, as he stretched out on her bed, trying to make the move look casual. He caught sight of her expression and sat up again.

'Hey, we're just hanging out, aren't we?'

'I suppose so.' Rachel perched primly on the edge of the bed, steadfastly avoiding eye contact. It didn't matter that she quite liked the idea of kissing him: she was not going to do it. Her mind was already flashing back to a similar scene in a hotel room in Edinburgh, when Giles Denton had stretched himself out on her bed. And that had not ended well.

Her mobile rang.

'Ignore it.'

But her instincts and training forced her to glance at the display, and when she saw it was Mike Perez's number she moved away from Rob and picked up.

'Hi?' she said, breathing a little more heavily than she would have liked.

'Hi to you too. Hope I'm not interrupting something?'

'No, no, I'm just… hanging out.' She felt her face colour, and was glad Perez couldn't see her.

'I have something for you. D'you want to maybe get dinner?'

Rachel laughed. 'Sorry Mike, I'm afraid I've already eaten.'

Rob disentangled himself and stood up. *I'll leave you to it,* he mouthed at her, and left the room. As Rachel's eyes followed him, she missed what Perez was saying.

'Sorry, what was that?'

'I said there wasn't a match. That photo – it's not the same girl as the one on the shampoo video.'

'Really?' Rachel straightened up. 'Damn. But I guess that's not so surprising. If you're setting up a fake profile it makes sense to use a fake photo.'

'Figures,' agreed Perez. 'I also got a buddy of mine to run the photo and a still from the video through the NGI-IPS. You don't need to know what all those letters stand for, but it's the facial database used by the FBI. They have access to thirty million mugshots, and driving licence photos from most states. No hit for the girl in the video, but we have a strong match for the profile photo. I'll email you her details.'

'That's fantastic. Thanks so much, Mike.'

'Be aware that the results sometimes throw up a false positive. It's not proof of anything at all, just someone who needs to be ruled out… so, you sure about dinner?'

What is it with these American men? Rachel wondered.

'I'm sure. Thanks,' she said firmly, hanging up.

She knew Rob's room number; she could go there now. She wanted to go there now. She picked up her key, walked to the door but stopped with her hand on the doorknob. She sat down on the bed again.

She wasn't going to go. That was definite. Tempting or not, she wasn't about to become entangled with either Rob McConnell or Mike Perez. As she walked into the bathroom to undress and brush her teeth, the room phone started ringing. It could only be Rob: he was the only person who knew her room number. She ignored it and eventually it stopped.

Her phone pinged.

It was the email from Mike Perez. She decided to read it in the morning when she was less tired and could give it her full attention. For a while she dozed in front of the TV, ignoring the phone by her bed as it rang once, twice, three times. Eventually, at nearly midnight, it stopped. Relieved, she switched off the light and crawled under the covers.

*

She was woken at eight by a knocking on her door. Rob was standing there with two cups of coffee, and seemed unfazed by the fact that she was wearing just T-shirt and knickers.

'Peace offering,' he held out a coffee.

'Do we need to make peace?' She took the coffee but did not invite him in. Fusty sheets and morning breath were not on her list of ways to impress.

'Calling you last night. I wondered afterwards if that was a bit…'

'Pushy?'

'Yeah. When you didn't pick up I debated with myself whether I should come over here in person. And while I was trying to decide, I fell asleep. Sorry.'

'Don't be.' She gave him a rueful smile over the rim of the coffee cup. 'I wouldn't have asked you in.'

'You have the prettiest eyes,' he told her.

'They're mud colour: that's what my dad used to say.'

'Used to?'

'He's dead.'

'I'm sorry.'

'Don't be; it was nearly eighteen years ago.'

Rob was still scrutinising her face. 'I'd say they were hazel. Kind of brown and kind of green.'

Rachel had already started backing away. She was starting to feel uncomfortable, and annoyed with herself for giving him mixed signals the evening before. 'Listen, I'm going to jump in the shower. I need to check in around ten, so I should get going.'

'I'll give you a ride to the airport.'

They didn't talk much in the car; Rachel watching the California landscape that slipped past her. Strip malls, distant hills and in between them a thousand palm trees pushing up towards the sky. Even when they were pinioned in one of the inescapable LA freeway jams, Rachel remained silent. They arrived at LAX dangerously late for the London flight, and she was forced to flash her police warrant card to jump to the front of both the check-in queue and the line for security screening. Rob showed his Interpol ID to gain access to airside, and together they ran to the gate. He stopped at the top of the jetway and waved her on.

'Go. Go! They're closing the goddam door.'

He reached forward to kiss her on the cheek, but she had already ducked away and was heading down the ramp, glancing over her shoulder as she went. He raised a hand in farewell, turning to go only once she had reached the door of the plane.

The female flight attendant took her boarding pass with one hand and ushered her firmly with the other.

'You're almost out of time.'

'No,' Rachel corrected her. 'I *am* out of time. Completely, one hundred per cent, out of time.

PART TWO

'There are times in life when people must know when not to let go. Balloons are designed to teach small children this.'

Terry Pratchett

SEVENTEEN

'Tinned peaches.'

Eileen Prince put two bowls down on the table. 'I've got evaporated milk if you'd like it?'

Rachel was at her mother's house in Purley for the weekend, ensconced in a womb-like space of familiar scents and sensations. Nubbly candlewick bed cover, Pledge furniture polish, china muffled by tablecloths, faded curtain fabric that let in sulphurous-yellow street lighting, the faintest cloud of dust when you sank onto the velour three-piece suite. She had been greeted equally enthusiastically by both her mother and Dolly the American Cocker Spaniel. Dolly had once been fostered by Brickall, but Eileen had ended up giving her a permanent home when it became obvious that Brickall's work schedule was not sufficiently dog-friendly.

'What?' Rachel looked up from checking her phone, absently fondling the pale gold fur on Dolly's skull as she waited for falling scraps. 'Oh, no thanks. Just the fruit is fine.'

'You should put that thing away at the table,' Eileen said firmly. 'It's bad manners.'

'Yes, you're right.' Rachel slipped it into her bag and turned her attention to trying to harpoon the peaches with the edge of her spoon as they slid around the china dish.

'You're not really here,' observed her mother. 'You've been like it ever since you arrived: twitchy, mind on something else.'

'It's the jet lag.'

'You've been back two weeks already!' scoffed her mother.

'Sorry Mum, it's been busy at work and I suppose I haven't had a chance to unwind properly yet.'

'Well, that's what you're here for,' said her mother, ladling out more peaches. 'A bit of R & R. Bit of looking after.'

'I'm here because Lindsay gave me a telling off,' Rachel said bluntly. 'And to give you your birthday present, obviously.'

There'd been no chance to shop in Los Angeles, but Rachel had grabbed the most expensive old-lady-friendly perfume she could find in the Heathrow duty free when she landed.

Eileen Prince sighed. 'It's different for Lindsay. She's very settled so she doesn't always understand how things are with your work.' Her mother gave another exaggerated sigh as she started to clear the dishes. 'It would be nice if you could settle down outside of work though. You need a nice boy.'

'Mum, I'm forty years old.' Since she was not a fan of parties, Rachel had let this milestone slip by a few months earlier with no more than drinks with a few colleagues. 'I don't need any kind of boy. Anyway, I've got a boy: he's called Joe. It's hard enough trying to find time to spend with him.'

'You know what I mean. You need to find yourself a nice man. Like that Howard. He was nice. I still don't understand why you saw fit to end it with him.'

Knowing that it would provoke, Rachel asked, 'How do you know I haven't already found one?'

'Have you?'

'No.' Rachel kept her head down, stacking plates in the dishwasher. She had never told her mother about her brief car crash of a relationship with Giles Denton, and she was not about to do so now. And she certainly wasn't going to mention her almost-involvement with Rob McConnell.

'Why don't you go for one of your jogs?' Eileen asked. 'That might blow away the cobwebs. You can take the dog.'

'Mum, nobody calls it jogging anymore.'

But she went upstairs and fetched her running shoes and pounded the twilit suburban streets of Purley with Dolly until tiredness started to set in. Then she and her mother settled themselves in the sitting room with the *Radio Times* (potential viewing ringed in red biro) and a bag of humbugs. They did the crossword together, watched a show about antiques and then a Danish drama, which Eileen insisted on having turned up very loud, despite the subtitles. This was followed by the ritual mug of Horlicks and a digestive biscuit, before retiring to the lumpy single bed she had slept in as a teenager. The following morning, after a cooked breakfast that she didn't really want, Rachel helped her mother weed the flowerbeds and drove her to a pub that boasted a Sunday 'carvery'.

'I'd better get back,' she told Eileen once they'd driven back to the modest 1930s semi on a pleasant tree-lined street. The very model of Middle England, one that had provided Rachel with both a stable upbringing and a burning need for excitement.

'I've made a Victoria sponge.'

'Oh, go on then,' Rachel conceded, allowing herself to be force-fed tea and cake, despite not being in the least bit hungry. The slabs of carvery beef and rubbery Yorkshires sat like concrete in her stomach.

'Make sure you bring that lovely grandson of mine to visit soon,' Eileen said as she reached up to kiss her daughter goodbye.

'I will,' Rachel promised. 'As soon as I can.'

It was dark when she drove back to Bermondsey. For once she wasn't looking forward to being back there, or to returning to work in the morning. When she had returned from California two Mondays ago, she had taken a cab straight from the airport to the office, as promised. Nigel Patten had called her in for a debrief, but he was officially still on paternity leave, and it had been short and perfunctory. Back at her desk, her caseload seemed to have mushroomed while she was gone, and little work had been done on her existing files. There were over 300 emails to answer, statements to read, endless updating, chasing, reviewing. For the foreseeable future she would be deskbound.

If Brickall was pleased to have her back, he went to extreme lengths to hide it. He was unusually subdued. His resentment, on the other hand, was out in the open. There were frequent references to 'people who skive off' and 'sunning yourself in foreign climes' (she couldn't hide her Californian tan). When she tried to discuss the Stiles case with him, he yawned theatrically or changed the subject. There was something up with him, and Rachel intended to call him out on it.

Meanwhile, she desperately wanted to talk to him about the case, to go through all the twists and turns and dead ends and find out what he thought. She had been plunged into an intense experience then yanked away from it, and was now expected to behave as though it had never happened. But it had happened, and it was still happening, spooling in her brain like an endless movie trailer. Scraps of images and scenes all sliced together: Washington's stately streets, Officer Brading's gun in its holster, a girl in a red dress laughing in the rain, the yellow sofas at CasaMia, Phoebe's coffin, San Diego's palm-fringed bay, Paige's tattoo needle, Matt Wyburgh's five o'clock shadow. Rob's expression as he tried to kiss her.

Rob was in her thoughts yet again as she swung into the office on Monday morning. She hadn't heard from him since she left Los Angeles, but since it was he who had taken responsibility for following up leads on her behalf, she would just have to wait for him to make contact. She pushed him from her mind as she sat down heavily at her desk, spilling coffee on her files as she did so.

'You're such a klutz,' observed Brickall. 'And you needn't have bothered sitting down – Patten wants us in the conference room in five.'

'Happy Monday to you too.'

'Human trafficking.'

Patten slammed a large file on the desk for dramatic emphasis. 'Specifically bringing young girls into the UK to work in the sex trade.'

Brickall rolled his eyes. Patten ignored him. 'We've had intelligence from the Nigerian Crime Commission concerning one Florence Obatola, aged forty-eight.' He pulled a mug shot out of the file. 'Apparently she approaches young girls in isolated villages in Nigeria, offering them the chance to study at a "college" in London.' He'd made air quotes, prompting another discreet eye roll from Brickall. 'They're scooped up and taken to the airport in Lagos and never seen or heard from again. The Met have had a tip-off about a property in North London where they believe girls are being held against their will. The witness says he saw some young women through an upstairs window who appeared to be IC3, and reported sounds of screams and loud cries.'

'So what's our involvement, sir?'

'Ultimately, if this tip-off proves correct, act as liaison when it comes to getting Obatola to court. But first I'd like you to do some onsite surveillance.'

Brickall groaned. 'Isn't that Plod's job?'

'I want us to have oversight from the start, and that involves building a picture of what's going on,' Patten told him firmly. 'You've both got plenty of tactical ops experience: grab yourselves an unmarked vehicle, vests and tasers and get yourselves over there.'

*

'Well this is a great way to spend eight hours,' Brickall observed, as they sat parked in a narrow street near Turnpike Lane.

Opposite them was the shabby terraced house that had been reported to police. The grimy windows were obscured by pieces of cloth that had been pinned up in place of curtains. There were no signs of life, nor had there been for the past hour. A couple of boys sped past on skateboards, the occasional pensioner shuffled past. Brickall was in the passenger seat, with his feet up on the glovebox. He leaned forward and started drumming rhythmically on the dashboard with his forefingers. When this elicited no response from Rachel, he took a box of matches from his pocket and started lighting them and blowing them out one by one. When he got to the tenth match, Rachel snapped.

'For God's sake, Brickall, you're not twelve! Why don't you go and buy us a coffee and something to eat? I'll be okay here for five minutes.'

Leaving his stab vest on the front seat, Brickall sloped off and returned with two milky coffees (he knew full well that Rachel drank hers black), a couple of chocolate bars and a packet of crisps, which he proceeded to eat noisily and messily, spraying the interior of the squad car with greasy potato dandruff. Once the food and drink had been consumed, Brickall amused himself collecting up the burnt matches, making holes in the box and sticking them in so that the whole thing resembled a bizarre carbonised hedgehog. Rachel kept her eyes fixed firmly on the front door of the house. Once or twice, the makeshift curtains twitched, but no one came in or out.

'Good weekend?' Brickall asked eventually.

'Went to my mum's house. So, pretty unexciting. Apart from Sunday lunch at the local carvery, which counts as exciting in my mum's book.'

Brickall started to dismantle the hedgehog. 'See Joe?'

She shook her head. 'Too busy with his social life. I think there might be a girl on the scene. You?'

He didn't reply.

'Look, Mark, I know there's something bugging you. Just tell me what it is.'

'Not now, okay? Not while we're on obs.'

Rachel sighed. 'Okay.'

They sat in silence for another two hours, then took it in turns to use the toilet in a local café, then ate the sandwiches Rachel had bought on her earlier visit. Buggy-pushing mothers returned from collecting their children from school. By now both Rachel and Brickall were both fighting cramp, shifting uncomfortably in their seats.

'Oh, go on then, you know you're dying to,' he said eventually.

'What?'

'Tell me all about what you got up to in Hollywood.'

'Blimey, you must be bored.'

Brickall found some chewing gum and offered her a piece. 'Well, go on then.'

She gave him a potted version, despite them not being short of time.

'So they found evidence on the boyfriend and charged him. Sweet: job done.'

Rachel sighed. 'Yes, but it's not that simple. The evidence against the boyfriend is at best weak, at worst suspicious. And then there's this other case that was strikingly similar.'

'Yeah, but you weren't assigned to the other case, were you?'

'But if this is a serial killer and the two are linked—'

'Prince, you know bloody well homicides only rate the term "serial" if there are three or more, each separated by a significant period of time.'

'We don't know there aren't more.'

The afternoon was fading into evening. A light went on in one of the upstairs rooms, then, as Rachel instinctively leaned forward for a better view, it was switched off again.

'"We"?' scoffed Brickall. 'There is no "we". It's not your case any longer. You need to get over yourself Prince, and move on. Case closed: forget about it.'

EIGHTEEN

It seems to take forever this time. Nowhere is just right, nowhere fits the bill. From time to time I take out my keepsakes and look at them for inspiration: the baseball cap and the cutesy keyring.

Time is ticking on, and pressure is mounting. People are starting to ask questions.

'Why haven't we seen you around?'

'Where have you been?'

'What's going on at work right now?'

'How are things with you?'

And finally, there it is. So I have to move quickly. I have to show flexibility over dates, otherwise it can't happen.

'There is one thing,' she writes. 'I will be there to meet you, but after that I have to be out of town for a while. Sorry!!'

She adds a kitsch little sorry face emoji. Whatever.

'But my boyfriend is around and he will be on hand to help you with any problems or issues you might have! I'll make sure and leave a note of his details for you!!'

She really likes exclamations marks. And emojis. They always do. They're always that kind of girl.

'Perfect,' I message her back, and I'm being genuine. This could not be more perfect.

NINETEEN

'I reckon this tip-off is bullshit.'

Rachel and Brickall were still in the car. It had long since gone dark, and lights in windows were being extinguished one by one as people went to bed. A steady drizzle was falling, so they were forced to keep the ignition switched on to intermittently clear the windscreen.

'If there's any movement it's going to be after dark.' Rachel reminded him.

'It went dark hours ago.'

Rachel checked her watch. 'Let's give it another hour and then head for bed.'

Brickall managed a faint grin. 'Best suggestion I've heard all day.'

'Don't be a twat.'

As the wipers cleared the screen, Rachel caught sight of a figure walking purposefully towards the house in question. Florence Obatola.

'That's her.'

Brickall reached instinctively for his radio handset and it bleeped into life. A light went on and there were figures glimpsed moving around behind the makeshift curtains. Then the sound of an unmistakable female scream, high-pitched and distressed.

'We should go in,' Rachel said, her hand on the car door.

'Don't be an idiot, Prince; we don't know who's in there or if they're armed. I'm calling for a PSU.'

Three minutes later an armed response vehicle roared into the street and four officers in full tactical gear jumped out, the letters NCA in large letters across the back of their jackets. Rachel and Brickall stood in the doorway as the door was broken down.

'Armed police!'

They emerged a few minutes later with Obatola and two men in handcuffs. 'There are five girls up there, three of them chained to the walls,' one of the officers told them. 'We're going to need more backup.'

Rachel and Brickall ran into the building and up the stairs. Two terrified girls crouched on the floor of one room, the door of which had been broken down by the armed officers. The other three were in a larger room, their wrists chained to a metal rings on the wall. A bucket in each room acted as a makeshift toilet.

Rachel crouched down next to one of the girls. 'My name's Rachel? What's yours?'

No response.

'Do you speak English?'

They stared at her dumbly.

'It's okay,' Rachel told them gently. 'She pointed to the chains and mimicked a cutting action. 'Someone's coming to take this off. You'll be okay now.'

An hour later, after the Nigerian girls had been taken to hospital and Obatola and her associates had been remanded in the cells in Wood Lane police station, Rachel was at home, under a hot shower. She stood there for a long time, trying to unknot her stiff joints and aching muscles. Nearly twelve hours sitting still in the front of a mid-sized saloon car would do that to you. She thought about going for a run through the deserted Bermondsey streets – along the Thames Path perhaps, but decided she was simply too tired.

And finally, there it was. A watched phone never rings was the adage, and the moment sheer exhaustion prevented her checking, there was an email from Rob. She made herself a cup of tea and climbed into bed with her laptop to read it.

From: Robert J. McConnell
To: Rachel Prince
Miss Tenacity,
Sorry not to have gotten back to you sooner: I've been waiting on various pieces of information to come in, and I figured feeding it to you piecemeal would get kind of annoying. So, here goes...
First, the DNA evidence from the dress, shoes and the lipstick. The dress gave two different samples of female DNA. (You mentioned that someone else could have worn it before or after our mystery girl.) Only ONE of those samples matches material found on both the lipstick and the shoes, which narrows it down neatly to one suspect. That's the good news. The bad news is that this DNA sample was not a match for anything held on any criminal databases here in the USA. I cross-matched it with every agency available. So we're not looking for someone with a long rap sheet. Or any rap sheet.
We received images from the security cameras at Valley Plaza mall from 21–23 February. There is indeed a female wearing a Padres baseball cap but her face is mostly obscured by the peak of the cap and large sunglasses, so we don't really know anything other than that this person purporting to be Ms Stiles is young and with slim build. I've attached a copy of the images.
The images of Tiffany Kovak's Toyota SUV are similar – there appears to be a young, long-haired female at the wheel but she's wearing sunglasses and the face shots are blurry. As you know, photos of a driver at the wheel are rarely distinct enough to stand up in court.

Last, there's the match with the CasaMia profile picture used by both 'Heather Kennedy' and 'Stacey Gunnarson'. This was identified by your co-worker at LAPD as belonging to Jennifer Van der Wieke, from the photo on a driver's licence issued by the state of Pennsylvania. I arranged for Van der Wieke to be questioned but she claims that the photo was lifted from her Facebook account. Her story and background check out, and there is no discernible link with Tiffany Kovak or Phoebe Stiles. It seems to be a straightforward case of cyber catfishing.

Rachel already knew this much. Jennifer Van der Wieke had been named by Perez in his final debrief email. Once she had arrived home, she had googled Van der Wieke and trawled doggedly through the girl's entire social media footprint, but this seemed to be no more than a pretty young blonde girl whose pouting selfie suited the suspect's purposes. A face that fitted. And a girl who was away travelling in Europe for three months.

She admitted that she favoured lipstick in a shade similar to the one we tested, and readily provided a DNA sample, which was not a match. So that bit seems to be a case of life imitating art. (Or maybe it's the other way around).
Of course it did occur that Van der Wieke herself could be a target, in addition to her image having been targeted, so her local police department have been informed and she's been advised on extra security in her home. She does not currently list her home on CasaMia and has never done so.
That's about all I have for now. Catch you later, Rob.

Rachel wanted to re-read the information and absorb it before replying, but was painfully aware that tomorrow would be a long, fractious day of dealing with Social Services and interpreters.

From: Rachel Prince
To: Robert J. McConnell
Rob, thanks for this – I'm very grateful for all your efforts. Please
do contact me if you find out more. Rachel x

She deleted the kiss, then reinstated it. As she was about to close her laptop, it pinged at her. The alert she had set up for mentions of Phoebe Stiles had been updated with a fresh result.

It was an article from the *Daily Mirror*.

TRAGIC PHOEBE'S DARK SIDE

A former classmate of tragically murdered actress turned reality star Phoebe Stiles, Lauren Mitchell, 25, has revealed that she has a mean girl past. 'Phoebe was a proper bully at school,' she told the Mirror. *She thought she was popular, but people didn't like her, they were scared of her.*

Some details about Phoebe's death followed, including the fact that her boyfriend had been charged. There was a paparazzi shot of Phoebe in her spray-tanned glory next to a picture of Lauren with arms folded and an indignant expression on her face. She was a plain girl with stringy hair, hoop earrings and a jailhouse tattoo on her upper arm. A meagre anecdote about Phoebe cutting off someone's ponytail and laughing about it was then padded to take up 200 words.

Rachel reached for her notebook and wrote '*Lauren Mitchell?*' before switching off the light and falling instantly asleep.

TWENTY

So much for the smooth check-in process. This time it doesn't exactly go to plan.

It has to be the swift, clean blow from behind. I don't want to look them in the eyes, see their reaction. That's not the point. I just want them gone, out of the way, so I can feel what it's like to be them. It also needs to be executed with something that belongs in that place; an object that's suitably blunt and heavy. And since I'm no bigger or stronger than they are – how could I be, right? – I have to rely on the element of surprise.

Only this time, as she opens the door, she says: 'I'm sorry, but I've literally only got a couple of seconds and then I've got to run.' She has her purse and her keys in her hand, her suitcase at her feet to show she means this. 'The instruction book is in the living room, along with a set of keys and the contact details for my boyfriend.'

I spot a heavy brass jardinière on the hall stand, and I pick it up as though admiring it.

'Oh, careful with that; my gramma gave it to me. It's kind of precious.' To make her point she wrests it out of my hand and puts it on a high shelf in the kitchen, out of reach. 'All righty then, I really hope you enjoy your stay.' She moves past me to the door.

I am now behind her and I take the only course of action available to me. I remove my fabric scarf and lasso her with it, looping it tight round her neck and twisting the ends around my hands. She's strong and somehow turns so she's facing me. I can see the panic in her reddening face, the slight bulge in her eyeballs. No, no, no, *I'm screaming in my head,* this is all wrong. *What if she manages to get free?*

I slide my hands down the scarf so that they're closer to her neck as I tighten it, but the flimsy fabric isn't giving me enough traction. In a split-second decision, I let go of the scarf and put my hands directly round the throat, feeling for the hyoid bone. Crushing it. It takes what feels like a very long time, but then it's done. I can let her fall.

Her face is an ugly purple, which is really not what I wanted. I like them to be tidy, to look as though they're just sleeping. She'd dropped the purse, but her fingers still cling onto the car keys. I put on latex gloves before prising them away and tossing them on the hall stand. Then I consult the instruction manual. 'Clean linen supplies are in the closet in the bathroom.' *I find a sheet and cover her with it. Disposal can wait; for now I want to explore.*

Her closet is organised in a rather prissy fashion by garment length and colour, but she has good taste, and there are lots of things I want to try on. Not too many though, because everything will need to be cleaned. At the end of the dress section there is a plastic garment bag containing an almond-green prom dress. It's long and elegant with thin shoulder straps and a small train. On the shelf above the rails there are some hats, Including a glittery beauty queen's crown. Of course she would have been prom queen. I put on the dress and crown, removing the latex gloves long enough to admire my reflection in the closet's full-length mirror.

In the bathroom, I pick through the well-organised trays and baskets of make-up. I add some blush, try a lipstick (taking care to set it aside to dispose of later), spray some of her perfume. It's a cloying, sickly scent; the kind that's packaged in a flower-shaped bottle and marketed to sixteen-year-old girls.

In the living room there's a handwritten note with the cell phone number of her boyfriend. Clayton Hill. It sounds like a place. There are framed photos on the shelf of the storage unit showing her in the arms of a muscular young man. He was almost certainly prom king. A jock. He looks a bit of a brute, but he's a handsome brute.

'Anything, you need,' *the note says,* 'just call Clayton!!' *I remove the new phone from its packaging and add his number to Contacts.*

TWENTY-ONE

The Nigerian girls made a heart-wrenching sight. They were huddled in one corner of the room that had been allocated to them at a north London women's refuge, like a flock of bedraggled birds. Flightless birds. They stayed closed to the wall, as though still chained.

After checking on them, Rachel went to speak to the refuge manager. It had been agreed that they would be interviewed there, rather than being taken to a police station, which could traumatise and frighten them.

'How are they doing?' Rachel asked the manager, a kindly but rather brisk woman in her fifties.

'Well,' she shrugged slightly. 'Obviously you've just seen for yourself: they're not great. But they have eaten and drunk a little.'

'Okay, that's something.'

'There is a problem though,' the manager went on. 'The interpreter that was sent speaks Hausa. That's the most prevalent Nigerian language apparently. But he said that these girls are Igbo speakers.'

Rachel sighed. 'I'll have to make some phone calls – I expect I can find an Igbo interpreter; the question is how long that's going to take. We need to start the interviews as soon as possible.'

'The Hausa interpreter knew some basic Igbo; enough to get their names and ages. Although you'll have to get Social Services to do a Merton age assessment to check they're telling the truth.'

She handed Rachel a piece of paper. One thirteen year old, two fourteen year olds, a sixteen year old and an eighteen year old. *Thirteen. Christ.*

Brickall was already on his way to the refuge, but Rachel phoned the Crime Support Unit and after a game of telephonic pass-the-parcel, spoke to someone who had two Igbo interpreters on their books. Both interpreters would be with them in around an hour.

Brickall arrived, accompanied by a video operator. He was in a bad mood, which usually indicated a hangover. When Rachel told him they were waiting for the correct language speaker, he swore colourfully.

'We can get the interview room set up in the meantime,' Rachel told him.

'But this is going to take forever as it is; we don't need delays on top. Not with the bloody headache I've got.'

Rachel reached into her bag and handed him paracetamol tablets. 'Tell you what; we've got two interpreters, why don't we request a second video operator and then we can do two sets of interviews simultaneously.'

'Fine,' said Brickall gruffly. 'You phone them while I'm finding a coffee.'

The interviews were laborious. Rachel started with the youngest girl, Ifeoma, who was so pathologically fearful that she would not even raise her head at first, let alone speak. It did not help matters that the interpreter was male, but Rachel thought it was more important for Brickall to use the female interpreter to temper his very masculine aura. Piece by halting piece, she and the interpreter coaxed her story out of her.

Someone had come to Ifeoma's village, spoken to her father, promising that she could go to London and study English, then get a well-paid job. She was not asked if she wanted to go. Did she want to, Rachel asked via the interpreter? No, she did not. She wanted to stay at home with her parents and her brothers and her grandmother. She had cried when they told her about it.

Then one night she was woken and put in the back of a large van. It drove through the darkness for many hours. A lady was with her who said she was called Auntie Florence, but she was not a real aunt. They went to a huge building with many aeroplanes and she was taken onto the plane with Auntie Florence and another girl called Essie. When the plane reached England they were not taken to a school or college, they were taken to a house. She kept asking why they were there, until Auntie Florence beat her. So then she shut up. She and the four others were kept chained to the wall most of the time, but sometimes they would be freed long enough to clean themselves up and be taken to another house, where strange men would do terrible things to her.

It took some time and a lot of very careful prompting to get Ifeoma to expand on this. Eventually it was established that they inserted their male organs into her, in more than one orifice. It made her bleed. Sometimes they were rough and bit and slapped her. Auntie Florence regularly beat her. Once when one of the other girls tried to run out of the house, Florence told the two men who worked with her to beat her too. These two men regularly raped the girls, whenever they felt like it.

After she had finished with Ifeoma, Rachel phoned the police surgeon who had examined them in hospital the night before, and checked that he had given a formal statement of his findings and that photos had been taken of any injuries. Then she interviewed fifteen-year-old Essie. Essie was a little bolder and more confident and seemed to welcome the chance to talk about what had happened to her. Her story was very similar to the younger girl's, save that in her case she had positively yearned to go to England and study. The subsequent shock and disillusionment had made her angry. She was the girl who had tried to run away.

Rachel checked the video recording, then went in search of coffee. She did not expect to bump into Brickall in the hallway, looking pleased with himself.

'Job done, thank Christ.' He waved a sheaf of paper in her direction. It looked suspiciously like a hand-written witness statement.

'Hold on, what's that?'

'The statement made by the eighteen-year-old. The video guy had to leave, but she's too old to require Special Measures so I did a routine pre-statement notice.'

Rachel stared at him. 'Routine as in you wrote down what the interpreter said and got them to read it back to her in her own language?'

'Yep.'

'And the witness signed it?'

'Of course. Don't worry, I took an accompanying statement from the interpreter too; it's all covered.'

Rachel was shaking her head.

'How do you know she understood it? These girls have had no education.'

'Because I told the interpreter to ask if the kid was able to read and she said yes.' Brickall scoffed.

'Back up the truck, Einstein…' Rachel was already checking her watch and taking out her mobile. 'These girls have been beaten and abused into compliance; they're going to say whatever they think we want to hear. We can't be sure she really does know how to read; not at any level of complexity.'

Brickall looked exasperated. 'I did the standard procedure we do with any non-native English speaker. She knows what's in her fucking statement: it was read to her in her own language!'

Rachel was shaking her head slowly. 'But there's something else you've overlooked. Something even more important.'

He looked blank.

'She says she's eighteen, but there's no documentation to back that up: she doesn't have a birth certificate or any genuine ID.

She might be younger. Considerably younger. And if she is, she needs Special Measures.'

'Shit.'

'You know how this works: if the fact we've just *assumed* she's of age comes out in court, the defence will try and use it to throw out her case. Belt and braces, Detective Sergeant.'

'Fuck, we're going to have to video her, aren't we?' Brickall covered his face with his fingers.

'Don't panic, I think my video operator's still packing up, and I can phone the office and tell them to send one of the interpreters back here. They can't have gone too far. They'll have to claim an additional fee, but I'll sort that with Upstairs.'

After a couple of phone calls, the female interpreter returned, cheerfully confessing that she had been having 'a cuppa and a cig' at a nearby coffee shop. An hour and a half later, and the video interview of the allegedly eighteen-year-old Augustina had been completed and Rachel and Brickall were in her car on their way back to the NCA offices.

'What a fucking carry on,' Brickall said. 'This is why I bloody hate trafficking cases.'

'Stop stressing: we got it done.'

'Thanks to you spotting the glaring error.' Rachel knew Brickall well enough to know that it pained him to acknowledge this. 'There would have been a right old shit storm if I'd submitted that written statement to the CPS. You can bet it would've got back to Patten.'

'No problem, fuckwit.'

They both let it go unmentioned that, after his recent six-month suspension for professional misconduct, Brickall could not afford to be caught making any more mistakes.

'Seriously, I owe you one.'

'Good, because I was going to ask you a favour.' They were at a set of traffic lights, so she could turn her head to the left and look at him. 'Quite a big favour.'

Brickall groaned. 'Suppose I can't really say no now, can I? Go on, what is it? You want me to set you up with that new guy in Child Protection, the one who's replaced You Know Who.'

He never mentioned Giles Denton by name, as though he was Lord Voldemort. There had been little love lost between him and Denton when they worked on cases together, but after the Irishman abruptly left his job at the NCA, simultaneously abandoning his romance with Rachel, Brickall was even more full of bile.

'I want you to come on a road trip with me.'

'Road trip? What the fuck, Prince?'

They were now turning into the basement parking area of the NCA. 'Come over to mine for a drink this evening and I'll tell you all about it.'

TWENTY-TWO

I take a handful of kitchen towel and throw it into the toilet bowl. Using the handle of the toilet brush, I push it down towards the U bend, then attempt to flush. It won't. Instead the water level swirls and rises queasily towards the rim. Then I text Clayton.

I check my phone every ten minutes or so, for the next couple of hours. Nothing. This is infuriating. She said that he would be on hand to help. That implies a certain level of responsiveness. I pace, unable to settle.

After more than three hours he replies.

Sorry, was at the game. Coming over now.

Of course this guy was at the game. That's where all guys like him are.

As I answer the door, he does a double take at the resemblance between me and his girlfriend. 'Wow,' he says, 'It's like she's still here!'

Technically she is, wrapped in a sheet on the floor of her closet.

'How'd the toilet get blocked?' he wants to know.

I tell him I was doing some cleaning in there and accidentally dropped the paper towel into the bowl. He accepts my explanation without question. 'Sure. The bathroom does look super clean.'

He clears the blockage by sticking his hand in and pulling out the towel. I could have easily done this myself, but this fact doesn't seem to occur to him. I offer him a cold beer, one of the six pack I bought specially. I don't drink beer, but I hold a bottle and pretend to swig. He doesn't notice that the level of liquid in my bottle isn't going down, because his eyes are focused on my chest. I'm wearing a sheer chiffon blouse that I found in the closet, through which my pink bra is clearly visible.

When he realises his staring is obvious he blusters about noticing my top, asking if it's his girlfriend's. I tell him it's mine. 'Weird; she has one exactly like it.'

'It's one of my favourites.'

'It's hot,' he leers.

We chat for a while. His small talk is leaden and predictable and I am bored. I can tell that he's thinking about going to bed with me.

'Guess I'd better get going,' he says eventually. 'But anything you need.'

I nod, already knowing what his next chore is going to be. He'll be back.

TWENTY-THREE

'Are you sure you actually live here?'

Brickall was standing in the living room of Rachel's flat, looking around at the bare walls, minimalist furniture and general absence of belongings, save the running shoes in the hall, a couple of pot plants and a colourful rug.

'What – just because it's tidy? Trust me, it doesn't look like this when Joe's been staying here.'

'But you tidy up after him?

'Of course.'

Brickall shook his head. 'Still can't get used to you being a mother. I don't think I'll ever get used to it.'

'It's only been six months: it's all still pretty new.'

She was slowly becoming accustomed to the practical and emotional demands of parenthood, but compared to most women with teenage children, she needed 'L' plates. Besides, Joe's adoptive parents were still his parents. She and her ex-husband Stuart Ritchie were content to play a peripheral role.

'Hasn't changed your design choices, that's for sure.' Brickall indicated the spartan décor. 'Still light on the personal touches.'

Rachel pointed to a framed photo of Joe that had pride of place, then handed him a can of lager. 'See – doesn't get more personal than that. Anyway, look how useful a bare white wall can be.'

She indicated the longest wall in the sitting area, where she had Blu-Tacked all the printable evidence from the Phoebe Stiles case. There were blown up photos of Tiffany Kovak, Phoebe Stiles and Jennifer Van der Wieke (aka Heather Kennedy or Stacey Gunnarson), crime scene photos, the CasaMia listings, stills from the Lovely Locks commercial and from the CCTV at Valley Plaza. She handed Brickall a file containing crime reports and forensic results, which she had attempted to place in some sort of chronological order.

Rachel poured herself a glass of wine and sipped it slowly while Brickall flicked through the papers.

'Okay, so the MO with Phoebe Stiles was a bash on the back of the head with a lump of marble… how about the first girl?' He flicked back to the crime report on Tiffany Kovak.

'She was hit on the back of the head with a Padres souvenir baseball bat. That's her local team. Their stadium's a couple of blocks from her apartment.'

'And afterwards they find the baseball bat in the apartment, but it's been completely cleaned using Citranox. That's a very… strange… touch.' Brickall pursed his lips with a sort of grudging respect. He put the file down and looked at the pictures on the wall. 'So this person here, wearing a Padres cap, who is this? Not Tiffany presumably.'

'That's someone a neighbour in Los Angeles identified as Phoebe Stiles. Except it can't have been Phoebe, because on the day in question she was definitely dead.' Rachel put down her glass of wine and joined him at the wall, pointing to the still from the commercial. 'It could be the same person as this girl, but it's hard to tell from the CCTV images.'

'Christ, talk about wheels within wheels. This is a right old hall of mirrors you've got here, Prince.'

'Mixing your metaphors after just the one beer,' Rachel grinned. 'Seriously though Mark, what's your gut telling you?'

He thought for a few seconds. 'That this isn't someone who enjoys killing. It's almost as if they want to get the killing bit out of the way so they can get to the good bit. So – what's the good bit? You'd think it could be robbery, except if I understand the reports correctly, nothing was stolen. And the places were left clean and tidy.'

'Pathologically clean,' concurred Rachel. 'Literally.' The doorbell rang and Rachel went to admit the curry they had ordered. She laid out the food on a tray with plates, forks and paper napkins and plonked it on the coffee table. 'Tuck in.'

As she bit into a poppadum, sending greasy splinters all over the front of her sweatshirt, she asked, 'So what about the CasaMia link? How does that fit in?'

Brickall was washing down a mouthful of rogan josh with his lager. '*Is* there a link though? I don't know how you can be sure, given that literally millions of people use the site. Isn't that like saying two crimes are linked because the victims both use Facebook?'

Rachel shook her head violently, covering her mouth to stop her pilau rice escaping. 'Not when the person who rented both girls' apartments used the same profile photo.'

'Unless you've got a forensic link, that's still just circumstantial.'

'The girl in the video is the key to this; I'm sure of it. She turned up at the shoot safe in the knowledge that the real Phoebe wouldn't show. She could only have done that if she knew Phoebe was dead. And the DNA she left in the dress and the shoes is the same as the DNA on the lipstick I found in Tiffany Kovak's apartment. *There's* your forensic link. You can't possibly say that's circumstantial.'

Brickall considered this as he chewed on a naan. 'Fair enough. So if the perp *is* the girl in the shampoo ad – or her accomplice – then she's targeting women who all have a very similar look to her own.' He pointed to Tiffany, Phoebe, Jennifer and the Lovely Locks girl. 'Look at them; from a distance they could be quadruplets. So what the fuck's that all about?'

'That's what I need to find out.'

Brickall siphoned lager from the can and wiped his mouth with the back of his hand. 'It strikes me that this is a hell of a lot of trouble to go to when the killing itself is so perfunctory, almost an irrelevance. She drives around San Diego in Tiffany's car, wearing a lipstick that she's copied from *this* chick,' He stood up and tapped Jennifer's photo. 'Then in LA, she turns up at professional shoot and does Phoebe's day job for her. It's a bit like that thing De Clerry… De Clarry…'

'De Clerambault's Syndrome.'

'That's the one. Where the sufferer believes they have a relationship with someone they don't know at all.'

Rachel considered this, picking bit of poppadum off her sweater. 'Kind of, but that's not quite it. There's a piece of the puzzle that we're missing, but I can't quite work out what it is.'

Brickall belched discreetly. 'What can you do about it from here? Not a fat lot.'

'Where Tiffany's concerned, no, but we can look harder at Phoebe. *Know your victim.*'

'And other great crime-solving clichés,' Brickall quipped. 'I'm guessing this is where the road trip comes in?'

Rachel nodded. 'This weekend. You up for it?'

'Go on then.' Brickall sat down on the sofa, closer to her this time, and put down his can. He scrutinised her face, and there was something in his gaze that made her hackles shoot straight up. 'You know something Prince, you're not a bad-looking bird when you make the effort. Quite pretty.'

Rachel indicated her curry-stained hoodie and tracksuit bottoms. 'I sincerely hope you don't think this is making an effort.'

'Maybe it's because your hair's down,' He tweaked one of the long blonde locks that fell around her shoulders. 'You always have it tied up at work.'

He didn't relinquish her hair, but wherever he thought this was headed, it was not somewhere she had any desire to go. In fact, his sudden change in manner sent curdling panic through her. *Not Brickall, for God's sake.* Never Brickall. That was the last taboo.

Keep the deflection light, she told herself. *Don't bruise his ego.* 'I sincerely hope you're not making a pass at me, Detective Sergeant?'

He jutted his chin defiantly. 'What if I did?'

'Don't be daft; you know you're not my type.'

'And why's that? You never did say.'

'You swear too bloody much.' She stood up and lifted the tray of dirty dishes to avoid having to overtly recoil. 'Now go on with you, it's a school night.'

TWENTY-FOUR

I love office supplies stores. They're full of interesting stuff, and the way they're laid out makes them feel neat and orderly. I like that.

So although this is a visit of expediency, I spend a happy afternoon pushing my giant cart up and down the aisles. I pick up a bale of air cushion packaging for void-filling, some heavy-duty tape and a large double-walled cardboard shipping box. 'Military grade!' *it boasts on the label.* 'Suitable for machinery and small engine parts. Recommended weight up to 150lb'. *This will be sturdy enough, I decide. I already have gloves and cleaning stuff.*

Back at the apartment I text Clayton. Need you to help me with something real quick. I have pizza!

I add a pizza emoji followed by a smiley emoji, because that's the sort of girl he's used to. Those *sorts of girls. He replies within seconds with a tongue-out emoji.*

I drag the sheet-wrapped body out of the closet into the hallway. I've had the aircon switched up high, but even so it's high time for it to leave before decomposition really kicks in. I fold it into the box (really hard to do single-handed; I'm sweating by the time I'm finished), press the air-pocket wrap into all the spaces and tape the box up tight. She can't weigh more than 125 pounds, so it should hold fine.

The doorbell goes as I'm fixing the last bit of tape. I shove the gloves out of sight, open the fridge and answer the door holding a 15" pizza box. This guy is sure to think bigger is better.

We decide we'll do the drop while the oven is heating, then come back and enjoy the pizza. I tell him it's some unwanted stuff from the apartment of my recently deceased aunt, which I'm donating. 'That's cool,' he says, as he hefts the box into the bed of his pickup. He doesn't complain about how heavy it is, because he wants to appear macho. Of course he does.

I tell him there's a special place the charity uses for people to leave donations, which they collect another time. As we pull up into the lot, the penny drops.

'Hey, I know this place!' he says, looking up at the facade of the theatre. 'This is where they held the Miss Carolina Teen USA pageant.'

It's a disused, boxy suburban theatre standing alone at the centre of a massive parking lot. The billboard at the front announces a residency by a third-rate country and western singer, but nailed on top of that is a makeshift sign. 'Closed for Remodelling'.

'You went to see it?' I ask, as he lifts the box out of the truck. I hope the air pillows are preventing the contents from shifting around too much. 'Well, yeah.' He has the grace to look embarrassed. 'My girlfriend, you know… she competed.'

I point to side of the building at the very back. It's in the shadow thrown by the overhang of the roof and away from the amber glow of the lot lighting. He puts the crate down and stands there staring at it.

'Pizza!' I grab his thick wrist and swing on it, my tongue caressing my top teeth, so he knows there's more than stuffed mozzarella crust on offer.

'All righty then.' He walks back to the truck without a backward glance.

Back at the apartment, he's eager, greedy. He wants sex and pizza, but definitely sex first. He grabs me, kissing me with too much tongue, which I find gross. I push him backwards onto the couch and straddle him, riding his erection like a metronome, back and forth, back and forth. I position him there because I know that while he's fucking me, he'll be able to see the photos of himself and his late beloved on the bookshelf, over my left shoulder.

The pizza is done at the same time that he is. I take it out of the oven and serve him three slices, placing one for myself on a plate but not eating it. He doesn't notice; shovelling the gooey cheesy bread down his throat as fast as he can, licking his fingers.

'Hold on a second, I just want to check something...'

I grab my iPad and look at an imaginary website while he chomps and slurps. 'Oh God, I totally got the address wrong. We left the box in the wrong place. It's not 208 East Broadway, it's 3208.'

'I thought it was kind of a weird place to leave stuff, by the theatre.' He grabs a kitchen towel and wipes his hands. 'But it's no big deal. We can go back and move it.'

'Are you sure?'

'Do you have ice cream?'

I shake my head.

'We can grab ice cream on the way back and eat it in bed.'

I grin. 'Great idea.'

I pick up my bag and my cap, he picks up another slice of pizza and we head back downstairs to where his truck is parked. My heart is thumping hard as we approach the theatre. What if the box isn't still there? But it is. Of course it is. Nobody's going to notice it in the darkness.

He jumps out of the truck before me, in a hurry for ice cream and more sex. There are latex gloves in my bag and I put them on, pick up the jack that I spotted on the truck bed when we loaded the crate and follow him. He's squatting to lift the crate when I bring down the jack in exactly the right spot at the back of his skull. Quick and clean. He slumps over the crate. I planned on sitting his body up against the side of it, like a broken action figure against a toy box, but this is kind of perfect. His body drapes over his girlfriend's in death, as it no doubt did in life. And he will be heavy to move, which will waste precious time. I need to leave.

I toss the jack back into the truck, pull down my cap, put on shades even though it's pretty much dark and drive his truck to some wasteground near railroad tracks. There are no security cameras. I leave it there with the keys in the ignition and walk quickly back to the apartment, tossing the vinyl gloves into the dumpster outside a fast food restaurant, where they will soon be obscured by half-eaten burgers and milkshake cups.

By the time I get back to the apartment, I'm starving. I sit at the table and eat the one slice of pizza that Clayton has left.

TWENTY-FIVE

The rolling hills and fields of Warwickshire gave way to dense suburban sprawl with a distinctly industrial top note.

Rachel's phone was propped on the dashboard with Google Maps open. As they turned off the motorway she had asked Brickall to navigate, but instead he was staring out of the passenger window, seemingly oblivious to Rachel's rising stress levels as she negotiated the intersection of the M40 and M42. It was the first time in a while that she had seen him out of a suit. He wore expensive branded jeans, a checked shirt, and twenty-four hours' worth of stubble.

'As soon as I leave the M25, my driving skills go to hell,' Rachel told him. 'The provinces put me into a panic.'

Brickall grunted, but made no comment. He was in a dark mood. This had become obvious by the time they were on the M40, but by then it was too late for him to unjoin their road trip.

'Which way now?' Rachel asked him.

'Why don't you just switch on the satnav?'

'Because it shafts the battery. And anyway, I've got a navigator – you.'

He picked up her phone with a sigh, and looked at the directions on the map. 'You need to continue up the A38 and then make a left down Middle Park Road. Which the satnav would tell you if you turned it on.'

Rachel shot him a glance, but said nothing. She'd experienced a fair few of his moods over the years, and knew not to poke the bear. She also had a suspicion that this time it stemmed from her awkward rejection of his pass, when he had come round to her flat for curry and crime analysis. And that was not a subject she wanted to examine.

They drove into a post-war estate of boxy townhouses. Brickall followed Rachel up the path of the scruffiest property: the front garden unkempt and the hung tiles slipping. 'This is Lauren Mitchell; she's a former classmate of Phoebe Stiles's,' Rachel told him.

'Right,' was all he said, reaching for his warrant card.

The door was opened by a plain girl with bad skin and long, straggly black hair. She wore the hoop earrings she had favoured in her interview, and badly fitting leisurewear that cut into her flesh, making her look bigger than she was. The tattoo on her upper arm was of a shooting star, and there was one just visible on her neck, that might have been a bluebird or a penguin; it was hard to tell.

'Awroight?' The accent was thickest Brummie.

'I'm DI Rachel Prince and this is DS Mark Brickall.' Brickall held up his card silently. 'Could we have a word?'

'What's this about?'

'It's about the article you did on Phoebe Stiles.'

Lauren looked wary. 'Am I in trouble?'

'No, we just need a chat.'

'But I won't get paid for it or nothing?'

Rachel shook her head. 'No,' she said with as much patience as she could muster. 'We're from the police.'

They went into a cramped living room, decorated in migraine-inducing fuchsia with a silver feature wall. There were some ornamental dried grasses in a pot in one corner, and a lot of silver and pink themed knick-knacks on every surface. The place had a sour smell blending stale biscuit crumbs and cheap perfume. Somewhere, a bin needed emptying.

They perched themselves on the black leatherette three-piece suite, Rachel and Brickall on the sofa and Lauren on the armchair.

She lit a cigarette and puffed the smoke up to the ceiling, cheap bracelets jangling every time she raised her hand to her lips.

'We're part of an investigation into Phoebe Stiles's death,' Rachel began. This was stretching the truth a little, but it would suffice. 'So we'd just like to talk to you a little about the things you told the newspaper.'

'Wanna cuppa tea?'

Rachel glanced at the grimy kitchenette. 'No, don't worry, we've just had some. Perhaps you could just start with telling us what sort of girl Phoebe was.'

Lauren curled her lip, smoke escaping in little tendrils. 'To be honest, I wasn't that surprised when I heard someone killed her. She was a nasty piece of work.' She emphasised the short Brummie 'a'.

'In what way?'

'She picked on people. Enjoyed it, you know. People she thought weren't as great as what she was.'

'Great in what way?'

'You know – pretty, nice clothes and stuff.'

'Was that what Phoebe was like?'

'She was spoilt rotten – anything she wanted, she got. Always had the latest clothes, jewellery, phone. Got her hair done in a posh salon, always had the most expensive make-up.'

'And she was pretty?'

'Suppose so. The lads all thought so, anyhow.'

'So what kinds of things would she do?'

'If she thought someone looked rubbish, she'd pick on them. Like there was this girl Nicky—'

'Were you in the same class as Phoebe?' Brickall interrupted.

Lauren looked surprised. 'Ooh, 'e speaks does 'e? Strong, silent type are ya?' She gave a flirtatious cackle.

'Go on,' prompted Rachel.

'This girl Nicky, she was really quiet, bit of a loner. Bless 'er.' Lauren tapped the ash off her cigarette. 'But she was really good at art. Phoebe deliberately knocked a pot of paint all over her art project. Ruined it.'

'Kids do stuff like that though,' Rachel offered. 'I'm sure I saw stuff at least as bad when I was at school.'

Lauren sucked her cigarette. 'That's not all though. When Nicky got a cold sore, she spread a rumour it was herpes, from giving the janitor a blowie. She'd be horrible to the younger girls too, the new Year Sevens. She'd tell them they weren't allowed to go into the toilets, and she'd get lads to stand there blocking their way until eventually one of them wet themselves. She'd take their phones off them and use them to sext the sixth formers.'

'You mean—'

'She'd send them mucky pics and pretend they'd come from the Year Seven whose phone it was.'

Brickall raised his eyebrows at Rachel. 'Thank God they didn't have camera phones when we were at school, eh?'

'And she was vile to anyone who was fat. There was this one time she nicked some sticky tape from the DT lab, wrote "Wide Load" on it and stuck it on Carly Taylor's back. Carly had a bit of a weight problem,' she added unnecessarily. 'Everyone was laughing and high-fiving Phoebe and she loved it. She loved being centre of attention.'

'Was she popular? Did she have friends?'

'The lads all fancied her. She had a great figure, to be fair.'

'And the girls?'

'She had her so-called mates around her, and they always did what she told them to. But I reckon most of them didn't really like her, they were just scared of her. If you didn't back her up, she'd turn nasty.'

'And how about you, Lauren? Were you friends with her?'

Lauren stuck her chin in the air. 'Not really, but I could look after meself, so she kept her distance from me.'

'And when did you last see her?'

Lauren thought. 'Must have been two or three years after we left school. Bumped into her with her mum down the shops. But then she got the job on that soap and she was always getting herself in the papers… don't think she bothered much coming back here after that. Too busy showing off.'

That was one way of summing up Phoebe's career, Rachel thought, *and not necessarily inaccurate.*

'Is there anyone else we could talk to, who might be able to corroborate this.'

'*Corr…* what?'

'Confirm what you've said. Someone from the school perhaps?'

'It's Saturday,' Lauren pointed out. 'You're not going to get much joy down the school.'

'Anyone at all you can think of who was there at the same time?'

Lauren chewed a cerise acrylic fingernail. 'Well, there's Miss Perry. She's retired now, but I know she still lives local; in a bungalow down Shenley Fields Drive. She was dead nice, so I expect she'd talk to you.'

'We'll see if we can catch her.'

'She'd be dead old now, so she's bound to be in. What else is she going to be doing?' Another cackle.

Brickall stood up, and Rachel followed his cue. 'Thanks Lauren, you've been very helpful.'

'You sure I don't get paid?'

June Perry's bungalow could not have been more of a contrast to Lauren's house. Pretty, well-kept garden, patterned carpets and heavy curtains, the smell of furniture polish and baking.

'We'll get a decent cup of tea here,' Rachel whispered, as they were shown into the lounge.

'Dead old' turned out to be a wiry and fit-looking seventy-something. 'Excuse the gardening clothes,' she told Rachel and

Brickall. 'I've been putting in the early annuals.' She fussed around them and, as Rachel had predicted, offered tea, which arrived on a tray lined with a linen cloth. Bone china cups and saucers and home-made shortbread.

'I made it this morning,' she beamed. 'I like to have something in the tin for when people come round.' Brickall took two pieces and slurped his tea noisily.

'It's just the most dreadful business, young Phoebe being taken from us like that,' Miss Perry said when they were seated on the mock brocade furniture in an open-plan lounge that had sliding doors onto the garden. A tortoiseshell cat wound its way round Rachel's legs, then jumped onto the arm of her chair and nudged her hand with its head, making her slop her tea.

'Can you tell us your memories of Phoebe?' Rachel asked, once the cat had been removed and shut out of the room. 'What kind of girl was she?'

June Perry considered this. 'She was always a bright spark, even though she didn't excel academically. And such a pretty little thing. Her poor parents doted on her. I wasn't surprised when I heard she'd gone into acting: she certainly had a flair for the dramatic.'

Rachel thought of the endless tabloid break-ups and make-ups.

'How was she with the other pupils?'

'She seemed to be always in the thick of things,' Perry ventured carefully. 'The centre of attention. I suppose she was popular.'

Brickall gave Rachel a sharp look, which she knew only too well after years of doing joint investigations meant *Get to the point.* Before she could frame her next question he said, 'There have been allegations that she was involved in bullying.'

June Perry put down her cup and saucer. 'I think bullying is a word that's overused these days. Darlington Road Comprehensive was a fairly rough and ready place then; there was behaviour throughout the school that fell short of desirable at times. Yes, Phoebe had a side to her, and she could be sharp, mean-spirited even. I would say that much.'

'Do you remember who her friends were?'

'She had a little gang, but I don't remember there being any one girl in particular.'

'Was there anyone who would carry a grudge?'

'I remember she was particularly… mischievous with Nicola Whittier, but she's a trainee accountant now and I hear she married recently. It seems unlikely.'

'How about Lauren Mitchell?'

June Perry shook her head. 'No. They weren't friends, but Phoebe knew better than to pick on Lauren. She was a tough nut. Difficult background, but I always had a bit of a soft spot for her. I see her sometimes; she works on the checkout in the local supermarket. Excuse me a minute, I'll show you something.'

She went over to her bureau and rooted through her drawers until she found a formal school photograph. 'I was their Year Eleven form tutor.' She handed the photo to Rachel and stood at her shoulder pointing people out. Phoebe needed no identifying: that perfect heart-shaped face, winning smile and mass of artfully backcombed blonde hair. Her uniform shirt was unbuttoned to expose her cleavage. Lauren Mitchell sported a Mohican and glowered into the camera. Nicky Whittier was a painfully plain child, who wore glasses but had by now lost the despised bunches.

'Obviously there's nobody in the school office at the moment, but I'm sure the current head would be happy to speak to you. Phoebe was before his time though.'

Brickall stood up and put his cup and plate back on the tray. 'That won't be necessary, but thanks.'

*

An hour later they were sitting in a motorway service café. Rachel toyed with a Diet Coke, watching Brickall tuck into burger and fries washed down with a can of lager.

Her phone buzzed with a text from Joe.

Can we get together soon? There's someone I want you to meet. Xx

She looked up again. 'You've been as much use as a vibrator in a nunnery today, Detective Sergeant. Care to enlighten me about the bad attitude?'

'We're off duty, remember?' He stabbed a chip into his ketchup.

She raised an eyebrow, waiting.

'Okay, if you want to know, I'm cheesed off because it's been a waste of my precious day off.'

'I disagree. We know a lot more about Phoebe Stiles than when we started. And we had some nice shortbread.'

'Don't be a smartarse. Okay, so we know this bird was a nasty little madam, but so what? It doesn't take you anywhere. And even if it did, what were you proposing to do with the information? Case closed, remember?'

'Not entirely. There are leads Rob's still following up.'

Saying his name out loud sent colour surging to her cheeks. Annoyed, she bit her lip and started pulling apart a paper sachet of sugar.

'Oh "Rob" now is, is he?' It was Brickall's turn to raise an eyebrow. 'I take it this is your Interpol bloke?'

Rachel nodded, poking at the loose sugar with the tines of her fork.

'Bit of a hunk, was he? Touch of the Jason Bourne going on?'

She shook her head, but his sceptical expression didn't change. 'There's just something about this case; I can't explain what it is. It's just under my skin, in my head.'

Brickall leaned back and looked at her. 'Prince, this bullying stuff – it's binary. Every schoolkid is either bully or bullied. So Phoebe was in the bullying camp along with fifty per cent of the population: so what? It doesn't narrow our focus in a meaningful way.'

Rachel didn't ask Brickall which camp he was in. She already knew the answer. She pictured him as a thuggish little boy, making up for his lack of height by being free with his fists. King of the playground.

'Which were you?' he asked, reading her mind.

'Bullied. Definitely.'

'I find that hard to believe.' He wiped his mouth hard with a paper napkin, then screwed it into a ball.

She sighed. 'Look, I'm sorry about today. I just had to keep digging. Rob and I, we—'

Brickall jumped up abruptly, spraying uneaten french fries over the floor. 'Stop banging on about it, okay? You're fixated, Prince! I'm telling you, you need to just let this go.'

He turned on his heel, throwing the screwed-up napkin at the bin and missing, then strode off in the direction of the car park.

Rachel went after him, grabbing him by the elbow as they reached the car.

'Hold on a minute, sunshine, I've had enough of this. Now, you need to tell me what's eating at you.'

He shook off her arm, turned away and opened the car door.

Rachel climbed into the driver's seat beside him. 'Don't tell me it's nothing: I've known you eight years. It's something.'

Brickall gave a long sigh and leaned his head on the dashboard. 'Shaun Rawlings,' he muttered.

Rachel was mystified. 'Shaun Rawlings?' Was this a case he was working on?

'He's the bastard who murdered my brother by driving four times over the limit.'

'What about him?' Rachel asked, though she could guess.

'He's out. He served nine months of his two-year sentence for killing Paul, then they let him out on licence. Because he's an animal he then committed an armed robbery and ended up serving the rest of the sentence plus another eight years.' Brickall scrunched up his shoulders. 'But… he's out now.'

Rachel put a hand on his shoulder. 'You always knew that was going to happen.'

'But he's moved back to south London, to my area. I've seen him in Tesco's and coming out of the betting shop. It's like he's trying to rub my nose in it.'

'I'm sure that's not true, but even if it is, you're going to have to find a way to rise above it and ignore him.'

'Easier said than done.'

'I know,' Rachel told him. But it's important you do.'

As she turned the key in the ignition, Rachel made a conscious effort to lighten the mood. 'For a moment there I thought you were going to say you were pissed off because I knocked you back last night.'

'Don't be so fucking daft, I was just messing around.' He gave a contemptuous laugh. 'As if I'd ever go there.'

Amen to that, thought Rachel. *That would be nothing short of madness.*

TWENTY-SIX

There's plenty of time to clean up. After I've finished eating, I sleep for a few hours. The blinds in the bedroom are open, so the early light wakes me. I climb into my Tyvek crime scene suit, cover my head with the hood and my shoes with paper covers. Two sets of gloves.

I don't rush it. The theatre's closed, my hostess is still officially out of town and I reckon I have at least twenty-four hours before anyone reports Clayton missing or notices his truck. I load every single item first into the washer, then the dryer. It takes several loads, all on the longest ninety-degree cycle, which is time consuming. While the washing machine is working, I tackle the floors, then every surface in the apartment. Slowly, thoroughly. I'm like the human equivalent of a fine-tooth comb.

While I'm waiting on the final drying cycle, I switch on the TV news with a gloved finger.

'Construction workers at the Fairfield Theater today made a grisly discovery when they found two bodies – one male and one female – on the site. The victims have not yet been identified. At this stage, Wake County Police say the deaths were not accidental and they're treating the discovery as a homicide investigation…'

I jump back from the TV as though I've been burned. Then I switch it off and start quickly but methodically gathering all my stuff, adding in the framed photo of the loved-up young couple. Clayton had his phone and his wallet on him, so he will have been identified. It's not going to take them long to figure out that the other one is his girlfriend, and then they'll be straight round here.

I step out onto the communal landing, still in my paper suit and shoes. I strip them off, bundle them into the garbage bag I've just removed from the kitchen bin and push it down the chute that's next to the elevator. Then I put on my cap and sunglasses and take the emergency stairs down to the parking garage. That was a lot closer than I had planned for. I'm going to have to be a lot more careful next time.

TWENTY-SEVEN

'Her Majesty's Inspectorate of Constabulary,' Patten addressed the officers in the Major Crimes Investigation Support meeting room, 'have decided in their wisdom to conduct another of their reviews into our effectiveness. Specifically, whether we are investing enough in equipment in order to support our officers. They also want to look at our extradition and fugitive protocols. So –' he slapped a file on the desk for emphasis; something he was fond of doing – 'we've got a lot to get through in the next few weeks.'

There was a collective groaning and eye rolling around the table.

'Obviously, it makes sense for International Division to cover Ins and Outs.' He used the favoured office slang for criminals crossing UK borders in one direction or the other – 'so DI Prince and DS Brickall: can I leave that with you? Retrospective summary of all our files going back to whenever the hell HMIC were last here.'

Rachel and Brickall slouched back to their desks like teenagers who had just been given extra homework.

'What do you want to do – Ins or Outs?' Brickall asked.

Rachel shrugged. 'I really don't care.' She realised as she said it that there were probably a lot more criminals coming into the country illegally than there were being shipped out.

'I'll do Outs then,' said Brickall, also realising this.

'Fine,' she smiled. His mood had improved somewhat since he had talked to her about Shaun Rawlings' release from prison, but she was keeping quiet about the American case anyway. She was, in effect, doing what Brickall had wanted and letting the matter go. He was right anyway; she was at a dead end. No more talk about Phoebe Stiles.

'Coffee?'

He nodded, eyes fixed on his computer monitor, and she headed off to the communal kitchenette to put on the kettle. Reflexively checking her phone while the kettle boiled, she saw she had a voicemail that must have been left while she was in the meeting. The associated missed call was from Robert J. McConnell.

Her hands trembled slightly as she called voicemail.

'*Rachel, something's… listen, you're definitely not going to want to miss this. It's probably best if I explain in an email, this is just a heads-up. Okay, take care now. Bye.*'

Back at her desk, she checked her inbox. There it was, intriguingly entitled '*You must see this*'. She glanced over at Brickall, who was watching her expression closely.

'What?' he demanded.

'Nothing. Just an annoying email from my sister.' She had indeed received an email from Lindsay that morning, demanding she disclose her plans for Easter, so this was not an outright lie. She closed her email down and stood up. 'I'm going to start pulling up some archived files.' She didn't want to risk another confrontation, so Rob's message was going to have to wait. But that didn't stop her thinking about it.

As soon as she got home, she curled up on the sofa with her laptop and started reading.

> From: Robert J. McConnell
> To: Rachel Prince
> Hey Rachel
> Hope all good in London?

Okay, so I've been regularly screening on homicides of women under the age of 35, and a few days ago there was one in North Carolina that caught my eye straightaway. The victim is blonde, pretty and not unlike our Heather/Stacey/Jennifer (who I now think of as Miss XX, given that all we know is that the killer has female DNA). I made some enquiries and – bingo. Sure enough this girl was renting out her apartment on CasaMia. I've not managed to get a look at the crime report, but I've spoken to the PD there and she was strangled, not struck, which doesn't fit the pattern. But this still has the potential to be more than a coincidence, so I'm currently trying to get the all the relevant police forces to talk to each other, but it's not easy from here at the Department of Justice. I'm attaching a link. Let me know what you think. Sending good thoughts, Rob.

Sending good thoughts? What on earth did that mean?

Rachel clicked on the link, which took her to a report on the Raleigh *News & Observer*'s site.

Morrisville resident and former beauty queen Melissa Downey (24) and her boyfriend Clayton Hill (26) were found brutally murdered on Tuesday. The grisly discovery was made by law enforcement officers outside the Fairfield Theatre, currently closed for refurbishment, where Miss Downey previously competed in pageants. Police have so far refused to comment on the motive for this double killing, but it is believed that Hill, who was Miss Downey's boyfriend, might have been going to her aid when he too became a victim of the killer. His Chevrolet Silverado was found abandoned a mile away. The investigation continues.

The photo of Melissa Downey, smiling and pouting for the camera, instantly put Rachel in mind of Tiffany Kovak. The boyfriend had the thick neck and heavy shoulders of an American football player.

She fired an email to Rob.

How was the boyfriend killed?

He replied a few minutes later:

Blunt force trauma to the back of the skull, same MO as Phoebe and Tiffany.

She emailed again. *CCTV images?*

Will work on that.

Rachel closed her laptop, changed into her running gear and headed for the Thames Path. It was nearly dark, and persistent drizzle made the air soupy and her face damp. The last of the office workers were hurrying to the tube station or over the bridge, some huddling outside bars and pubs to smoke.

I have to go out there, was the persistent thought in her head. She had tried to forget about the case – not perhaps as hard as Brickall would have liked her to – but it was no use. She could not, would not, let go.

As soon as she had parked her car the following morning, she went straight to Nigel Patten's office. The desktop photos of Danielle and toddler Jack had now been joined by pictures of the new baby, as bald as his father.

'Sir, you remember the Phoebe Stiles case. In Los Angeles?'

He steepled his fingers and looked at her wearily. 'It was only a few weeks ago. I'm hardly likely to have forgotten.'

'Interpol in Washington have been in touch, and it looks like there's another related case.'

'Where? You mean in the USA?'

'Yes, sir.'

'And is this another UK national?'

Rachel shook her head. 'American this time.'

Patten frowned. 'So why on earth is Interpol contacting you about it then? I'm not sure I follow.'

Rachel hesitated. He had a point. It wasn't strictly a matter for an international agency. 'I suppose because it has links to the Stiles murder, and she was British,' she extemporised. 'And I'm not convinced the man they've arrested killed Phoebe. In fact, I'm pretty sure he didn't.'

'So why exactly are we discussing this now, DI Prince?'

'Because I'd like permission to go out there and continue helping with the investigation, sir.'

He dropped his palms hard onto his desk and sat upright, giving her the steely look he usually reserved for insubordinate constables. 'Out of the question, not when we're so busy. Permission most definitely denied.'

'But sir—'

'I said no, Detective Inspector. I need you here.'

TWENTY-EIGHT

It's definitely becoming harder to find candidates. This makes me antsy. I know they are out there; hundreds of them, thousands probably. More. But getting all the requirements to line up seems harder. And I'm not prepared to lie low and wait any longer; I have to do it again. Right away. The patience I used to pride myself on is running out. I believe this is what the crime experts call escalation. I try to calm myself by spreading out the key, the cap, the photo of the loving couple, and looking at them.

There is one, but it's quite a long way north. Part of the impatience is not wanting to deal with the travelling. But then, some geographic distance could be a good thing right now. The dates work. The profile works. I press 'Request Booking' and wait. An hour later: 'Pack your bags Kelly, your trip is confirmed!'

I'm at Logan Airport, waiting to pick up a small-but-not-too-small rental car, when I see, to my dismay, an updated message on my phone.

'So sorry, I'm afraid I can't be there myself to meet you. The doorman will let you in the building, and the key will be in a lock box to the right of the front door. Code is 6719. Everything you need to know is in the folder. Enjoy!'

This is a major hitch, there's no doubt about it. But she has to come back sometime, right? She would always have planned on returning to the apartment. I'm just going to have to wait for her to return home. And in the meantime there's plenty of other things I can be doing.

Her perfect life is all mine right now.

TWENTY-NINE

'Do you think they're after the total number of EAWs issued, or just those where an extradition hearing has actually taken place?'

'Sorry – what?' Rachel looked up at Brickall with a start.

'I'm talking about European Arrest Warrants. What's the matter with you? Your head's completely missing today.'

'Nothing.' She went back to staring at her screen.

He shot her a sharp look, but Rachel ignored him and kept her head down. A few minutes later, she abruptly shut down the screen she was looking at and marched back to Nigel Patten's office, rapping smartly on the open door.

'DI Prince. How can I help you?' His expression was not one of a person who wished to help.

'Sir, I've just been checking my leave card, and I've got nine days carried over from last year. Which, if I don't take them in the next five weeks, I won't be able to use at all.'

'Go on,' he sighed.

'So I'm going to take them now.'

'Now as in…?'

'Today, sir. You can count the rest of the afternoon as a full day.'

Patten grimaced. He looked tired, but then he'd looked permanently tired ever since his paternity leave. 'You are aware, Detective Inspector, that you need me to sign off on this. And also that with this inspection coming up, we're at our busiest.'

Rachel kept her gaze level and her tone neutral. 'I am sir. But can I remind you that I haven't taken any time off in over seven months. Since before Scotland.'

'I know you've worked hard, DI Prince. And you did a good job on the Nigerian trafficking case. But—'

'I came in early this morning and worked on the fugitive figures.' By early, she meant five thirty, fuelled by two double espressos. 'I've got a spreadsheet and PowerPoint presentation all prepared. I'll send them to you and copy in DS Brickall.'

'What about your DCI board? Isn't that about to happen?'

'Still a couple of weeks away. I'll be back in time.'

'What if I say no?' As she stood her ground, Patten continued: 'No, don't answer that. But have it on the record that I'm only agreeing with extreme reluctance. And I want you back here at the end of your nine days leave.'

'That's thirteen days, sir. If you add weekends. Which means I'll be back in the office the day before my promotion board. So it all works out perfectly.'

She left the room before he could change his mind and almost skipped back to her seat, plonking herself down and scanning her inbox for any last-minute loose ends, while stuffing her things into her bag.

'What are you doing?' demanded Brickall. 'Did somebody die?'

'I'm taking some leave.'

'What the hell for? You never take leave. Oh, hold on –' he slapped his hand to his forehead – 'this is about that bloody case, isn't it?'

Rachel ignored the question, standing up and shouldering her bag. 'See you a week next Monday.'

Brickall very pointedly turned away and absorbed himself in his computer screen. Rachel waved to his back. She didn't like leaving him when he was so down, but he was an adult after all, and she wasn't going for long. 'Well… bye then,' she called.

He did not reply.

*

After booking her flight for first thing the next morning, and wincing at the last-minute prices, Rachel reached for her suitcase and started filling it. She was interrupted by the doorbell.

Joe stood there, his tall figure looming over a tiny, pretty girl with masses of wavy brown hair and huge brown eyes.

'Er… hi!' Rachel said.

Joe spotted the suitcase through the open bedroom door. 'You're not off somewhere again? Only we were having a drink in Bermondsey Street and I thought we might as well pop by.'

'No problem, I'm flying first thing tomorrow, so I've got a couple of hours before I need to get some shut-eye. Come in… come in.'

Joe placed his arm protectively round the waist of the girl as he steered her into the flat. 'Great. I wanted you to meet Sophie. Sophie – this is my mum.'

'Hi,' Sophie said, with a shy little wave.

Rachel felt a little ripple of pleasure at his use of the 'm' word. He usually addressed her as Rachel. 'Mum' was his adoptive mother, Jane.

'There are beers in the fridge, or I've got wine?'

Sophie accepted wine, Joe helped himself to a beer and Rachel poured herself a mineral water and set out a bowl of crisps. They chatted happily for forty-five minutes about Rachel's work, Joe's internship and Sophie's fine arts course, then Rachel packed up a carrier bag with all the viable fridge contents and gave it to Joe, along with a set of spare keys to the flat before returning to her packing. She whistled tunelessly to herself as she threw clothes in the suitcase, happiness making her light-hearted. Seeing her son always left her like this. Happy, and so very grateful.

*

As the taxi pulled away down a near-silent Jamaica Road the next morning, Rachel phoned Rob's number. It went to voicemail. She quickly checked her watch – it would late evening there, and she'd hoped to catch him before he went to bed. Then she cleared her throat.

'Listen, it's me. I know this is a bit sudden, but I've managed to take some time off and I'm coming over. To Washington DC; it makes most sense to start there and I got a seat on an early flight. So, guess I'll see you soon. I'll call when I arrive.'

Once she was in the departure lounge waiting to board, she texted Brickall.

I'm really sorry Mark…

She hardly ever called him by his first name.

I know you're pissed off with me, but please understand I just can't not finish this. I'll see you very soon. R x

He was surgically attached to his mobile and always replied to texts instantly, unless he was driving or asleep. She checked her phone every few minutes, but there was no response. There was, however, an email from an address she did not recognise.

From: Abigail Harris
To: Rachel Prince
I hope this is okay. I was talking with Paige Chen about Tiffany and she gave me your card because she told me you were trying to find who would want to kill her, and I said I wanted to say something about that. I don't know who killed her, but I'm not surprised somebody did want to. Tiffany Kovak was really mean. At school she was the biggest bitch. When we were in eighth grade and I got my period, she stuck her phone

under the cubicle door in the toilets and took pictures of me. In tenth grade she told Tyler Roth that I was in love with him even after I begged her not to. She was absolutely awful to Mindy Poole, just because she was heavy. Used to call her a fat pig and to her face too. Anyhow I just wanted to tell you this, she was not a nice person. It was not me that killed her but I kind of wish I had. Sincerely, Abbie Harris.

Rachel read and re-read this. *I'm not surprised that someone wanted to kill her.* Exactly what Lauren had said about Phoebe.

The flight started boarding, but as she walked to the plane there was still no response from Brickall. *Asleep, then? Fair enough.* When she landed at Dulles and switched her mobile on again, she knew he would be only be sitting at his desk, going through arrest warrants. Still no reply.

She continued checking her phone screen intermittently while she was at baggage claim, and as she walked through the arrivals hall.

'I said hi!'

She looked up. Rob was standing in her path.

'I figured you'd be on this flight, so I thought I'd come and meet you.' He swept her up in a hug. She surrendered to it completely. It felt good.

'You came back,' he said into her hair.

'I did.'

They straightened up, and he took her bag from her, leading the way through the milling arrivals hall traffic. 'Come on Miss Tenacity, you and I have got work to do.'

THIRTY

She describes herself as 'Part-time model and beauty blogger'. I read her blog and watch her YouTube videos. Product reviewing, tips for contouring and smoky eyes, fake wellness advice... yawn. You and all the millions of others, sweetie. She has a Pomeranian called Dorothy who appears in some of her vlogs, and Dorothy has her own zone in the apartment's impressively stocked closet, featuring diamanté collars, tiny sweaters and even a miniature tutu.

In my opinion she's not especially good at being a vlogger, and her mediocre follower numbers bear this out. There's no evidence of any commercial sponsorship. Nor is she tall enough or distinctive enough to be a successful model. So how is she supporting herself? I sit at her desk, take out the file she's helpfully labelled 'Tax and Invoices' and start looking through the paperwork. And there it is. A bunch of pro-forma time sheets, dated at fairly regular intervals, from an office temp agency. So, in reality, she's a secretary.

The great thing about this is that it means she doesn't have a fixed place of work. Every few weeks or so, when she's not vlogging or 'modelling', she shows up to work at a place where no one knows who she is. They know nothing about her other than name and social security number; they're unlikely even to have seen a photo. I take the agency's number from their payment slip and call them, telling them I want to work now. This week. Today even. I should go to the Elite Staffing website and log into my account, they tell me, and fill in an online request with the dates and hours I'm available, along with any preferences for type of work. I tell them my internet is down. The woman on the other end of the line, whose name is Marianne, bitches and moans that this messes up their paperwork, but eventually agrees to see what's available and get back to me.

Marianne calls me back after a couple of hours. I spend the intervening time going through the contents of the overflowing closet, trying on and co-ordinating potential workwear outfits. I can start that afternoon at a downtown law firm, but they only need help with filing and general clerical duties. Marianne stresses it's not the kind of executive-level PA work they normally find for me. I tell her that's just fine: it's only short-term. It occurs to me that if they'd found me something where I had to take shorthand I might be in trouble. Do people even do shorthand any longer? I've never worked in an office, so I don't know. I dress in a silk blouse, a tight pencil skirt and high-heeled pumps, and I really love the effect. Like Rachel Zane out of Suits.

People in a commercial law firm are far too busy to notice temps, or care what they do. Only the woman who shows me where I'll be sitting speaks to me; to say I might like to wear more comfortable shoes next time, as I'll be on my feet going through filing boxes a lot of the time. I'm well suited for the work, given that I'm very methodical and I like to organise. I like the light, bright offices, the super-clean staff kitchen, the soothing background hum of noise. Occasionally the male lawyers walking past my desk give me a curious second look, and after I've relaxed a little I allow them brief eye contact, give a half-smile in return. I don't talk though. The less I say, the safer I am.

The same woman comes to me at the end of the day and says I'm doing a great job and would I be prepared to stay for the rest of the week? I say I would.

THIRTY-ONE

'Time to join up the dots.'

Rachel and Rob were in a coffee shop next to the budget hotel she had booked, and he was arranging photos on the table in front of them, much as Rachel herself had done when Brickall visited her flat, only this time a photo of Melissa Downey joined the gallery of pretty young blondes. Rachel showed him the email she had received the day before from Abbie Harris.

'She's no wordsmith, but I think we get the picture.'

'Phoebe Stiles's classmate had something very similar to say about her. Almost identical, in fact.'

Rob took a sip of his coffee and thought about this. 'That's very interesting.'

'Is it though?' Rachel remembered Brickall's bullying statistics. 'Clearly neither Tiffany or Phoebe were very nice people...'

'Little bitches, you might say.'

'Exactly. But that's hardly a sub-sector of society. There are a hell of a lot of little bitches out there.'

'Trust me, I know.' Rob grinned. 'But it implies a type, and in victimology that's significant.'

'Victimology? Is that even a thing?' Rachel asked, even though she knew full well it was.

'Sure it's a thing. There are loads of studies and books on the subject. And d'you know why?'

'I'm sure you're about to tell me.'

'Because the victim leads us to the criminal. Victimology tells us why there is a link between two otherwise unconnected parties, and in a case like this, which isn't about spontaneity or gratuitous violence, we need that.'

Rachel was shaking her head slowly over the rim of her mug. 'I'm still not sure how we move past mere coincidence.'

Rob tapped the picture of Melissa. 'That's where this young lady comes into it. The serial killing rule is at least three. So, the way I see it, if Melissa Downey fits the same type then we move from coincidence to a definite pattern.'

Rachel leaned back, sipping her coffee and staring at the photos. 'So we obviously need to know more about Melissa.'

'You got it.' Rob started shuffling the papers together. He stopped long enough to place his hand lightly on hers. 'How long did you say you were here for?'

'It's Wednesday. Allowing travel time to the UK I have to leave no later than a week on Saturday. Eleven days.'

'Then we don't have time to waste.' He finished gathering up the exhibits. 'Go and get your stuff, we need to make a move.'

'But I haven't even checked in yet.'

'Even better. We're going to pay our respects to Miss Teen North Carolina.'

For most of the forty-five-minute flight from Washington DC to Raleigh–Durham – her thigh pressed up against Rob's, her arm brushing his – Rachel was not thinking about Melissa Downey, but about sleeping arrangements. Rob had said something vague about checking in somewhere. Surely he didn't mean the same room? She thought she'd made her position clear at the end of her last trip.

The idea disturbed her. Of course, he was gorgeous. Brickall had not been far off the mark about him being Jason Bourne made flesh.

But too much proximity was not going to work. It was too much of a risk. If she allowed anything or anyone else into her headspace, everything stopped working. Or you ended up drastically compromising the investigation, just as she'd done with Giles Denton. They were investigating parties held by a child grooming ring in Edinburgh, only for Rachel to discover that Giles had attended one of the parties as a guest. It became messy, to put it mildly.

She needn't have wasted the time worrying. At the bland, cookie-cutter airport hotel that they drove to in their rental car, Rob requested two rooms. 'Keeps things professional,' he said with a brief smile, as he handed her the key. 'Meet me in the lounge in five.'

He was on the phone when she returned to the reception area, and she hovered awkwardly, waiting for him to finish.

'That was the Raleigh PD,' he said when he hung up. 'They're emailing me a copy of the crime report right now, and I'll print it off in the business centre here. I think we need to read that before we go any further? Agreed?'

Rachel nodded and waited while he strode off, returning a few minutes later with two printed copies of the report. It made grisly reading. Melissa had died from ligature strangulation and an estimated thirty-six to forty-eight hours later, her body had been packed and sealed inside a heavy-duty shipping crate. Clayton Hill had died later, probably soon after the packing process had taken place, and had been found at the deposition site, bent over the crate. Rachel scrutinised the crime scene photos. It looked as though he was embracing it, or shielding her.

'So what do we think?' demanded Rob. She liked that he read and absorbed information as quickly as she did. She liked so many things about him.

'If this was our Miss XX, then I think the strangling was an unintentional departure, probably because the blow to the head method failed for some reason.'

'I agree. But what do you make of the difference in the times of death?'

Rachel considered this for a while. 'The boxing-up before disposal and the choice of site are very deliberate, very staged. We saw the same thing with Phoebe and Tiffany. Does Clayton suspect something and follow Miss XX and then she manages to bash him when she's confronted?' She frowned. 'I don't know… that doesn't feel right. I don't think she would allow for a mistake like that.'

'He's surely more likely to call law enforcement? And if someone confronts you, someone much bigger than you are, how do you conveniently get behind them and hit them? It just doesn't work, in my mind. She needs the element of surprise.'

'He can't have suspected anything. He must have been lured to the location somehow.'

Rob was nodding. 'And then his truck's dumped elsewhere. Also by Miss XX, presumably. So if he drives himself there, how does *she* get to the location of the theatre?'

'Did you find any CCTV footage. That's what we need.'

Rob shook his head. 'The main office was closed.'

Rachel stood up and shouldered her bag. 'So what are we waiting for, Agent McConnell? Time to pay a visit to the scene of the crime.'

They left the confines of the airport and headed towards the CBD. Rob drove while Rachel stared out of the window, enchanted by the spring blossoms beneath a forget-me-not blue sky: magnolia, dogwood, cherry and a reddish-purple tree she'd never seen, that he told her was called redbud.

'They thought long and hard about the name of that one,' she laughed.

The Fairfield Theater was a brick cube of a building standing alone in a parking lot the size of a football pitch. The police had done their work and left, and the place appeared deserted.

'This is where they found them.' Rachel pointed to the rear left-hand corner of the building. Rob was scanning for cameras. There were none at the rear of the building where the packing crate was placed, but there was one at the front, facing the parking lot. He tried the front door, which opened.

'Let's see if we can find someone; if the door's open there must be someone around.'

The foyer was carpeted in brick dust, and there was plastic sheeting everywhere, loose wiring hanging from the ceiling.

'Hello!' Rob called. Silence. They looked into the auditorium, which was completely empty, all the seats removed. Eventually, after fighting their way through cabling and piles of loose floor-ing, they made their way to a back office where a solitary security guard was swilling Mountain Dew with his feet up on the desk.

'Already gave a copy to the police,' he grumbled when Rob showed his badge and asked to see footage from when the bodies were dumped.

'You'll have the original on here though?' Rachel said, pointing to the hard drive. 'We only want a very quick look.'

The security guard found the right digital file and disappeared for a cigarette break. The grainy images showed the front of a pickup truck. It was only just in shot, with not much more than the bumper visible. Then after a few seconds, the back view of Clayton Hill appeared, carrying the large box, swaying slightly under the weight. Behind him was a smaller, slighter figure in jeans and T-shirt, hair covered by a baseball cap.

'She's got something in her hand – look!' said Rachel, pointing.

Rob rewound the tape and they watched again. It was a tubular metal object, like a wrench or a tyre iron. Then both figures disap-peared from shot, heading past the camera towards the left side of the building. Less than a minute later, the nose of the truck could be seen reversing out of shot. There was nothing more.

Rob sat back in the security guard's chair. 'Wow. She makes him carry his own girlfriend's corpse. That's so fucked-up.'

'Do you think he knew?' Rachel mused. 'Could it even have been him who strangled Melissa, at Miss XX's bidding?'

'No,' Rob shook his head. 'That doesn't fit. I'm pretty sure she killed them both. From what we know so far, using an accomplice isn't in her wheelhouse. She's a lone operator.'

'So…' Rachel breathed out slowly, 'in that case he had no idea what was in the box.' The room felt suddenly cold. The two of them sat for several seconds in the chill silence.

As they walked back to the car, Rachel asked, 'Do you think we can take a look at Melissa's apartment?'

'It's probably still undergoing forensics, but I guess it's worth a try.'

They headed for Fayetteville Street, an inner-city neighbourhood packed with bars and galleries. Melissa's condo was in a pre-war building, and their access to it was barred by an officious uniformed security guard.

'Uh uh,' he said shaking his head. 'Oh-ficial crime scene.'

Rob pulled out his Interpol badge, Rachel even produced her NCA warrant card, but the concierge remained unmoved. 'I don't have the authorisation to let you in. You'll have to come back with a warrant from Wake County.' He retreated huffily into to his cubicle.

'Oh crap,' said Rachel, turning back to the building's foyer.

'Hey, Miss Tenacity, you're not giving up?' Rob pulled a lighter from his pocket. 'Watch this.' He struck it and held the flame under the smoke detector. Within a few seconds the lobby sprinkler system kicked in, with a squealing alarm accompanying the jets of water. The concierge came running, but not before Rob had grabbed Rachel's wrist and pulled her through the fire door. They collapsed, laughing, against the wall.

'That was a pure Bonnie and Clyde moment,' Rachel said. 'I'm impressed. Although not so much that you're a closet smoker.'

'I'm not.'

'Why carry a lighter then?'

'Let's just say that's not the first time I've set off a sprinkler system. Come on.' He led the way up the stairwell. 'Just be thankful that we only have to go up to the third floor.'

The condo was screened off with crime scene tape, and its front door had a polished nickel doorknob with an inbuilt deadbolt. Not that this discouraged Rob, who squatted down with his penknife and jiggled the lock open.

'Proper little boy scout, aren't you?' Rachel observed drily. She held up her own Swiss Army knife. 'I was about to offer to do the honours.'

'Those locks cost about ten bucks and they're not even worth that much; a seven year old could pick one.'

They stepped into a well-proportioned three-room apartment with polished floors and crown mouldings. The décor was at odds with the surroundings, betraying a twenty-something who had not yet developed taste. Rachel looked at the photos on the shelves. The way they were arranged suggested one was missing from the group. She picked one up and looked at it. Clayton Hill, draped around his pretty girlfriend, just as he had been in death. She shuddered, and moved on to the closet. The clothes were ordered by colour, apart from one flimsy top, which hung alone. She picked up the clothes hanger and sniffed it. There was a distinct chemical smell. She smelled the other clothes on the rail, but none of them shared it.

'This one's been recently washed,' she observed. 'Not with the same laundry detergent all the others share.'

They checked the bathroom and the kitchen. 'Like an operating theatre,' said Rob.

'Phoebe's apartment was just the same.'

In the bedroom, the linens had all been stripped, and the mattress gave off a similar chemical odour to the top. It made Rachel feel nauseated, and she was suddenly aware that, after a transatlantic flight sandwiched between two work days in two different time zones, she was starting to feel very tired.

'Come on,' said Rob, noticing her expression. 'You need a margarita.'

'I'm not sure about that.' She wanted to lie down and sleep for twelve hours.

'Sure you do. Everything's better after a margarita.'

He took her by the hand and led her down the stairs and out onto Fayetteville Street. The happy-hour crowd was starting to fill the bars, and Rachel and Rob joined them. Despite her protests, he ordered a jug.

'Better now?' he asked, as she sipped the sour, icy liquid through a straw.

'A little,' she conceded, then asked. 'How did you even know Melissa had shared the apartment on CasaMia?'

'The detective I spoke to said Melissa's mother mentioned it. She said that Melissa was supposed to be travelling to Florida for a few days, and had rented it out while she was gone to help cover the bills. Of course, the police here saw no particular significance in that, but then they don't know what we know.'

Rachel sat silently for a while, letting the tequila numb her.

'So what are you thinking our next move should be, Miss T?'

'I think we need to talk to Melissa's mother.'

Back at the hotel, she told Rob she needed a shower and a nap, and headed to her room. Taking out her phone, she texted Brickall.

Hey, loser, what's with the radio silence?

There was no reply. Not that she had expected one, but she worried about Brickall nonetheless. What he was going through was tough. She showered, turned down Rob's offer of ribs and fries downstairs in the grill in favour of a room service salad, and just as she had done in Los Angeles, lay on the bed watching CNN until she drifted off to sleep.

She was woken a couple of hours later by a gentle tapping on the door. She switched off the TV and stumbled to answer it.

'Room for a small one?'

Rob was standing there in sweatpants and a tight white T-shirt that showed off his muscular torso.

Rachel smiled. 'There's nothing small about you, Agent McConnell… what can I do for you?'

'I was wondering if I could come in.'

Rachel hesitated. It was an appealing idea. But that wasn't really the issue. She pursed her lips, and slowly, reluctantly, shook her head.

'No?' he asked, not hiding his disappointment.

'No.' She gave a heavy sigh. 'We've been over this. It's really not a good idea.'

'Sure there's nothing I can do to change your mind?'

But she was already closing the door, quickly, before she weakened. Once she was in bed, sleep eluded her. She tossed and turned for a couple of hours, her mind continually running to Rob, and what they could have been doing. Eventually, just as she was dozing off, her phone bleeped with a text. She snatched it up and checked it.

From Lindsay. *Lamb or chicken for Easter lunch? I need to know!.*

As if it bloody matters, Rachel thought, but restrained herself from replying.

THIRTY-TWO

The home share period ends today, but all she does is message me asking me to empty the trash and put the key back in the lockbox. I check her Instagram feed for clues. There are some selfies of her clutching a green juice and fake-smiling with a bunch of other similar beauty blogging morons.

The tag reads: Hi everyone, having an amazing time at the awesome Wellness Convention in Portland, with fellow influencers @KandeeGirl2, @MissBubbles23 and @LisaGG89.

'Influencers'. The word curdles my stomach. It seems that's what they're calling Mean Girls these days. I google the convention. It ends this evening, so maybe she's flying back tomorrow. That's okay, I can arrange to be here to greet her. No problem.

In the meantime, I'm still enjoying my job in the law firm. I'm punctual, professional and super-efficient and they can't get enough of me. Patty, the woman who gave me my induction, asked me yesterday if I would consider a temp to perm move. In other words, they want me to stay on indefinitely. I say I'll think about it, but of course it's not going to happen.

When she phones me and asks me to step into her office, I'm guessing she wants my answer. I stalk confidently down the hall in my nude Louboutin pumps, teamed with a buff pencil skirt, striped Breton top and a wide scarlet belt. It's a look I pulled out of the closet last night; one that steers the line between classy and sassy. A couple of the male associates look up as I walk by, which confirms I'm hitting the right note.

Patty isn't smiling.

'We seem to have something of a problem.'

'Oh, really?'

'I phoned Elite Staffing yesterday to discuss a possible change to your contract – we have to pay a fee if we take on one of their workers permanently – and according to them, you've been signed off as unavailable this week. Because you're out of town, travelling.'

There's a sharp lurch in my stomach, as though I'm in an elevator and it's just fallen several floors.

I smile cheerfully. 'That can't be right... who did you speak with?'

'Donna. Apparently she handles all your work.'

I shake my head. 'No, that's changed. Donna was unavailable, so Marianne covered. I called her to tell her I'd changed my plans and wanted to work after all, but she must have forgotten to tell Donna. I'm sorry.'

Blaming someone else then apologising for their mistake is the best I can come up with on the spot. Patty seems unconvinced, suspicious even.

'Well, all right,' she says reluctantly. 'I guess I can speak to them again. In the meantime I'd like you to bring your ID in with you tomorrow.'

'My ID?' I ask stupidly.

'Your social security card, and either your passport or driver's licence.'

'And you need it tomorrow?'

'Tomorrow, first thing. If that's okay.' She smiles, but that suspicious look hasn't left her eyes.

'Sure,' I smile back. 'No problem at all.'

THIRTY-THREE

When Rachel woke up, the room was silent apart from the faint drone of a vacuum cleaner in the corridor outside.

She checked her mobile again. No new messages. She deleted the text from her sister without answering it.

The phone rang. 'Morning, Miss T.'

Rachel scrunched her eyes, pushing her hair back off her face. 'Is it?'

He laughed. 'I take it you didn't sleep too good? That's what comes of sleeping alone.'

She groaned.

'Grab yourself some coffee and meet me downstairs in half an hour, okay?'

She groaned again.

'Okay, an hour. And bring your stuff. We're checking out.'

Cameron Park was a gracious neighbourhood of manicured lawns and stately older homes, its streets lined with more trees in blossom, reminding Rachel of the American small towns in old black-and-white movies. It could have been Bedford Falls. The Downeys lived in a small, neat white colonial with a porticoed porch.

The door was opened by a young woman of around thirty. She had mousey hair scraped up in an untidy pony tail, and her freckled face was pale and drawn.

'Is Melissa Downey's mother here?'

The woman shook her head.

'Her father?'

'They're staying with relatives right now. She just lost her daughter.'

'Yes, we know that. So sorry.' Rob flashed his badge. 'And you are?'

'Meghan Downey. I'm Melissa's cousin. I'm just here taking care of things for them. Minding the dog, while… you know…' A fat, wiry-haired dog appeared at her side to prove the point.

'Could we come in for a moment?' Rachel asked. 'I promise we won't take too much of your time.'

'Okay,' Meghan sighed wearily. 'Can I get you coffee?'

They refused the offer, but she led them into the kitchen and switched on the coffee machine anyway. The dog followed them, its claws clicking on the wood floor.

'He knows there's something wrong,' Meghan patted him sadly. 'Don't you, boy?'

'We were hoping to talk to Mrs Downey about Melissa,' said Rob. 'It's come to light that she sublet her apartment through CasaMia. Do you know anything about that?'

Meghan poured coffee. 'You think that has something to do with…' Her voice trailed off.

'It's a line we're following,' Rachel nodded.

'Supposedly Lissa was on her way to a Miss Glamour pageant in Florida. From what my aunt said, she had someone taking the apartment for a few days while she was gone. She travelled a lot to pageants, so when that CasaMia app started she was quite excited. She told me she planned on renting out her place as much as she could to cover the expenses… there are entrance fees, hair and make-up, and those fancy sequinned gowns can run to, like, thousands of dollars. My uncle and aunt helped her out too.' Her voice grew thick. 'They were so proud.'

'Was she successful?' asked Rachel.

'You know what: I don't know much about that whole pageant world, but she seemed to win quite a lot, yeah.' Meghan pointed them to the dining room, where professional portraits of a glossy, groomed Melissa lined the walls, wearing elaborate tiaras and sashes, holding sparkly trophies.

'See that one,' Meghan pointed to a very young Melissa in a shiny lilac coloured gown. 'That was the first one she won: Miss Teen North Carolina. It was at the Fairfield Theater.' She hesitated. 'Where, you know…'

'Where her body was found,' confirmed Rachel.

Meghan nodded slowly. 'It weirds me out. It's like they knew.'

They went back into the kitchen. 'What kind of a girl was Melissa?' Rachel asked. 'Apart from the pageants.'

'She was just a regular kid, you know… bubbly, fun, outgoing, just a sweetheart.' Tears welled up in Meghan's eyes. 'Sorry.'

Rob waited a few seconds for her to compose herself, and then asked, 'How about at high school?'

Meghan found a well-used tissue in her pocket and dabbed her eyes. 'I don't know all that much; she was younger and we were at different schools anyway. I mean, she wasn't the brightest academically. Not a straight-A student by any means.'

'And with the other kids?' persisted Rob.

'I think she was pretty popular. She seemed to have loads of friends.'

'Do you know if she was ever involved in anything… negative?' Rachel asked.

Meghan looked confused. 'Negative?'

'Bullying, for instance?'

She shook her head vigorously. 'No. Nuh uh. Not Melissa; never. She was one of the kindest people I knew. A total sweetheart.'

In the car afterwards, Rachel said, 'I suppose it's logical when you dissect it. Phoebe's working as a model-slash-actress and her body is dumped with a load of shop dummies. Tiffany is the school sports star, and hers ends up in her high school gym. And Melissa, the pageant queen…'

'… fetches up at the theatre where she won a beauty queen title.'

'So the killer's hatred or resentment is targeted at what they did with their lives.'

'Like I told you; it's a case of the victims pointing us back to the killer. Victimology 101.' Rob turned and grinned at her.

Rachel was quiet for a few seconds. 'I'm trying to focus in on what these three girls have in common. They're good-looking and conform to a certain physical type. Phoebe and Tiffany were the school mean girls… but apparently not Melissa.'

'It didn't sound like it.'

'It doesn't seem to fit,' Rachel mused. 'I guess her adoring, grief-stricken cousin might not have been aware. Or not believed her capable of being nasty. I guess we'd need to talk to her friends.'

Rob shrugged. 'I don't think that's a priority. For right now, let's think about the stuff the three murdered girls *do* have in common.'

He turned the car off the freeway at the exit for Raleigh–Durham International Airport.

'Such as?'

'Okay, come up with some adjectives that describe all three of them.'

Rachel considered this. 'Pretty. Popular. Spoilt. Self-centred.' She paused a beat. 'Entitled.'

'Exactly. The killer is sourcing victims from a group that could roughly be described as entitled.'

They were at the rental car drop-off now, and Rob took their bags from the boot and handed the keys to a waiting agent. 'Come on,' he said, taking Rachel's hand, 'the shuttle to the terminal is just over there.'

'Are we going back to DC?'

He shook his head.

'Where then?'

'Think about it, Detective. What's the other glaringly obvious thing that all three victims share?'

The shuttle bus pulled up, air brakes hissing. They climbed on, dumping their bags in the luggage rack and finding seats for what seemed like an absurdly circuitous journey to the terminal.

'They all rented out their homes using CasaMia.'

'Precisely, my dear Watson. We're taking a little side trip to San Francisco.'

THIRTY-FOUR

Today's outfit: a bodycon dress in a heavy navy-blue jersey, burgundy patent Valentino T-bar pumps. Matching Prada bag. Miss Beauty Blogger has the best wardrobe so far. Maybe she gets sent free stuff, even though she's not that big a deal as an influencer.

'Looking good, Miss!' the elevator man greets me as I head to the thirty-first floor. I am just about to sit down and start in on the pile of depositions and non-fiduciary agreements that require assignment to the correct files, and a backlog of citations that need to be checked on Westlaw, when Patty appears in the doorway.

'I have my ID,' I say brightly, reaching into my bag and pulling out the Social Security card and passport that I turned up the evening before after an extensive search of Beauty Blogger's filing system. There was no driver's licence; she must have taken that on her trip.

Patty takes the proffered documents and checks them, looking at the name on the card and on the front of the passport. Then she flicks to the photo page. She looks at the picture, then at my face, then at the picture again.

She hands the documents back, thrusting them at me roughly as though she can no longer bear to touch them. 'You've been suspended,' she says. 'Pending an enquiry. I'm going to have to ask you to go home.'

'An enquiry?' I make myself sound puzzled rather than upset. 'What kind of enquiry?'

'I'm afraid I can't say, not right now. If you'd please just go home, someone will be in touch.' Patty waits long enough to see me pick *up my bag and walk back to the lift, then she turns on her heel and walks away.*

In the elevator I run through some potential scenarios in my head. It's fairly obvious which is the most likely. It would be Patty going back to Elite Staffing, reporting that Donna seems to have got it wrong: that I'm here at the law firm, not out of town. In order to clarify for themselves, either Donna or Marianne would then have phoned Beauty Blogger's cell phone to check. And she's told them that she's in Portland, Oregon. I've heard her squeaky little voice on her vlogs and I can hear it now: 'Whoever that is, it isn't me.'

It isn't me.

I go back to the apartment, take off the blue dress and the heels and force myself to think. I don't care about the job. Today would have been my last day anyway. Beauty Blogger is on her way back and I was planning on being there to surprise her. But now she's coming back with a whole load of questions about what the hell has been going on in her absence. She might have made the connection between the imposter at the temp agency and the stranger who's ensconced in her home. It may not be the obvious conclusion to draw, but it's a possibility. Depending on what Elite told her, she might be spooked. She might not come back here alone.

But as for the 'enquiry'; if they've spoken to Beauty Blogger and know she's fine, it's not going to be a matter of any urgency. They'll wait until she gets back to town before taking things further: that's only common sense.

On her Instagram she's just posted a cheesy airport selfie (of course) from Portland International: Woohoo – flying back to Beantown. Can't wait to get home. See you in a few hours! *She doesn't come across in the least bit upset or worried, which is in my favour. If she's not worried, then she'll come back here on her own.*

I start to look around the apartment for something to use. There's a brass candlestick on the fireplace that caught my eye when I first arrived. I pick it up, testing the weight of it in my hand.

Heavy enough.

THIRTY-FIVE

'What do you think?'

Rachel stood looking out of the window from twenty-one floors up in the Loews Hotel. Beneath her, as though glimpsed from an aeroplane, was the pale sweep of the San Francisco Bay. The twin russet towers of the bridge surged through the thin layer of white mist, bold and solid. The combination of the dizzying height and yet another time zone was making her lightheaded. It had taken five hours to fly from North Carolina, but having gained three hours in the time shift from east to west, it was now some time in the middle of the afternoon. Immaterial, given that her body still thought it was in London, where it was now the middle of the night.

Rob came and stood behind her, placing his hands lightly on her waist.

'This place is amazing,' Rachel said. 'But we seem to be one room short. I'm not about to start sharing now.'

He raised his hands on her shoulders and spun her round to face him. 'It's okay, you can relax. They only had one room available for tonight, but the views from this place are so spectacular I thought you'd be happy to trade two so-so rooms somewhere else for one great one here.'

Rachel suppressed irritation at being manipulated. 'I suppose so.'

'And we have two queens.' He indicated the generously appointed space with its pair of huge beds. 'Really, it's okay, I got the message last night. We can stick to our own side of the room.'

'Okay then,' Rachel nodded reluctantly. She disliked sharing her space at the best of times. Her brain worked better in solitude, and she liked her own routine. 'I suppose so.'

'Besides –' Rob gave her his most charming smile – 'is the prospect of spending a night in the same room as me really so terrible?'

She shook her head. 'No, it's just… the time difference… I'm really tired.'

'Go ahead and take a nap. I'll be quiet as a mouse, I promise.'

When she opened her eyes again, Rob was asleep on the other bed, breathing quietly. She eased herself up and tiptoed to the window. The shades were still open, and to her dismay an inky night sky looked back at her, the lights of Marin County twinkling in the distance. She glanced at the bedside clock. It was 7.45 p.m.

Rob stirred. She walked over and prodded one of his feet. 'Hey – we've overslept!'

He rolled onto his side and checked his phone. 'I guess jetlag is catching.'

'Rob, this isn't a joke! We were supposed to go to CasaMia.'

'So we can go first thing tomorrow. It's not going to make a real difference if we leave things another twelve hours.'

'Try telling that to our killer!' Rachel snapped as she reached for her shirt. 'Sorry,' she added, seeing the expression on Rob's face. 'It's because I'm hyper-aware of the clock ticking. I can't afford delays when I only have…' she counted her fingers 'Eight full days including tomorrow.'

'So extend your trip. Stay longer.'

'I can't. I have to be back for a job interview. A promotion.'

Rob sat up. 'Okay, but for God's sake don't start beating yourself up. You only got here yesterday morning and look how much we've done. Give yourself a break.'

He climbed off his bed and went into the bathroom. 'Let's clean ourselves up and go for a nice dinner. A friend of mine owns a great oyster bar on Sacramento Street. It's just around the corner.' He grinned at her as he closed the door. 'And you know what they say about oysters…'

'That they give you food poisoning,' offered Rachel, but the noise of the shower drowned her out.

Rob's phone bleeped with a message, lighting up the home screen. Rachel glanced over at it, then picked it up. The wallpaper was a photo of two cute blonde children. One boy, one girl. A reminder flashed up on the phone as she held it in her hand: 'ANNIE BIRTHDAY'. She placed it onto the bedside table again, and to distract herself from her discomfiture, checked her own phone. There was a cheery text from Joe – mostly about Sophie – but Brickall still hadn't replied. Not even to give updates about the HMIC inspection. It made her uneasy.

When Rachel had taken her turn in the shower, she came out to find Rob dressed in a white button-down shirt and tweed jacket. 'If you're expecting me to put on a dress,' she said, keeping her tone light, 'you'll be sorely disappointed.'

'No problem; I just thought I'd scrub up a little for our date.'

Rachel walked over to him, first making sure that the expensively fluffy white towel was secured tightly around her. She put her hands on his shoulders and looked straight into his eyes. 'Rob, this isn't a date. We're going out to get dinner.'

He looked straight back at her. 'Right. That's a dinner date.'

'No it's not.' She stuck out her chin stubbornly. 'Because we're not dating. We're not sleeping together. We're working on a case. And solving this case – or at least doing everything within my power to solve it – is all that matters.'

Rob pulled his arm up into a salute. 'Yes, ma'am.'

'And I'm not eating oysters either. I'm under far too much time pressure to spend two days staring down the bowl of a toilet.'

*

It was strange to be back on the yellow sofas in CasaMia's Brannan Street lobby. Even stranger to be greeted like a long-lost friend by Paulie Greenaway, who was wearing bright green dungarees and had her hair twisted up in a shocking-pink scarf-cum-turban arrangement.

'Detective Prince!' she swept Rachel into a hug. 'So good to see you. Although I guess you being here means you have bad news for me.' She ushered them into one of the adult soft-play areas and organised coffee for them. 'Now, tell me what we can do to help.'

'I'm afraid there's been another homicide.' She handed Paulie a printed copy of the information they had on Melissa Downey.

'So you're just going to need me to get you the client account details like before,' said Paulie hopefully.

'To start with, yes.'

After Paulie had disappeared to find the relevant information, Rachel turned to Rob. 'Surely now we can make a case for them suspending the site, or at least going public with the potential dangers?'

Rob rubbed his chin. 'Problem is, there's an issue of jurisdiction here.'

'Not if it's a nationwide issue, surely.'

'No, I mean…' He squeezed her hand. 'I need to come clean about something.'

'Go on.'

'I'm not here officially. I mean I'm not officially on the case. I can't be: it's not an Interpol matter. I took time off to be here, to do this. Just like you did.'

Rachel stared at him.

'As far as the Department of Justice are concerned, I took some time off to visit family. Because I want to find the person who's doing this. Just like you do.' Rob smiled. 'And yes – I admit it – because I wanted to get to spend more time with you. But it does affect what we can get done now. We can ask them to do it, but we're not empowered to order.'

'I see,' Rachel tried to quell her frustration.

Paulie came back and handed them a printout. 'This was the home sharer who booked Melissa Downey's apartment for those dates.'

The profile photo was not the same one used for Heather Kennedy or Stacey Gunnarson's accounts. This time the girl – still young and attractive – was a redhead. Nicole Maher.

'Was this the only reservation under that name?' asked Rob. Paulie nodded.

'Damn.' Rob read the details again. 'And this credit card? Was a payment processed?'

'Same story as before. When it was time to charge the customer at the start of the reservation period, we received notification that the credit card account had been closed and the payment had bounced.'

'Miss XX isn't stupid. Quite the opposite. She's going to use as many fake names and cards as she needs.' Rachel addressed Paulie. 'Okay, this is what we need you to do. I know it's a lot of work, but there are potentially more lives at risk. You need to try and pull out all your hosts who are in the target group. That's Caucasian women over the whole of the USA –'

'And Canada,' Rob interjected

'– and who are under the age of thirty-five and blonde.'

'But we have around half a million hosts in this country, and probably thousands in that demographic,' protested Paulie. 'Tens of thousands even.'

'Under thirty then,' conceded Rob. 'And leave out Canada for now. Your IT guys must be able to create an algorithm that will pull up a filtered list. Then you have to suspend those accounts from making any un-vetted reservations.'

'Okay,' Paulie sighed. 'This is going to take a ton of work though. And a ton of time.'

'Please try and get it done as quickly as you can,' said Rachel. She realised she sounded starchy, and added an ingratiating smile. 'But the first priority needs to be searching on this profile photo,' she waved Nicole Maher's details, 'and making sure it doesn't crop up again under a different name.'

'And pass on everything you have on Melissa Downey to Wake County Police Department in North Carolina.' Rob flashed Paulie a winning smile. 'Please.'

'Do you guys want to wait here?' asked Paulie as she reached the door. 'If so, feel free to jump on to the Wi-Fi and help yourself to goodies from the snack room. We have matcha cookies and vegan cinnamon buns.'

'Of course you do,' muttered Rachel, *sotto voce*.

Rob caught her eye and grinned. 'We could go back to the hotel for an hour. Have some breakfast? Real breakfast: bacon, eggs and pancakes. With gluten.'

She shook her head firmly. 'I'm going nowhere. Not till this is done.'

Paulie came to find them about forty minutes later. She had been running and was red in the face, which sent a thrill of alarm shooting down Rachel's spine. She jumped up. 'What's happened?'

'We found this,' Paulie panted. 'Oh God, this is really scary.' She collapsed on a bean bag, thrusting a piece of paper at Rachel. Rob leaned over her and they read it together.

There was Nicole Maher's face, only this time she was using the name 'Kelly Castellano'. The words 'ACTIVE RESERVATION' leapt out at her, above an address in Boston.

'Hold on, that started Tuesday...' said Rob.

'… and ends today.' Rachel looked up at Paulie, already knowing at least part of the answer to her next question. 'Whose apartment is this?'

Her hand shaking, Paulie held out another piece of paper. The profile page of one Talia Schull.

Young. Pretty. Blonde.

'I already tried calling her cell number, but there was no reply.'

Rob had his phone out in an instant. 'I've got a counterpart at the DoJ in Boston; I work with him a lot. I'll ask him to get someone from the US Marshals Service to the address as a matter of urgency.'

'Oh Jesus,' wailed Paulie. 'What should I do? I think we need to pass this onto Legal & External Affairs.'

'Forget that; just keep trying Talia's number,' Rachel told her sternly. 'And don't stop until she picks up.'

Rob hung up his call, as Paulie obediently dialled, redialled, redialled again. 'A couple of marshals are heading over there now, and they'll feed back to me as soon as they know anything.'

An agonising ten minutes passed, the silence in the room punctuated only by the repeated tapping of the buttons on Paulie's phone. Then she abruptly twitched into life.

'Talia? Am I speaking with Talia Schull?'

Paulie promptly burst into tears. Rachel wrestled the phone from her.

'Talia, my name's Detective Prince. I'm from the police. Can you tell me where you are right now?'

A bemused voice said, 'I'm at my mom's house. Why are you calling me?'

'Are you okay?'

'Um, I'm fine. I just flew in from a conference in Portland and I stopped at my mom's on the way back from Logan to pick up my dog. What's wrong?'

'Can you please just stay at your mother's for a while longer. Don't go back to your apartment. Not until we've had a chance to check something out: it's really, really important – you could be at risk. I'm afraid I can't tell you any more than that, but someone will get back to you right away, I promise.'

'Well, okay. I guess…' Talia sounded irritated. But alive, thought Rachel. That's what matters.

'She's fine.' She told the others.

Paulie started crying again, but Rachel barely noticed. *One life saved*, she was thinking, *but how many more are at risk?*

THIRTY-SIX

Her flight must have landed by now. I wait for her to arrive, but nothing happens.

I pass the time by searching for my next assignment. As ever, the process is painstaking and the possibilities limited. I hear a car draw up outside. Maybe this is her. I look out of the bedroom window to the small parking lot at the rear. The car belongs to the county sheriff. The doors open and the officers haul themselves out, hands on holsters. There's a guy in US Marshal body armour with them too.

I stare for a split second, then leap into action. I run out onto the landing and call the elevator. It's a small building so there's only one. When it arrives, I jam open the door with a book, so nobody will be able to call it. Once they press the button several times and eventually realise it's not working, they'll have to take the stairs. But that's only going to detain them about ten minutes, maximum.

Back in the apartment I look around, forcing myself to be thorough, methodical. My Los Angeles key ring, my San Diego cap and my North Carolina photo are all still arranged where I can see them. I scoop them into my bag, along with the clothes I was wearing when I arrived. I also grab Talia's toothbrush and hairbrush, since I've used them both, and my favourite among her shoe collection: the burgundy Valentino T-bars. My cleaning stuff is still in the bag, because I'd only have needed it after she got here. I grab a sani-wipe and wipe down the computer mouse, the key fob and any other obvious surface, but there simply isn't time to do everything.

I run into the bedroom, wrench the sheets from the bed, grab the towels from the bathroom and hurl the whole lot into the washing machine with detergent and bleach and switch on a hot wash. Then I take my bag, pull out the book wedged in the elevator door and press the button for the lobby, just as pounding footsteps reach the top of the fire stairs.

THIRTY-SEVEN

'Surely we get forensics involved?'

Rachel and Rob were back in their room at the Loews Hotel. The official check-out time had been and gone, so they were gathering their belongings with efficiency if not outright haste.

Rob shook his head. 'The county sheriff went round there, accompanied by the marshal, and they say they found nothing amiss. When they got up to Talia's apartment it was empty; there'd been no robbery or criminal activity. Everything was quite in order. No crime: no need for a forensics team to be deployed.'

'But it looked like the apartment sub-letter had left in a hurry, isn't that what you said? So she could have left something behind this time.'

Rob placed himself between her and her suitcase. 'Rachel, there's nothing more we can do. We did the right thing intercepting Talia like that; that's something we can be proud of. We could even have saved her life. Probably we did.'

Rachel turned away from him, screwing up a sweater and thrusting it roughly into her bag.

'This is a huge country.' Rob went on. 'And our perpetrator is quite happy to criss-cross it at will. She knows how to stay one step ahead.'

Rachel stomped into the bathroom, grabbed toothbrush, toothpaste and face cream and hurled them into her bag.

'So she probably knows to lay low for a while now,' Rob went on. 'In fact, she might even stop now…'

The underwear on the floor was scooped up briskly and scrunched into a pocket of space in her case.

'… and we still have no knowledge of who she really is. You can't identify someone who has no identity.'

'She has many identities.' Rachel grabbed her trainers from the side of the bed and pushed them down the sides of her bag.

'It amounts to the same thing. We have to face it: we've done all we can. And CasaMia are on the case now.'

Rachel clenched her jaw and tossed her make-up bag on top of her case.

'I tell you what – how about this? I've got a buddy at the *Washington Post*. I'll get him to run a piece on the CasaMia murders, without mentioning me as a source. That'll spook our killer; keep her away from the site.'

Rachel zipped her case and turned to face him. 'You mean you'll leak the story?'

'Exactly. Although you could argue that it's in the public interest.'

'I suppose that would be a result of sorts. Even if it's not how I envisaged this ending.' Rachel took one last admiring look at the Golden Gate Bridge, then turned and asked, 'Are you going to go back to DC?'

'Yep. You coming?'

She shook her head. 'I've still got a week of leave. I think I might go back to Los Angeles for a while. I'll retrace Phoebe's steps, see if there's something I missed.'

'Share a ride to the airport then, Miss Tenacity?'

They went through security together. When they reached the departure gates, the flight for Dulles was a left turn, and the one to LAX to the right.

'I guess this is it then.' Rob put down his case to sweep Rachel into his arms, just as he had when she arrived in Washington two days earlier. 'Time to say goodbye.'

'I never say goodbye.'

'Not in your nature, right?' Rob laughed, and patted her shoulder. 'Thanks for being such an amazing teammate.'

She smiled, reaching up and kissing him swiftly on the cheek. 'No, thank *you*. You've been an incredible sport about all this. I truly appreciate all you've done.'

Before he could say more, she turned on her heel and walked off to her gate without looking back. Sitting in the waiting area with twenty minutes to kill before her flight boarded, she pulled out her mobile and tried calling Brickall. Perhaps he would be mollified if she told him she might be heading back to London sooner than planned. The call rang a few times, then was cut.

'Rachel!'

She swung round. A slightly breathless Rob stood there beside her.

'If you think you're going to get a goodbye out of me at the eleventh hour, forget it. I told you; I don't do them.'

He was shaking his head vigorously. 'No, that's not it, I've just had a call. From my co-worker. A familial DNA match has come through on CODIS.' Rob reached down and pulled her to her feet. 'This is huge! We've got someone related to Miss XX.'

PART THREE

'Who in the world am I? Ah, *that's* the great puzzle!'
Alice's Adventures in Wonderland, *by Lewis Carroll*

THIRTY-EIGHT

'A twenty-five per cent match? What does that mean for us?'

Rob and Rachel were sitting in a fast food concession in the San Francisco International Arrivals area, both of them no-shows for the flights they had been about to catch. A plastic basket of fries sat between them, and they were taking it in turns to pick at them, even though the food was cold and unappetising.

'Okay, so from what the guy told me, only an identical twin shares one hundred per cent of an individual's DNA.' Rob took a gulp of his soda. 'A parent or full sibling shares fifty per cent. For twenty-five per cent it's going to be either a grandparent—'

'Unlikely.'

'Exactly. Or an aunt or uncle.'

'I suppose that's possible. If they were young enough.'

'Otherwise it's either a half-sibling or a first cousin.'

Rachel stirred her paper cup of watery coffee with slow, deliberate movements as she absorbed this. 'So, let me get this straight: the woman whose DNA was found on that lipstick and also the dress and shoes from the shampoo shoot, is either a cousin or a half-sister of someone on the national criminal database?'

'Correct. Well, the science is a little bit more complex than those numbers suggest, but that's the crux of it.'

They looked at each other a moment. Rachel was unable to suppress an excited grin. 'Narrowing down our pool of suspects from around a hundred and fifty million to… what?'

'At most, ten?' supplied Rob. 'Probably no more than five.'

She fished in her bag, pulling out her notebook and pen. 'As breakthroughs go, this is pretty significant. So what do we know about the relative on the database.'

'He's called Ethan Rowe. Twenty-five years old. Caucasian. A long rap sheet of petty misdemeanors; arrested three weeks ago for felony arson, which resulted in his fingerprints and DNA being logged on CODIS.'

Rachel wrote this down. 'And where is he now?'

'Pine Ridge Correctional Facility, awaiting trial.'

'Which is… where?'

'It's in Oregon. Near a city called Madras.'

Rachel smiled. 'Well, we're on the right coast, at least.'

'It's about five hundred miles from here. Close enough.'

'So, assuming we can go and talk to him, what are we going to say? We can't blow our cover by telling him we're cops, because it would only take one phone call to his half-sister or cousin and…'

Rob looked down at his hands.

'What?'

'Rachel, I'm not going to be able to come with you. I have to fly back to DC today.'

'Can't you at least come with me to see Rowe? Twenty-four hours more?'

'I can't. It's… family stuff.'

Rachel remembered the reminder on his phone. Annie's birthday.

'It's your daughter's birthday?'

He examined his fingernails, avoiding eye contact. 'Not my daughter. My wife. We're separated, but the kids really want me to be there. It's…'

'Complicated?'

'Exactly.'

'I see.'

Rachel sat silent for a few seconds while she digested this. She had initially assumed from the absence of a wedding ring that he was single. Then – when she'd seen the picture of his children – divorced. But he was technically still married.

'There's something else, too,' Rob went on. 'You know I've been doing this on my own time, because it's no longer an Interpol matter. Just like you have.'

She nodded.

'Now we have this break, and a there's a real chance of proving our theory, I have to hand over the evidence to the FBI.' He looked into her face. 'I have no choice Rachel, you know that.'

'I'm still going to go and see Ethan Rowe,' she said stubbornly, forcing herself to forget about Rob's private life. 'But I'm going to need your help to get in there.'

He shook his head. 'I don't know, I'm not sure I can.'

'Please Rob. I know you want to solve this case as much as I do.' She gave him a half-smile. 'Otherwise why would you even be here?'

Madras, Oregon called itself a city, but with a population of only 6000 souls it felt more like a large village, marooned on a flat valley floor. There was a broad main street with a couple of gas stations, a drugstore and a supermarket, a small park and little else.

There were no hotels either, but Rachel found herself a room at the Sweet Briar Inn; the town's only bed and breakfast. It overlooked a park and had roses in the front garden with a deep porch that featured a swing seat. The interior was a riot of overblown faux-Victoriana; all fussy chintz and lace with a 'parlor' downstairs and 'boudoirs' upstairs. Rachel took a photo of the lace-draped four poster in hers and sent it to Brickall with the caption '*I keep expecting Norman Bates's mother to appear.*'

She whiled away an hour or so checking through Melissa Downey's social media pages. The content was predictable and innocuous enough, but she did find a comments thread on a pageants forum where she and one of her friends were mocking a contestant who was very overweight. Melissa had used a whale emoticon, followed by a laughing face. So, superficially sweet Melissa was a fat-shamer after all. Not a surprise, perhaps, but oddly disappointing.

The ornate mahogany cabinet turned out to be concealing a TV, so after a long soak in the claw-foot tub, Rachel lay in front of the news sipping her turndown glass of cherry wine, and thinking about Rob arriving home to his estranged wife like the perfect civilised co-parent. Helping wrap his daughter's gifts, blowing up balloons, greeting guests. As though he hadn't just chased halfway across the country with an Englishwoman he barely knew.

But this was who Rob was, and she was in no position to change things, or even to be shocked. Someone of his age was going to have baggage, just as she did. That was something Rachel had taken as read when she met first met him, despite the lack of wedding ring. His situation was complicated, so it was just as well she had followed her professional instincts and avoided getting involved. *No regrets*, she told herself. *Well, maybe just a few.*

She consoled herself by eating the home-made truffles that had been left on her pillow. They shed crumbs of chocolate which melted and left dark smears on the lace bedclothes when she eventually drifted into a restless sleep.

THIRTY-NINE

Saturday afternoon was family visiting time at the Pine Ridge prison. Rob had taken the time before his flight to make phone calls to his contacts, with the result that Rachel would be permitted to visit on Saturday morning. According to his email, it would be more 'convenient' for her to be there on Monday, but she was adamant that she couldn't wait a further forty-eight hours. Her time was a precious commodity.

The cover story, constructed with the prison governor's collaboration, was as follows: she was an academic conducting research into the effect of incarceration on the families of inmates. It was decided that this would explain her English accent, among other things. The prison authorities would tell Ethan Rowe that he had been randomly selected to take part in the study. His cooperation would be encouraged, but could not be forced. The challenge for Rachel would be to get as much information as possible from him without raising his suspicions.

After turning down the absurdly indulgent 'Sweet Briar Break-your-Fast' of fruit compote, coffee, muffins, omelettes, hash browns and pancakes with syrup, Rachel helped herself to a take-out coffee and an apple. As an afterthought she grabbed a couple of packets of M&M's from the entrance hall's self-styled 'Treat Table' as she headed out to her car. Madras had had an airbase during the war and retained a tiny airport. That tiny airport had a single rental car franchise whose sole available vehicle was hers for the duration of her trip.

She headed due east out of Madras, and after driving for fifteen minutes came to a halt at the wire fence surrounding the Pine Ridge Correctional Institution. You couldn't really miss the place.

'Nature of your business?' enquired the corpulent corrections officer in the bulletproof reception cubicle. He had a thatch of silver hair with a matching beard, and wore a badge that said 'C.O. Ernest Dwyer'. If the guards' uniforms had been red, he would have been a dead ringer for Santa Claus.

'I'm here to see Ethan Rowe.'

'Ah…' He gave Rachel what bordered on a wink. 'You're the lady that's coming to talk to Rowe. Come with me, Miss.'

Ernest led her down the corridor to a windowless, featureless interview room. The place smelt of disinfectant, urine and despair. She sat on one of two plastic chairs and waited. Ten minutes later, Rowe shuffled in, wearing leg irons and handcuffs. The corrections officer removed the hardware and left the room with a small nod at Rachel. 'I'll be right outside.'

Rachel gazed at her subject with ill-concealed curiosity. He was around her height and his build was slight; his orange jumpsuit hanging off him. His hair was thin and mousey, and an unconvincing fluffy goatee beard covered a weak chin. The only striking thing about his face was his eyes, which were a startling jade green.

'Hello, Ethan,' she extended her hand.

He refused to take it, looking down at his lap.

'My name's Miss Prince. I'm studying inmates and their families, and I'm here today to talk to you about yours.'

'They said I din't have to talk to you.' His voice was thin and hoarse, with a faint hillbilly twang.

'It's not going to take very long; I only have a few questions.'

Rowe slouched back in his chair, ankles crossed, chin thrust up.

'Can I start by asking you about your parents?'

He did not reply, half closing his eyes.

'Ethan?'

Silence.

Rachel tried another tack. 'How are things in here? How are they treating you?'

There was no response. Rowe affected a catatonic state, his eyes now mere slits. She rummaged in her bag for one of the packets of sweets she had taken from the B & B. Tearing it open, she pushed it across the table to him. 'Go ahead, help yourself.'

He rocked forward in his chair so that he could slide his hand into the bag and take a fistful of the garishly coloured treats. Leaning back again, he opened his mouth and dropped them in one by one. Then he repeated the process. Rachel waited patiently for the sugar surge to take effect.

'So waddya want to know?' he asked eventually, chewing with his mouth open.

'Tell me about your parents. How do they feel about you being in here?'

'Mom died when I was nine.'

'And your father?'

He gave an insouciant shrug. 'Never knew him. He split when I was a baby.'

'Do you know his name at least?'

'Raymond. Raymond Rowe.'

'And your mother was?'

'Kathleen.'

'Tell me what happened when your mother died. Where did you go.'

'My gramma raised me mostly. Was in foster care a bit.'

'And how about siblings?'

He stared at her blankly with those disturbing green eyes.

'Brothers and sisters.'

'Don't have any.'

'Are you sure?'

'Well, my mom had a couple of babies with my stepdad. Don't really know 'em.'

'Boys or girls?'

'Two boys.'

'So you have half-brothers?'

Rowe had returned to his heavy-lidded stupor. Rachel reached for the second bag of M&Ms and pushed it towards him. 'How about half-sisters?'

He frowned. 'Not that I know.'

'And cousins. Do you know how many you have?'

Rowe filled his mouth with sweets and chewed for a couple of minutes. When he had swallowed he said. 'There's my cousin Rainey. She used to stay with Gramma too sometimes.'

Rachel paused, pen over on the page. 'And how old is Rainey?'

He shrugged again. 'Don't know for sure. Around the same age as me.'

'Do you know where she lives now?'

'No, I don't.' Rowe checked the bag, and realising he'd eaten all the available sugar, turned and bellowed 'Guard!' in the direction of the door. When the prison officer came in, Rowe stood up. 'I don't want to talk no more.'

'Just a couple more questions,' Rachel pleaded.

But Rowe was holding up his wrists in readiness for them to be re-cuffed. 'I said, I'm not going to talk no more,' he enunciated slowly. 'This stuff is stupid.' The prison officer gave Rachel an apologetic look and led him out of the room.

'Get what you need, Miss?' beamed Officer Dwyer as Rachel returned to reception.

'Not really. But I don't think I'll get any more out of him.'

'He's a tricky little weasel, that one,' sympathised Dwyer, checking her bag and then opening the main gate for her.

'Does he get any visitors?'

'His grandmother comes on Saturday afternoons. Lives quite near here. Nobody else.'

'And visiting hours are?'

'Starts 1 p.m. She's pretty much here on the dot of quarter after one every time.' He reached out his visitors' logbook and looked up the relevant page. 'Norma Starling's the name.'

Rachel checked her watch. It was still only eleven fifteen. Did she really want to wait here for another two hours? She could always drive the nine miles back into Madras and return again later. On the other hand, what was there to do in Madras when she got there? And if she ended up missing Ethan Rowe's grandmother by a few minutes, she was certainly not in a position to return again the following Saturday.

Her policing instincts kicked in. She would sit and wait. She occupied herself by sketching out a basic family tree with the limited information she had. Norma Starling was almost certainly Kathleen's mother. She drew a line from Raymond Rowe to Ethan, and placed cousin Rainey off to his right, two rungs down from Norma, with a big question mark next to her name. One of her parents would have to be a child of Norma's too. There were five names on the tree, for now. A fair start, she decided.

There was a knock on her window. Santa Claus stood there with a cup of coffee and a doughnut. She rolled the glass down.

'You look like you could use these.'

'Officer Dwyer—'

'Call me Ernie.'

'Thank you, Ernie. Very kind.'

'And if you need it, come find me and I'll take you to the staff bathroom.'

The coffee was very welcome despite being lukewarm and slightly acid, and Rachel drank it straight away. She had not intended to succumb to the doughnut, but after an hour passed she was not only bored but genuinely hungry, so she polished it off and followed it up with her breakfast apple.

First rule of stakeouts, she heard Brickall's voice saying in her head. *If you've got it, eat it.* This prompted her to check her phone, but there was no response to the photo she had sent him. She photographed her empty coffee cup, the sugary doughnut wrapper and the apple core and sent it to him captioned '*The stakeout diet.*' She fully intended to keep the message-bombing going until he caved in and replied.

She had intended to start researching cousin Rainey, but the sun coming through the car window was warm, and the prattle of the radio soporific. Despite herself, she started to doze. She was woken by more rapping on her window.

'Miss, thought you'd want to know that Miz Starling's just gone in to visit her grandson. She'll probably be out in no more'n twenty minutes. He's no talker, as you know.'

'Thank you, Ernie. Very kind.' Rachel straightened herself up, then climbed out of the car to stretch her legs. She waited, leaning on the bonnet for fifteen minutes until a scrawny woman with wispy, greying hair walked out of the gate and towards one of the parked cars, leaning on a stick. She wore a floral top, polyester trousers that were several sizes too large for her, and open-toed slides which revealed painful-looking bunions.

'Mrs. Starling?' Rachel called out to her. 'Could I have a word with you?'

She was expecting hostility, but was met with a beaming smile. 'You're the young English lady: Ernie told me about you.'

Rachel extended a hand. 'Rachel Prince. Nice to meet you.'

'Call me Norma, dear.' She pointed to one of the cars with her stick. 'You better follow me.'

FORTY

'Now my dear, what can I fix you?'

Rachel was perched awkwardly on the edge of the sofa at Norma Starling's house. She had followed her there in her own car, hanging back patiently while Norma ignored green lights, stamped randomly on her brakes and swerved across lanes to avoid imaginary objects.

The house was a modest three-room, single-storey dwelling – little more than a trailer – on a scrubby, unfenced lot in the tiny, featureless town of Ashwood. There was disorder and dirt everywhere, from the heaps of clothes on the furniture, to the discoloured carpet tiles and the milky film of grime on the windows. Norma had changed into a pair of pink fluffy slippers when they arrived, and her second order of business had been to feed the two vulpine German Shepherds that circled round her thighs. The small living room was pungent with the scent of cheap canned dog meat, but at least their meal was keeping the animals confined to the far end of the kitchen.

Rachel accepted a glass of iced tea, and cast around for a clear surface on which to place it. 'Let me do that,' said Norma, jumping to her feet and clearing space on a side table, which she wiped with a sour-smelling cloth. Next to the glass were two photos; one of a gap-toothed Ethan as a child and one of a young bride with lank mousey hair and hazel eyes. The pale green ones must have come from the Rowe side of the family.

'Is that your daughter?'

'Yes, that's my Kathleen, may God rest her soul.'

'You must miss her.'

'Yes dear, yes I do.' Her eyes grew misty. 'Now, let's have a nice chat. Tell me all about yourself.'

She's lonely, thought Rachel, feeling bad about having to tell this woman lies. But she was at least in a position to give her some much-needed company. She spun the party line about doing academic research on prison inmates, giving herself credentials from Berkeley, which Norma accepted without question.

'And are you married, dear?'

Rachel shook her head.

'Well, that's a pity, good-looking girl like yourself. Maybe you'll find yourself some handsome college professor. Have yourself a house full of babies.'

'I don't think so,' smiled Rachel. 'But I do have a son. He's eighteen.'

'How precious.' Norma beamed. 'And you went to talk to my Ethan?'

'Yes, yes I did. This morning.'

'Not that I expect he had much to say. He was never very good with his words, even as a little boy.'

The giant dogs had finished inhaling their meat, and sat themselves either side of Norma's chair like heraldic beasts. Norma fondled their ears.

'What can you tell me about Ethan's father?' Rachel asked.

'Not a whole lot. On account of he didn't stick around long.'

'Raymond Rowe, is that right?'

'Yes, that's right. Handsome devil he was, but that made him a poor sort of a husband.'

'And he and Kathleen only had one child together?'

'Yes, just Ethan. After Ray left, Kathleen took up with a man from out Willowdale way, Billy Turner. She had two more babies with him.'

'Ethan said they were boys?'

'Yes, Tyler and Drew. When Kathleen passed they were only three and five, and they went to live with their daddy. He remarried, and moved away, out of state. I never see them no more.' She pointed sadly at a photo of two small boys, darker in looks that Ethan.

'And Ethan came to you?'

'Yes, that's right.'

'And do you know if Ray had more children?'

'I don't know what happened after, he never kept in touch. Not with me. He left Oregon for a while and went east. I do know that he was married before he met Kathleen, and they had a daughter. Harley, I think she was called. Harlowe?'

'But you never met her?'

Norma shook her head. 'No. I don't think Kathleen did either, even though it was her stepdaughter. I'm not even sure where she lived. Apparently, she was the smart one. She got the brains in the family, instead of the good looks.'

Rachel shifted her weight to free the soles of her trainers, which were sticking to the carpet tile. She took a tentative sip of her iced tea.

'Can I refresh that for you darlin'? Get you something to eat?'

Rachel shook her head, even though she was hungry. 'Ethan mentioned his cousin to me. Said she stayed with you too?'

Norma nodded, patting the back of one of the dogs. 'That'd be Rainey. She's my son Charlie's youngest.'

'And how old is Rainey?'

'Twenty-three. Two years younger than Ethan.'

'Do you have a photo?'

'Somewhere I do, yes.' She shuffled into her bedroom and came back with a picture. Rachel sat straight up in her chair. Rainey was an attractive female version of Ethan, with fair hair and a winning smile.

Young, blonde, pretty.

'Do you still see Rainey?'

Norma shook her head. 'Haven't seen her in several years. Not since she was around eighteen or nineteen. She went to Portland.' She said this as though it was the moon. 'I get a Christmas card from her. A birthday card too, when she remembers.'

'And what is she doing now? Do you know?'

Norma shook her head. 'She seemed to just move from job to job. Didn't graduate high school, so she just had to take work where she could find it, you know?'

'And what kind of girl is she, would you say?'

Norma sighed. 'She was always feisty. My little hell cat, I used to call her. She ain't of much use to your study though, seeing as how she and Ethan haven't had contact since they were little. She's never visited him.'

'Do you have an address for her, anyway?'

Norma heaved herself up and searched through heaps of papers in a bureau until she found what looked like a birthday card.

'Last one she sent me, I believe.'

She handed it to Rachel, who copied down the name and address on the back of the envelope.

Rainey Starling, 2725 NE 14th St, OR 97212

'And your son Charlie,' Rachel asked as she scribbled, 'Is Rainey his only child?'

Norma shook her head. 'Middle of three. He's got Steven, who's twenty-four, and Brianna.'

Another female cousin. 'And Brianna is?'

'Just turned eighteen, this last week. She's a senior at high school, but she's going to be graduating this summer.'

Rachel looked down at her notes. 'Did you just have the two children yourself, Charlie and Kathleen?'

'I've got Lynette too, my youngest, but she's never married, never had kids.'

The sad-eyed dogs had become restless, weaving round Norma's legs, nudging the arms of her chair.

'If you'll excuse me dear, I really ought to take these darned critters for a walk. They've been shut in the whole afternoon. You'd be welcome to join me, and then stay for some dinner.'

Rachel stood up, peeling the seat of her trousers from the greasy chair cushion. 'That's very kind, but I really need to get back to Berkeley and start writing up my notes.' She was already envisaging a cleansing soak in the claw-foot tub back at the Sweet Briar Inn.

She put her hand over Norma's and gave it a squeeze. 'But thank you so much, you've been very helpful.'

As she drove back in the direction of Madras, she stopped and took photos of direction signs to places named 'Horseheaven' and 'Antelope'. After her bath she would send them to Brickall, accompanied with a suitably witty quip that did not betray just how desperate she was to hear from him. Sooner or later he would have to reply.

FORTY-ONE

Since Boston I've been keeping my head down. Lying low.

Outwardly I stick to my regular daily routine. Work, chores, trips to the store. At home I continue with my research, mentally prepping for a new opportunity. I'll have to be patient after what happened last time. I can't afford to go drawing attention to myself. But I'm prepared to wait.

I'm also waiting for law enforcement to come knocking at my door. I accept that it has to be a possibility, however remote. But day after day goes by, and nothing happens. I'm left to my own devices, to my own dreams and desires.

I've got away with it. Again.

FORTY-TWO

On this Sunday, Rachel decided, she had earned a lie in.

She reclined in her lacy four-poster, filling in the Rowe/Starling family tree. The names Harley/Harlowe, Charlie, Steven, Brianna and Lynette were all added on their respective branches. It should have been a calming, even therapeutic activity, but her heart was racing and her limbs felt taut. She had slept fitfully, unable to stop thinking about Rainey Starling. Rainey fitted the physical type. She was the right age. If any of them was Miss XX, then she was in the running.

After indulging in a calorie-dense *Break-your-fast* in the inn's chintzy dining room, Rachel checked out and began the two-hour drive across the featureless plain towards Portland. *This must be what they mean when they talk about Badlands*, she decided, as she passed abandoned mines and fenced-off ghost towns.

The landscape made her uneasy, and she was relieved when she arrived in Portland a little before one. Tree-lined, brick-paved streets and trams gave the city a vaguely European air, and there were coffee shops, wholefood stores and bookshops everywhere she looked. The atmosphere of urban civilisation re-energised her. Despite growing up in suburban Purley, Rachel thought of herself as a city girl.

The address Norma had given her was on the north-east side of the broad Willamette River; a neat brick Arts and Crafts bungalow on a pleasant suburban street.

A man of around forty opened the door. 'Yes? May I help you?'

'Could I speak to Rainey Starling please?'

He frowned. 'Rainey… who?'

'Rainey Starling. I believe she lives here.'

The man shook his head. 'Not now she doesn't. I've been here the past year and a half. It must have been before then, I guess.' He moved to shut the door.

'Wait –' With her ingrained police instincts, Rachel whipped out a hand to stop him – 'did she leave a forwarding address at all?'

'Not that I know of. Sorry.'

Rachel returned to her car to sit and brood for a few minutes. Her time on the beat had instilled in her that you didn't abandon a lead without at least doing some door to door. Asking around. She spoke to an elderly woman in the house next door, who said she remembered Rainey, and her keeping some questionable company, but didn't know where she had gone. There was no reply at the house on the other side of number 2725.

A small neighbourhood café and bakery was the next port of call. The young man behind the counter, who had dreadlocks and impressive flesh tunnels in his ear lobes, remembered Rainey too.

'Yeah, she was cool. Came in here with her boyfriend quite a bit.'

'Do you know where she moved to?'

'I don't, like, know the address, but I think she stayed in Portland.'

This news was only a very minor triumph, but Rachel celebrated by taking a seat in the café and ordering the house cold-press coffee and a surprisingly good lentil salad.

She took out her phone and called Rob McConnell's cell. He did not pick up, and she didn't leave him a message. He was probably still celebrating Annie's birthday, she thought, suppressing irritation. It pained her to admit it, but after only a couple of days she was missing him. Missing his physical presence, but also his perspective and his input with the case. The ease with which they had bounced their ideas and theories to and fro had been extremely satisfying. It was a bit like working with Brickall, only without the mood swings and the swear words.

There was no time to sit and mope. She scrolled to Mike Perez's number and tried that.

'You really need to stop calling me on the weekend, Detective Prince.'

She could hear the smile in his voice, and found herself smiling too.

'Good to hear your voice, Perez.'

'Likewise. How's my English buddy?'

'I'll come straight out with it: I'm in a bind, and I really need some help.'

'Where the hell are you, anyway?' Perez asked.

'Portland. Oregon.'

She updated him on her return to the US after the third murder of a CasaMia host, and that she was now on a hunt for relatives of Ethan Rowe.

'So I went to his cousin's address here in Portland, only she's moved.'

'You want me to find another address for her.'

'Please.'

'Okay…' Perez sighed. 'I guess I could either spend my Sunday afternoon at the gym, or I could unofficially hack into the DMV and social security records of your suspect.'

'You're the best, Mike.'

'Don't think I don't know you're only using me for my access to government databases.'

'Let it never be said.'

He laughed. 'Leave it with me, Prince. Or should that be Prince-ess? See what I did there?'

'I do. Like I said, you're the best.'

*

An hour and a half later, Perez phoned her back.

'Apartment 3, 1315 North West Upshur Street. Only you never heard that from me, okay?'

Rachel scribbled the address on the back of a paper napkin. 'Never. But I still owe you one.'

'Yeah, you keep saying that.'

She programmed the new address into the hire car's cheap satnav and set off. The building was in the Slabtown district north of downtown Portland; a tired 1980s block that housed several apartments. She rang on the bell for Apartment 3, but there was no reply. Thrash metal music was audible from one of the apartments on the first floor, but when Rachel rang the bell for the other apartments there was no response bar the testy barking of a dog. It was back to waiting in the car.

After a couple of fruitless hours her bladder was bursting from all the coffee she had drunk. Rachel capitulated and drove to a Holiday Inn a few blocks away, where she reserved a room for the night. This allowed her to drop off her bag and use the bathroom. It now was six o'clock and starting to go dark. She returned to the apartment block on foot this time, more than ready to get some exercise. As soon as she approached she could see that there was a light on in Apartment 3. She rang the bell.

The intercom squawked. 'Hullo?'

'Is that Rainey Starling?'

'This is she. How may I help you?'

'My name's Rachel Prince. Can I come in and talk to you please?'

There was a short pause. 'No way, sorry. I don't let in people I don't know. Not when it's dark.'

'Please, Rainey. I'm a friend of your grandma. Norma.' This was almost true.

'My gramma doesn't have no friends that talk like you do. You're probably some kind of crazy person.'

Rachel quelled her rising frustration. 'Okay, I tell you what, just open the door a crack and talk to me. You don't have to let me in if you don't want to.'

'You might rush me. You might have a gun, like a mugger or something.'

Rachel rested her forehead on the door. She was tired and she was hungry, and she was close to losing her rag. Or blowing her cover. Or both. 'I won't. I promise. And I don't have a gun.'

There was a silence of several minutes. Rachel leaned on the bell again.

'All right, all right. You can come up, but you've got thirty seconds and then I'm going to call the cops.' The door was buzzed open. Rachel walked up the stairs and tapped lightly on the door of Apartment 3. It opened a few inches. All Rachel could see were heavily kohled eyes.

'Hands where I can see them.'

Sighing, Rachel raised her hands.

The door was pulled back several inches more, and there stood Rainey Starling. Young, pretty and blonde. And heavily pregnant.

FORTY-THREE

'When's the baby due?'

Rainey opened the door fully. 'On Wednesday.' She pressed a hand to her rotund abdomen, the bulge of the baby sitting low, poised for its arrival. 'Can't come soon enough, I'm telling you.'

'You must be very uncomfortable.' Rachel thought back to the last few days of her own pregnancy, and how every hour had seemed like a week.

'You got that right. I'm exhausted. You got kids?'

Rachel nodded. 'One.'

'Well then you probably remember this bit ain't much fun.' She looked Rachel up and down and seemed to relax a little. 'I guess you may as well come in. Standing makes my back ache.'

Rachel followed her into the apartment and sat down at the table in the neat, homely kitchen. Through the doorway that led from the hall into the bedroom she glimpsed a white bassinet, a heap of tiny pink clothes and a huge packet of newborn disposable nappies.

Rainey put the kettle on and made them each a herbal tea. 'So you know my gramma?'

Rachel gave a brief summary of the fake research study. 'I went to talk to Norma yesterday.' When she could have saved me a lot of time and effort by telling me about the baby, she thought, exasperated. 'I'm sorry; she didn't mention you being pregnant.'

'She doesn't know,' admitted Rainey. 'I guess I should call her.'

'Before Wednesday might be a good idea,' smiled Rachel, as Rainey put a Japanese teapot and two matching porcelain cups on the table and lowered herself heavily onto a chair.

'What about the father?' asked Rachel. 'Does he live here?'

Rainey nodded. 'Luke. He's at work.'

Rachel showed her the family tree in her notebook and then wrote in Luke's name to the right of Rainey's, which seemed to please her.

'The baby's going to be called Lark,' she told Rachel. 'Can I put her in too?'

'Of course.' Rachel handed her the notebook and pen. Rainey wrote the name slowly, in a clear, childlike hand, then held it up and admired it.

'This is so cool… oh, wait, you haven't put in Cadence.'

'Cadence?'

'Cadence Rowe. Ethan's sister.'

Rachel frowned. 'Really? I could swear Ethan and Norma told me Kathleen only had boys.'

'I guess I mean half-sister.'

Rachel took the notebook back and looked at her drawing. 'I thought his half-sister was called Harley?'

'Harland. That was his daddy's little girl from before Ethan was born. But my mom told me that the reason Ray dumped Kathleen and took off was because he got another woman pregnant, right around when Ethan was born. And that baby was Cadence.'

'Ah.' An alternate suspect, thought Rachel, her heart speeding. She wrote the name down on the family tree. 'Do you know her?'

Rainey shook her head. 'But I heard plenty about her. From my mom, and my gramma.'

'What do you mean?'

Rainey grinned. 'You know what; I was no angel growing up, but from what I heard, Cadence was way worse. I mean *way* worse.' She caressed her belly with satisfaction.

'Go on.'

'In trouble with the law.'

'What – drugs?'

'Worse stuff. Violent stuff. She's a quite a piece of work from the sound of it. And now Ethan… they must get it from the Rowe side. Ray was a dark character I heard; you wouldn't wanna trust him.'

'Well, thank you, that's all interesting material.' Rachel gave a tight smile. 'For the study. Do you know where Cadence lives?'

Rainey shook her head. 'On the east coast somewhere I think, like Harland.'

'Are the two of them close?'

'I doubt it. Knowing the way Ray was with family, they probably never even met.' Rainey was shifting uncomfortably. Rachel stood up and cleared the tea things into the sink. 'I'll leave you to rest, but thanks so much for seeing me. And if you think of anything else…'

Rachel reached reflexively for her wallet to take out a card, then remembered that her cards said she was a police detective from the National Crime Agency, International Division. She ripped a sheet from her notebook and scribbled her mobile number on it. 'And don't forget to call your grandmother and tell her about the baby!'

Rachel's instinct was to phone Perez as soon as she had returned to her hotel, but it was Sunday evening and she reluctantly decided she should leave him in peace until the morning. There was no further investigative progress she could make until then, even though the kaleidoscopic picture had shifted, making the delinquent Cadence Rowe the most promising lead.

After another fitful night's sleep, she waited until the sun was up then reached for her phone and dialled.

'It's a little early, Prince-ess.' His tone was good-natured.

'Sorry.'

'So what happened – didn't that address check out?'

'It did, thanks. But it wasn't the girl I'm looking for, so now I need you to find me another one.'

'You have a name and date of birth?'

'Not a date of birth, but I know she's around twenty-four.'

'You know what: I'm on the freeway right now. Email me what you have and I'll get back to you after I've checked in at work.'

'Be sure and give my love to Frank Gonzales.'

Perez laughed. 'I'm sure he remembers you fondly too.'

An email from Mike Perez appeared in her inbox around an hour later, after she had done some circuits in the hotel gym, showered and had coffee.

No record of a Cadence Rowe anywhere. Is there another relative who might be able to fill in the gaps?

Rachel consulted her amateur attempts at genealogy, and wrote:

Only two possibilities, I think – father Raymond Rowe, born in Oregon, and his older daughter Harland Rowe. Born 1980s? That's all I have. Do your best x

She checked out of her room, stowed her bag in the car and walked through the Fields park on the edge of the river. A light breeze blew wisps of cloud through a hazy spring sky and she strolled briskly, feeling energised and purposeful. Although if Perez could not help this time, she was not sure of her next move. Five days of her trip down, only six to go.

Perez phoned her as she reached her car again. 'I've found Raymond Rowe.'

'Fantastic, thanks.'

'That was the good news. The bad news is, he's dead. Died two years ago.'

'Oh.' Rachel stopped in her tracks, her heart thumping. 'And the sister?'

'I only found one Harland Rowe. Aged thirty, living near Baltimore.'

'That must be her.'

Perez read out the address.

'Hold on…' Rachel scrambled in her bag for her pen and wrote it down.

'So I guess it's next stop Baltimore, Ms Prince?'

She gave a theatrical sigh. 'Another day, another city: that's how I roll.'

The rental car was due to be returned in Madras, but Rachel was not about to drive for two and a half hours to hand it over, only to turn straight round and fly back to Portland. She phoned HandyCarz and explained that due to circumstances beyond her control she would be forced to leave the vehicle at Portland International Airport. A disgruntled employee informed her that an additional 'relocation' charge of $450 would be placed on her credit card. Time is money, she told herself, and it seemed hers was currently rated at $200 per hour. On leave meant not on expenses.

Direct flights between Portland and Baltimore were another time saver, as was the available seat on one due to leave at midday. Rachel sprinted down the jetway and buckled herself in with the same sort of excitement she remembered from childhood car journeys to the seaside.

She was getting closer, she could feel it.

FORTY-FOUR

The difference between time zones was not in Rachel's favour this time. When the plane had finally taxied and emptied its passengers into the terminal and she had queued to collect yet another rental car – so many now, she could barely keep count – it was after nine in the evening. The map on her phone estimated that the drive to Harland Rowe's address would take around forty minutes. So by the time Rachel arrived, Rowe might well have turned in for the night. The visit would have to wait until Tuesday morning. For now, a room in another airport motel beckoned.

Pikesville, where Rowe lived, was a pleasant outer suburb north of the city. The nine-storey block was bland 1960s red brick – rectangular windows flanking rectangular balconies – but well-maintained and prosperous-looking, surrounded by mature trees. And it had a doorman.

Rachel waited while he went into the office area behind his desk twice to fetch spare apartment keys for visiting workmen. When she finally had his attention, he informed her politely that Miss Rowe was out at work.

'I believe she works at Johns Hopkins,' he told her, naming the world-renowned centre of medical research, adding, 'She normally leaves like clockwork at five before nine, gets home quarter after five. Can I give her a message?'

Rachel smiled. 'It's okay, thanks.' She didn't tell him she would be back later, in case this was relayed to 'Miss Rowe', and she in turn was minded not to be in to callers.

The area around Baltimore's inner harbour was lively and tourist-friendly. Rachel whiled away a pleasant couple of hours drinking coffee and wandering aimlessly in and out of shops whose contents didn't really interest her. She ate some lunch in a seafood restaurant, admired the boats and visited the modern aquarium building. When she passed a bowling alley called 'Strike Three', she sent a photo of the sign to Brickall, captioned *'Guess I'm buying the drinks.'*

And this time, finally, her phone buzzed with a reply.

You're still not funny, Prince

And you're still a grumpy git

As she stuffed her phone back in her pocket, it rang.

'No good trying to deny you're grumpy,' she said, grinning into the handset, 'Not after that epic two-week sulk.'

'Excuse me?'

It was Rob.

'Oh… hi. Sorry, I thought you were someone else.'

'Is this a bad time? Only I can call back later.'

'No, this is fine,' she said levelly. 'How was your maybe ex-wife's party?'

He paused a beat. 'Well, I guess I deserved that.'

'Just a bit.'

'You're mad at me.'

She sighed. 'No Rob, I'm not mad. But I could use your help.'

'I know, I'm sorry I couldn't take your call over the weekend, I was—'

'Look, I don't care about that. I want to talk about the Stiles case.'

'Where are you now? Still in Oregon? Or back in California?'

'Baltimore, actually.'

He took this in. 'Not so far away then.' When she failed to respond to this, he went on, 'So what's been going on? Fill me in. How was Ethan Rowe, blood relative of a serial killer?'

So she did fill him in, about the Pine Ridge Correctional Institute, and Norma and Rainey.

'Wow, you're quite the bloodhound. This Cadence girl: it sounds like you may have found our suspect.'

'Identified her: yes. Found her: no. Not yet. But I'm going to.'

'Well if there's anything I can do to help, let me know.'

'Tricky, if you don't pick up the phone.'

'Next time I will, I promise.'

'Okay, well, I'd better go—'

'Wait. Rachel… friends again?'

'I'll think about it.' They probably could still be friends, she reflected as she hung up, and walked back to retrieve her car from the multi-storey. After all, she handled the situation better than with Giles Denton. She and Rob hadn't ultimately crossed the professional line, so she had no right to feel disappointed over his personal life.

It was five thirty when she arrived in Pikesville, and the doorman had left the condo building and locked up his office. Clearly the service charge did not extend to twenty-four-hour cover. She called the elevator and headed straight up to the sixth floor.

The brains, but not the looks.

Norma's assessment of Harland made glaring sense. The door was opened by a plain, dumpy woman in baggy black trousers, a shapeless roll-neck sweater, and the sort of orthopaedic footwear favoured by the elderly. Her hair was a dull mid-brown and worn in an unflattering bowl cut and she looked much older than thirty.

Only the Rowe green eyes stood out, from behind thick-rimmed glasses. She reminded Rachel of someone, but it was neither Ethan nor Rainey.

Rachel's research cover story was met with a look of scepticism.

'Do you have your academic credentials with you?' she demanded.

'Well, no, they're back at my hotel. '

'You have tenure where, did you say?'

'At Berkeley. In California.'

'I'm aware of where it is. So you'll know Professor Roger Goodman.'

This threw Rachel completely. She groped for a response.

'He used to work with one of my colleagues at Johns Hopkins.'

'What is it you do there?' Rachel blindly went for a change of subject.

'I work in the medical center. So, you know Professor Goodman?'

'I believe I may have met him, yes.'

Harland folded her arms across her doughy chest. 'Well that's strange, because I just made him up.' She stared, those unsettling eyes magnified by the fishbowl lenses in her glasses. 'So, who are you really?'

Rachel hesitated. The truth was, she could not come up with a sufficiently convincing lie, not when her interrogator was already one step ahead. She was only left with the one card to play: her warrant card. With a sigh, she pulled it out and held it up for inspection.

'Police. I thought so,' said Harland with satisfaction. To Rachel's surprise, her smile became friendlier. 'Come in.'

Harland led the way into an open-plan living and dining room, with parquet floors and a view over a golf course. The furnishings were spare and functional, but with a few feminine touches. Floral blinds, matching cushions, an arrangement of silk flowers, a linen runner on the dining table. The old-fashioned hall stand had just one coat hanging on its row of pegs, and one pair of frumpy low-heeled pumps on the shoe rack. It reminded Rachel a little of her mother's house.

'May I get you a coffee, Detective?' she asked politely. Rachel nodded, and Harland disappeared into the small kitchen off the hall. Her gait was awkward, limping. She reappeared carrying a tray neatly set with a coffee pot, cups, a jug of cream and a bowl containing paper sachets of sugar and sweetener. There was a plate arranged with chocolate chip cookies.

'This is a nice apartment. Is it just one bedroom?'

'Two,' Harland informed her equably. 'Do help yourself to a cookie. I made them.' She offered the plate with some pride, and to make sure the ensuing interview ran smoothly, Rachel took one. Brickall would have taken more than one, she thought, suppressing a smile.

'So,' Harland spooned sweetener into her coffee and stirred it. 'I'm guessing that if you're here from law enforcement, then this is probably about my sister. Cadence.'

FORTY-FIVE

Harland Rowe was not just prepared to talk, she seemed to positively relish the opportunity. She topped up her coffee – not touching the cookies, Rachel noted – tucked her feet under her ungainly body and said, 'Shoot – anything you want to know.'

Rachel took out her notebook. 'I appreciate you giving me your time like this.'

'No problem.' Harland smiled. 'I'll give you all the time you need.'

'Okay, first: how well do you know Cadence? Did you grow up together?'

'Not really. But my father moved back here to Baltimore after he left his second wife.'

'Kathleen.'

'Yes, Kathleen. He moved here with Debra, the woman he left Kathleen for. Cadence, their daughter, was born here. He left when she was quite little and went back to Oregon. She would have been around three or four at that point, I was in my late teens. Cadence stayed here with Debra.' Harland paused. 'I saw her quite a bit when my father was still here. After he left, not so often.'

'So… what was she like as a little girl?'

'Extremely pretty.' Harland smiled to indicate lack of rancour, but the smile didn't quite make it to her eyes. 'Gorgeous-looking kid. But a handful. Debra could never control her.'

'And now?'

Harland looked down into her coffee cup. 'You know, I really don't want to bad-mouth her…'

'Anything you can tell me is important.'

'Let's just say we're very different people. Cadence started getting into trouble with the law as a teenager. Just small incidents to start with: shoplifting, DUIs, public order offences. But then she fell in with a bad crowd and got into worse stuff.'

'Drugs?' asked Rachel.

'Probably. That wouldn't surprise me. But I'm referring to even worse stuff.'

Rachel's pen remained poised over her notebook. 'Can you be more specific?'

'Voodoo. Black magic.'

Rachel stared. 'Really? You're sure about this?'

Harland nodded, then sipped her coffee. 'Of course I am. She belongs to an occult society. Called The House of Spirits. They believe in rituals, and fetishism, and sacrifices. That kind of thing.'

Harland's tone was matter of fact, rather than shocked or disapproving.

'You mean animal sacrifice surely? Not…' Rachel's voice tailed off.

Harland shrugged. 'I really couldn't say.'

'So if the two of you aren't close, how do you know about this?'

'She told me.' Harland refilled her coffee cup, holding the pot out to Rachel, who shook her head. 'She was quite open about it.'

'Do you have a picture of her?' There was not a single photo on display in the apartment as far as Rachel could see.

Harland took an album from the bookshelf and removed a picture, handing it to her. 'It's quite an old one I'm afraid.'

It showed a stunningly pretty teenager with an angelic smile, revealing perfect teeth. It reminded Rachel at once of Rainey. And of Phoebe's school photo.

'Could I keep this?'

Harland considered for a moment. 'All right. But I want you to tell me why you're looking for her.'

Rachel was absolutely not about to start confiding in this oddly self-possessed woman about the CasaMia murders. 'I'm afraid I can't discuss the case at this stage.'

'But why an overseas police officer? Why not the FBI?'

'We're working with the FBI,' Rachel told Harland pleasantly. Rob had almost certainly handed over the file by now, so this was technically true.

'Oh really?' Harland's expression was unreadable. 'Well then I guess the FBI will be able to find her for you. That's their job, isn't it?'

Rachel ignored this. 'So you don't know where she is?'

Harland paused, as if holding her breath. It was clear that this was for dramatic effect rather than genuine reluctance. 'The truth is, she's on the run. I guess that's the best way of calling it.'

'Why?'

Harland shrugged. 'Cadence is always in some sort of trouble with the authorities.'

'And you don't know where?'

'I do not. I haven't heard from her in over a year. But my best guess would be she's back in Daytona Beach. She lived there for a while when she first left home.'

'Any idea where?'

'The boardwalk area, most likely. That's a favourite spot for criminals to hide out. Although…' she met Rachel's gaze with a slight smile. 'Apparently the crime rate there is not as high as it is here in Baltimore.'

There were no available flight connections to Daytona on Tuesday evening, so Rachel was forced to stay on at the airport motel until Wednesday morning. Four days of her leave remained.

As she handed over her credit card to yet another ticket sales clerk to purchase yet another flight, she made a quick mental calculation of how much she had spent on this investigation so far. At least £2000, if she included the transatlantic trip, her share of the five-star San Francisco room, the car hire charges and petrol. The Madras vehicle relocation. She would not be able to claim any of it back on expenses, as she had done with her visit to Los Angeles. But she was so close now. She could feel it.

In Daytona, Rachel followed Harland's advice and headed for the beach. She had envisaged a more exotic version of Blackpool, but this was a beach resort on a stupendous scale. Twenty-three miles of white sand fringed by ice-cream-coloured high-rise hotels, amusement arcades, funfair rides and water parks. She had no idea where to begin looking for her criminal needle in a holiday playground haystack, but decided to begin with a door to door on the main drag, focusing on the seedier, less glossy reaches of Atlantic Avenue. She called at tattoo parlours, sports bars and gaming arcades, but with only a name to ask for, her efforts met with limited response.

Only one man in a pool bar claimed to know Cadence Rowe. He asked to see a picture for confirmation.

'This is the only one I have, but it's not recent.'

The teenage photo left him sucking his teeth.

'Yeah, that could be her. But I don't know where she's at now.'

The temperature was well over thirty degrees Celsius and it was very humid. After a couple of hours, Rachel was sweaty, exhausted and no further forward. Time to regroup.

After she had indulged in a long cold shower and a long cold beer, she stretched out on her hotel bed with her laptop and searched for The House of Spirits. She was taken to a website with a blood-red background and a slide show of images featuring skulls, animal bones, shrines, blank-faced dolls and pentagram symbols.

The House of Spirits is led by master occultists and obeah priests, and has gained worldwide recognition for our work with Voodoo, Black Magic and Pharaonic witchcraft. We offer our members assistance with ritual castings, calling on the sacred spirits to harness the power of the universe and lead them down the path they desire.

For a fee, members could gain access to a list of secret rituals and prayers, purchase 'powerful' bracelets, rings and amulets or 'special' books. Without paying the membership fee of $400 and a processing fee of $50, Rachel was unable to penetrate these offerings any further. But the page featured clickable links to all major social media networks. So far, so not secret. This was a mere commercial exercise, and about as arcane as any other organisation with an online presence.

And then it occurred to Rachel that she was missing a very obvious trick. Just because Perez had failed to find an official record on his government databases, that did not mean Cadence had no digital footprint. If Rachel could find The House of Spirits on Facebook, then perhaps Cadence had done the same and friended, commented on or liked their site. She opened Facebook and typed in 'Cadence Rowe'.

A profile popped up. *Kaydance Rowe.*

Rachel stared at her screen, then slapped her forehead with her palm. Of course. She had been spelling it wrong. She had copied it down in her notebook exactly as Rainey had said it: C-A-D-E-N-C-E, and that was also how she had written it in her email to Mike Perez. So he in turn had been searching for someone who did not exist.

And now, here was Kaydance Rowe's own page. A pouting, scarlet-mouthed selfie, which if you squinted slightly could almost have been Phoebe Stiles. A few dozen friends who favoured poses with aggressive dogs, gangster jewellery and guns. And in the list of friends was Harland Rowe, whose photo was just a blank avatar, and whose account settings were private.

Kaydance's geographical location was given as Florida, so she could indeed be in Daytona. The remainder of her content was also hidden by the privacy setting, but someone with Mike Perez's technical skill might be able to unlock it.

Excited, Rachel grabbed her phone and tried calling his number, but it went straight to voicemail. It was late afternoon in Florida, so would be lunchtime in California. She tried again, repeatedly, but his phone appeared to be switched off. She turned back to her laptop and emailed him.

From: Rachel Prince
To: Mike Perez
I screwed up monumentally. It's not Cadence Rowe, it's KAYDANCE Rowe. Can you search again for me? Thanks so much. R.

Her phone rang, and she grabbed it. *Lindsay calling*, the display informed her.

She cut the call and sent her sister a text instead.

In the USA. Back Sunday, will call then x

Unable to settle, she opened Contacts and tried Rob's number, but it rang out. She emailed him the same message that she had sent to Mike Perez about the Caydence/Kaydance error, opened the bottle of wine in the minibar and sat on the balcony overlooking the vast expanse of beach, waiting for either Rob or Mike to get back to her to her. At this stage it didn't matter which one did so first: she needed all the help she could get.

FORTY-SIX

The man in the bed stirred and rolled over onto his back, kicking the covers to one side. He was completely naked, his genitals brazenly exposed below the white tan line where his shorts normally began.

Rachel looked at him as she towelled her hair, trying to remember what his name was. Don? Dan? Dale? He did definitely tell her when they met in the cocktail bar near her hotel, but by then she'd chased down a beer with most of the minibar wine and two margaritas, and hadn't been paying much attention. He was meant to be her holiday distraction. A small compensation for having the willpower to resist Rob McConnell, but of course it hadn't worked that way. It never did.

And now that she was sober and a headache was squeezing her temples, she was full of regret and just wanted him gone. Rachel prodded his bare foot. 'Hey!'

He stirred slightly, but did not wake up.

Her phone rang shrilly, and this time he opened his eyes. Rachel looked down at the display. Rob.

The nameless man opened his jaw as though he was about to speak, and she had a flash of memory from the night before. He had a loud, strident voice. She clicked *Accept*, simultaneously positioning herself by the side of the bed and holding her hand over his mouth. His eyes flashed with surprise.

'Morning!' Rob sounded cheerful.

'Morning to you too.' Rachel released her palm from Don/ Dan/Dale's mouth and motioned to the door, indicating that she would like him to leave. Then she took the call outside on the balcony.

'Where the hell are you?' Rob asked, picking up the screech of the sea birds harmonising with the wail of a car alarm.

'Florida. Daytona Beach to be precise.'

'Fancied a little R & R before you left, huh?'

'Not exactly.' Rachel peered through the French windows. Don/ Dan/Dale had disappeared, but she couldn't tell whether he was in the shower or had set off on the walk of shame. Where had he dropped his clothes the night before? But no, that was a detail she couldn't remember.

'In that case, it's a question of d'you want the good news or the bad news.'

'Go on,' said Rachel cautiously.

'The good news is I've located Kaydance Rowe for you.'

Rachel punched the air silently.

'The bad news is that she's not in Florida. She's in Maryland.'

'Wait, what?' Rachel attempted to re-run the conversation with Harland Rowe, but her pounding head was not cooperating. 'Rob, I don't want to be rude, but can I call you back when I've showered and I'm on the other side of a cup of coffee. It sounds like I need to focus.'

'I'm in meetings all day, which is why I'm calling so early. I can easily email you what I have. Which is not a whole lot, but it's possibly significant.'

'Okay. But let's try and talk again after I've seen the email. Thanks so much Rob.'

'We still friends?'

'Possibly. Maybe.'

*

From: Robert J. McConnell
To: Rachel Prince
Re: Kaydance Rowe.
Now we have the correct spelling, I've managed to track her to
an address in Madison, Baltimore (attached). It's worth noting
that the property is owned and run by a charitable housing
project, as part of a re-entry program. In other words, it's a
place that gives accommodation to ex-offenders. Although it's
the last known address, there's no way of knowing if Rowe is
still there. But if I know you, you'll want to check it out anyway.
I've also accessed her records and she has quite the rap
sheet for someone so young. A cross-check with CODIS
database is ongoing, so I'd advise holding off until I have
results. Best, Rob.

Rachel digested this as she sipped a double espresso in the motel coffee shop. Don/Dan/Dale had departed without the need for an awkward goodbye, and Rachel had just checked out. She was steeling herself to drive to the airport as soon as she had finished her breakfast. *The last time*, she told herself. *This is the last internal flight I'm going to take. We've narrowed the list of suspects to one, and I'm possibly, maybe, about to bring her in.*

There was another email in her inbox, from Mike Perez. He too had been able to track Kaydance easily once he had the right spelling. He forwarded a copy of her State of Maryland driver's licence, showing an angry but still beautiful Kaydance scowling at the camera. It recorded a Baltimore address, though not the same one that Rob had found. Either way, it looked like a return to Baltimore. Rachel shut her laptop, shouldered her bag and prepared to take what she hoped would be her final domestic flight.

*

The Francis Merritt Residential Re-entry Center was in a run-down suburb on the eastern edge of the city.

'You sure you want to go there?' the car rental clerk had said dubiously, when she asked him to show it to her on the map. He looked her up and down, frowning. 'I have to tell you, it's kind of rough. Tourists don't go there.'

'That's okay; I'm not a tourist,' Rachel said pleasantly. Now that she was here, against Rob's advice, she could see exactly what he meant. The wide streets had an impersonal air, their pavements ill-kempt and lined with boarded-up row houses. On a fenced basketball court, teenagers stopped their game and stared at her as she parked. Rachel had watched a few episodes of *The Wire*, and this could easily be a scene from that show.

The centre was in a modern low-rise block opposite a second-hand car lot. It smelt of cheap carpet and had jarring fluorescent lighting. There was an overweight woman with bobbed steel-grey hair and winged glasses sitting behind the reception desk.

'May I help you?' she asked, cocking her head to one side to reinforce her helpfulness.

Rachel flashed her warrant card. 'I'm looking for a Kaydance Rowe. Is she a resident here?'

The woman checked a clipboard. 'Yes, she is. She's room eighteen. Would you like me to show you where that is?'

'Yes, please, if you wouldn't mind.'

'Surely,' said the woman pleasantly, squeezing out from behind her desk and beckoning Rachel to follow her down a long corridor lit by flickering, buzzing fluorescent bulbs. They stopped outside number 18, and the woman knocked on the door. 'Kaydance?'

There was no response.

'Kaydance, somebody to see you dear.'

The woman opened the door and stuck her head in. 'Looks like she's not here.' Before she closed it, Rachel got a full view of the chaos inside. A grimy, unmade bed was strewn with clothes and at its centre was an overflowing ashtray and a plate of congealing food. The floor was a mess of shoes, make-up, coins, used tissues and dirty underwear.

'She may be in the recreation room,' the woman told her, pointing to the far end of the corridor. Rachel followed the noise of a blaring TV and raised female voices. A handful of residents, who all seemed to be dressed in sweats, were watching the TV. Several were smoking. There was a pool table in the corner, and a game was in progress, amidst much swearing and dispute.

'Kaydance Rowe?'

Kaydance was among the spectators, but Rachel spotted her before she moved free of the group. Her beauty was just about discernible, but dulled by her unwashed hair, nicotine-stained fingers and the prominent pentagram tattoo on her neck. She stepped forward from the group of pool spectators.

'Who's asking?' She dragged belligerently on her cigarette.

Rachel held up her warrant card. 'I'd like to ask you some questions, if that's okay.'

'Fuck you,' retorted Kaydance. 'I ain't talking to you. Not unless you got an arrest warrant.'

'I just want an informal chat.'

'Well that's too bad, because I don't.' Kaydance turned her back and motioned to the pool players to continue.

'Kaydance—'

A tall black girl squared up to Rachel, invading her personal space. 'She just said she don't want to talk to you. Now don't make me show you what that's about.' She placed two fingers on Rachel's sternum and pushed her, reinforcing her message.

Rachel gave Kaydance a long look, then turned and walked to the reception area, where the grey-haired woman was back at her desk.

'You okay, honey?'

Rachel showed the warrant card again. 'Can you look in her record and see how long Kaydance Rowe has been here.'

'Let me see now…' The woman reached into a filing cabinet. 'She arrived here at the centre five weeks ago, from MCIW. That's the Maryland Correctional Institution for Women.'

'And how long had she been in there?'

The woman chewed her lip as she flicked through the pages of the file. 'Looks like she served eleven months on a three-year sentence for felony battery. Prior to that incarceration she was out on parole for felony animal cruelty for four months, and then prior to that—'

'That's very helpful. Thank you.' Rachel turned to go, then stopped. 'One other thing, does she ever get any visitors?'

'One woman comes sometimes. Think she's the only one.'

'Fuller-figured woman with short dark hair and round glasses?'

'Yes,' smiled the woman. 'That's her. Walks with a limp.'

FORTY-SEVEN

Rachel needed to run.

It had always been the most effective way of calming herself and clearing her head. She drove back to the Howard Johnson near Pikesville, where she had booked a room, and changed into her running kit, heading along the highway until she came to a green space. It turned out to be part of the golf course, but there was a trail around its edge that she could pound along. Her headphones were not plugged in for once. She needed to listen to her thoughts.

Kaydance was not their killer. There was no doubt about that. Even before the woman at the residential centre had confirmed her recent incarceration, Rachel knew it to be true. There was the small matter of the neck tattoo, of course. But one look at her room had been enough. Kaydance was a slob with little control over her own life. Their killer was highly organised, meticulous and clinically clean. And Rob's check would surely confirm that Kaydance Rowe's DNA was one of the nine and a half million offenders on the CODIS database. So she couldn't have left the traces on the dress, lipstick and shoes, or the match would have been picked up straight away.

Which brought her back to Harland. She had to be the woman who visited Kaydance, and so she had known exactly where her sister was. Yet she had deliberately obscured this fact, inventing a very plausible wild goose chase that sent Rachel scurrying off to Florida. If Kaydance had been convicted and served time for her most recent crime and been released on licence, why would Harland claim she was on the run? It was a classic obstructive move, one people made when they had something to hide.

She phoned Rob as soon as she got back to the motel, before taking a shower or even removing her sweaty kit. As he had promised, he took her call. By now her agitation had dissipated a little, and she was able to give a clear and logical timeline of the last two days.

'What we have to do now is go back to the family tree and fill in the blanks. There must be more cousins, half-sisters, aunts of Ethan Rowe that we haven't accounted for.'

Rob was silent for a long beat.

'What?' demanded Rachel.

'I was just thinking. You've only got a couple of days before you need to fly back to London. Back to your job. I admire your sticking power, I really do, but realistically what can you do in that time?'

'I could come back to DC now – today – and we could get our heads together. My return flight to London leaves from Dulles anyway, and it's so close to here. I've got a car so it'll only take me an hour.'

The pitch of her voice rose to a squeak, and she was aware that this made her sounded desperate. So be it; she *was* desperate.

'Rachel,' Rob's voice was gentle but very firm. She found herself picturing him talking to his children. He was probably a great father. 'Rachel, I've handed the case over to the FBI. And if we can't make this Ethan Rowe link stand up, then it's looking like whoever filled in for Phoebe's job on that commercial has no relevance to her killing. We're back to the evidence against Wyburgh, and treating the murders as unconnected.'

'But you know the same DNA was on the lipstick in Tiffany's apartment,' Rachel pleaded. 'That proves the two cases are linked.'

'Only if the DNA testing was one hundred per cent accurate, and on a potentially contaminated sample like the lipstick, we can't be sure. Very occasionally, DNA results are wrong.'

'Rob, can't we at least have this conversation face to face in Washington?'

'Rachel... I'd be happy to see you; you know I would. I'm just not sure it would achieve anything. I think we've reached the end of the road on this one.'

Rachel screwed her eyes tight and counted to three to slow her breathing. 'I'm heading back to DC tomorrow anyway, so please just think about it. Okay?' She hung up before he could refuse her again.

After a shower and some food, Rachel felt calmer. She sat down with her laptop and composed an email to Mike Perez in the hope that he, at least, would still be willing to help her. Then, after checking the time in London, she did something she had been wanting to do for a while. She video-called Brickall.

He was at home in his flat, eating pizza and watching a Champions League match.

'Well, well, look who the digital cat dragged in.' He muted the TV, but continued eating the pizza. 'How's life being AWOL?'

'There's no WOL; that would imply 'Without Leave', you moron. I'm *on* leave.'

'Whatever.' Brickall took another bite of pizza, sword-swallowing the long, greasy strands of mozzarella.

'What's that?' enquired Rachel. 'Let me guess – ham and pineapple with extra chilli?' Brickall's love of spice was extended to the blandest of foods.

'Quattro formaggi, actually. With extra chilli. Hang on a minute.' He vanished from shot and reappeared with a can of lager.

'How are things?' Rachel asked. 'Have you seen Shaun Rawlings again?'

Brickall shrugged. 'Not recently. But that doesn't mean anything. I'm just trying not to think about the little scrote… So what's going on over there? You'd only be phoning me if you wanted something. And if you'd cracked the case you wouldn't want anything. So you can't have cracked the case.'

He leaned back and swigged from his can, looking pleased with this analysis of the status quo.

'I'm bloody close actually. I've managed to narrow the potential field of perps from the population of one of the biggest countries in the world to a handful.'

Brickall frowned. 'How the fuck did you manage that, Prince?'

'Hold on, let me send you a visual aid.' She took a photo of the family tree and sent it to him from her phone. 'This will help you make sense of what I'm talking about.'

She ran through the familial DNA match with Ethan Rowe, and her encounters with the female relatives she had found so far.

'So it's not Rainey – about to give birth. Or Harland – overweight, a bit of a cripple and dead plain. Or Kaydance – in prison during the critical time period.'

Brickall consulted the family tree. 'Brianna?'

'She's a teenager. Hardly seems likely she could pull off something like this.'

Brickall nodded. 'Probably, but look at her anyway.'

'I wondered if Lynette, Norma's allegedly childless daughter, had a baby no one knows about. I've asked my contact at the LAPD to check.'

'More cousins seem a possibility. Raymond Rowe could easily have siblings. Any number of them. So there could definitely be female cousins on the dad's side. Or he could have had other children we don't know about, given he was putting it about a bit.'

Rachel dropped her chin onto her hand with a sigh. 'True. Problem is, it will take time to trace them and they could be anywhere. Realistically, I can't do much about it in less than forty-eight hours.'

'And you've got to be back for your promotion board next Tuesday,' said Brickall cheerfully, tearing a chunk off his pizza. 'So basically you're stuffed.'

'Thanks a lot. Very validating.'

'Seriously though, Prince –' Rachel was sensitive to his changed tone of voice. Thanks to their long-standing partnership she could tell when Brickall's brain was engaged – 'If you phoned me because you want my advice—'

'It was hardly to admire your face.'

'What does your gut tell you?'

'To talk to Harland Rowe again.'

'Well listen to your gut; that's what you always tell me. She's told you a load of porkies to keep you away from her sister. Who is a criminal. Why, that's what I'm wondering. Is there someone else with links to both of them that she's shielding?'

'I might as well. She's just up the road from where I am now. I don't need to catch another bloody plane.'

'She's hiding something: that much is obvious. Maybe something she knows about cousins on her father's side of the family? At the very least, before you get your arse back here you need to try and find out if that's the case.'

Rachel nodded slowly. She had been thinking the same thing; she just needed to hear someone confirm her hunch.

'So do what you can, and at least you have a chance of returning with some questions answered. And when you become a Detective Chief Inspector, this will all be a dim and distant memory.'

'Thanks, Mark.'

'And don't be late on Monday morning or Patten'll have yet another baby. And not in a good way.'

There was a strangled electronic gurgle as he cut the connection.

A few seconds later, an email alert appeared on her screen.

From: Mike Perez
To: Rachel Prince
What a smart cookie you are, Prince-ess. I've been through a heap of birth records, and it turns out that Lynette Starling did indeed have a daughter, twenty-six years ago. The baby was given up for adoption. Now known as Melody Burr, and living in Colorado Springs. So she would also be Ethan Rowe's first cousin. Hope this helps. Sincerely, Mike.

Colorado Springs. That rang a bell. Something Paulie had said the first time she visited CasaMia. Heather Kennedy had used an address there. Excited, she ran a Google search on Melody Burr.
About 295,000 results.

This was someone who was hiding in plain sight. And someone whose exposure instantly ruled her out. Melody Burr's Instagram account announced her as a 'Plus Size Model and Body Positivity Icon'. A stream of images spilled onto the screen, of a stunningly pretty redhead with huge blue eyes, blowing kisses and seducing the camera. There she was in a burlesque corset, a fifties prom dress, even naked apart from a coyly draped sheet. And she must have weighed getting on for 300 pounds.

She moved on to searching for Rainey's younger sister Brianna, but all she found was an unremarkable teen's social media activity, full of dental retainers, Snapchat flower crowns and torrid crushes. From the banal commentary posted by her and her friends, this was no sociopathic criminal.

Rachel snapped her laptop shut and lay back on the bed with her eyes closed. She was too disheartened to email Perez and thank him, even though his help had been invaluable throughout her wild goose chase. The light was fading outside; another day almost over. There was just Friday and part of Saturday left before she went back to London. She could give up now and try and enjoy the rest of her time. Drive to Washington and do some sightseeing, with or without Rob's help.

Or she could listen to her gut.

She grabbed her bag and headed out to the car park.

The apartment block was peaceful, as the residents settled in for their evening. The parking lot was almost full, and there were lights on in most windows. A faint murmur of TV sets was carried out on the evening breeze, along with the smells of dinner cooking. The lobby area was quiet, the doorman gone, leaving a security light on in his booth.

Rachel walked up the fire exit stairs, not wanting the pinging of the elevator bell to announce her arrival, and tiptoed the length of the corridor. There was light visible under Harland's door, and the almost imperceptible sound – more a sense – of someone moving about. She pressed the button to the right of the door and heard the electronic 'ding-dong' inside. There was no response, although the moving stopped. This time she rapped smartly on the door. Nothing.

'Harland!' she called. 'It's Rachel Prince. I need to speak to you.'

As she had anticipated, she was ignored.

'Please, I need to ask you some more about Kaydance.'

Nothing.

'Why did you lie to me?' she shouted, slapping the door for good measure. It was solid, with no handle, only a couple of heavy duty deadlocks. As a police officer, assessing front doors became second nature, and this would need either a battering ram or a set of keys. Without either, all she could do was head for the elevator.

There were two women in fitness gear waiting to get in when it arrived on the ground floor. They were engaged in animated chat about their recent trip to the gym, smiling briefly at Rachel as they passed her, then continuing their conversation. Once the elevator had gone, the lobby was deserted. Rachel peered through the glass entrance doors, but could see no one heading into the building.

Moving quickly, she tried the door of the security booth. It was locked. Of course. Her twenty years in the police force had pitted her against hundreds of locked doors. She pulled her Swiss Army knife from her bag and selected the reamer tool.

You need two things to pick a lock, her old sergeant had told her when she was a rookie constable. *A straight pin to poke at the tumblers and a tension wrench to twist the plug to the shear line.* He had shown her how a reamer, which was designed to stitch leather, would act as a pin, while the hook tool would act as a wrench. She had carried a Swiss Army knife with her ever since.

This was a flimsy partition door, and the lock a basic one, so it took her no more than twenty seconds. The drawer under the desk was also locked. As she reached for her knife again, a man walked in through the lobby door. He was distracted by his phone screen long enough for Rachel to duck down below the front window of the booth. From her squatting position, she prised the locked drawer open, and once he had gone, clambered to her feet again. The drawer was full of spare keys, but they were all jumbled up, and the paper labels attached to them so faded they were hard to decipher. It was going to take time to sort through them, so Rachel crouched out of sight on the floor and used the torch on her phone to help her read the faded pencil marks.

Eventually she found it. 714. Harland's apartment. She switched off the torch, closed the door of the booth and used the reamer to lock it again. Then she sauntered out of the lobby and walked to where her car was parked. If Harland Rowe wouldn't open her door, then Rachel would have to do it herself.

FORTY-EIGHT

She's back. The smug British cop.

She called round a couple of days ago looking for Kaydance. Kaydance? Don't make me laugh. As if she could pull this off. The girl's way too dumb, and too flaky. Anyhow, she came back to the apartment demanding to talk to me. I pretended not to be in. Not that she was fooled by that, but it bought me a little time. Time to think about how to handle things when she comes back. Which she will.

Time to decide what to do with her.

FORTY-NINE

Rachel's plan for Friday was the essence of compromise.

She would check out of the hotel, stow her luggage in the car and make a last detour to the apartment complex in an attempt to probe the undiscovered branches of the Rowe family tree. Just for her own satisfaction. And to do as Brickall had instructed; follow what her gut was telling her.

Then she would be content to admit that Rob was right, and that this was the end of the road, and she would hit the interstate to Washington DC in readiness for her flight the following evening. She would return to work and go through her DCI promotion assessments, having first feasted on the generous helping of humble pie which would no doubt be served up by both Brickall and Patten. There was a point at which a wild goose chase became less wild and more goose, and she had reached it.

She already knew from the helpful doorman that Harland left at 8.55 every morning, so Rachel reasoned that if she arrived soon after 9 a.m., apartment 714 would be empty but there would be enough commuter footfall through the lobby for her to blend in. She left her bag in the boot of the car and took just her phone and the spare keys to Harland's apartment.

Sure enough, there were several people waiting to talk to the doorman about Amazon packages and dry-cleaning deliveries when she entered the building at 9.10, so nobody paid any attention as she called the elevator and went upstairs.

'Hello?'

She called out as she unlocked the door, but as expected there was no reply. The apartment was as bland and orderly as the last time, and smelled of cleaning fluid and air freshener. In the kitchen, the breakfast dishes had been cleared and the counters wiped down. The dishwasher was sloshing quietly, and the tumble dryer hummed. Rachel went into Harland's bedroom. The bed was made with starched blush-pink linen, smoothed and plumped like a hotel bed. There was nothing on the bedside tables, and only a hairbrush and a tube of hand cream on the dresser. The closet was half empty, with just a modest collection of elasticated waist trousers, tops and cardigans in size XL. A beige padded anorak hung alone in a corner, with a pair of sensible fur-lined boots on the floor below it, and a small black suitcase on the shelf above it. The en suite bathroom had white sanitary ware, counter and tiles. Off-white towels and bathrobe. Basic brands of shampoo and face cream, one toothbrush. Like Phoebe's apartment, it was giving nothing away.

Like Phoebe's apartment.

To her right as she came out of the bedroom there was a guest bathroom, opposite were the doors to the living room and kitchen, and to her left there was another door. The second bedroom.

She opened the door and stared.

The room was a mirror image of Harland's in layout, but the antique iron bed was covered with a gaudy quilted bedspread in burgundy satin. The dressing table was crowded with make-up, brushes, hairspray and jewellery. Several pairs of high-heeled shoes lay discarded on the carpet and there were clothes draped on the bed. This was not Harland's room. So whose was it?

Rachel sat down gingerly on the edge of the bed and examined the clothes. A green sequinned miniskirt, a sheer chiffon blouse, a strappy black dress with cut-out panels, all US size 6. The beauty products on the dresser would not have disgraced the collection of a professional make-up artist. There were highlighter powders and bronzers, palettes of shimmering eye shadow, primers, false lashes and hairspray; all premium brands. And a lipstick in a rose-gold tube. She twisted it up and stroked a slash of colour against her inner wrist. Orangey red.

Tangier Nights.

Her heart hammering in her chest, Rachel went into the walk-in closet. More clothes; sexy, glamorous size-6 clothes. Baskets full of plunging Victoria's Secret bras and matching wispy knickers. Court shoes and strappy sandals and high-heeled boots neatly lined up against the wall. In the far corner of the top shelf there was a large black lacquer box. Rachel took it down and lifted off the lid, then stumbled back against the shelves, her head swimming with shock.

Inside there was a keyring in the shape of a metal P. P for Phoebe.

She waited for the pounding in her chest to subside a little and looked inside the box again. A Padres baseball cap. A framed photo of Melissa Downey and Clayton Hill. A pair of burgundy Valentino T-bar courts.

There it was: all of it. The key was the spare that Matt Wyburgh had given to Phoebe, the cap – from Tiffany's local team – worn by the killer on CCTV, a photo from Melissa Downey's apartment and the shoes. Rachel took them out and examined them. Size 9. They almost certainly belonged to Talia Schull in Boston, she of the lucky escape.

Here was her incontrovertible proof. Harland was linked to whoever carried out the CasaMia killings. But she wasn't operating alone, and the size-6 accomplice couldn't possibly be her sister Kaydance. It wasn't Rainey, or Brianna or Melody. So who the hell was it?

Rachel waited for her breathing to calm and her detective instincts to kick in. She pulled out her phone from her trouser pocket and took photos of the souvenirs, and the lipstick, then placed the box back on the shelf. Something propelled her back to Harland's closet, only this time she took down the black suitcase and opened it. Inside were bottles of Citranox, Tevlar suits, latex gloves.

Slamming the case shut, she dialled Rob's number, fingers still trembling.

'I promise I'll pick up next time…'

He did not pick up.

She dialled again, and again, and again; the last time leaving a message demanding he call her urgently. Then she went into the living room, where she remembered seeing a laptop on the desk. It was password protected, naturally.

She phoned Mike Perez, and he answered on the second ring.

'It's not even the weekend yet, and you're already—'

She cut across him. 'Mike, this is urgent. I'm at Harland Rowe's apartment.' She was speaking like a speeded-up recording, trying not to waste time. 'And I've finally found the evidence. Real, not circumstantial, and—'

It was Perez's turn to interrupt.

'Slow down.'

'I'll explain later, but for now can you tell me how to get past the password protection on a laptop? Quickly.'

He sensed the urgency in her voice and dropped the playful tone. 'Okay, press Control R or Command R and wait for it to reboot in recovery mode.'

She watched the screen go grey and a loading bar appear. 'Okay, now what?'

'Go into Utilities, select Terminal and then type in "resetpassword" – all one word. Got that?'

Rachel's fingers felt thick and sausage-like as she typed incorrectly then tried again. 'Now?'

'That should pull up a password reset box. Yes?'

'Yep.'

'Okay, you just need to select the user account you want to get into, then the "Enter new password" option. Leave it blank and press enter, and you should be in.'

There was only one user account, helpfully called HRowe. Rachel did as instructed, and there she was on Harland's desktop.

'Did that work?' Perez was asking her.

'Yes, it did. Thanks, I really owe you one.'

'I think we're up to at least three now… what's the address there, so I can—'

'Gotta go.' Rachel hung up and shoved her phone back in her pocket, already pulling up Harland's browser history on the laptop. The most recent hit was some online shopping, then Facebook and Instagram hits. Lots of them. She scanned further down the list. There it was. CasaMia.com.

Rachel went straight to account avatar in the top right-hand corner.

Welcome, Linda!

Harland was currently logged on to the site as someone called Linda Ruffner. The account profile photo was of a girl who was young and pretty. A girl who was not Harland, and whose image was undoubtedly pilfered from her cloud storage. Linda Ruffner had not been on any trips yet, but she had saved several properties as favourites, accessed by clicking on a red heart icon. Rachel paused, and listened. It felt as though hours had passed, but it was still only ten o'clock. While the list was loading, she used the guest cloakroom, being careful not to disturb anything. Then she returned to Harland's laptop to scrutinise her choices, although she already knew what she would find.

There was a shabby chic apartment in Austin, Texas, belonging to Jacqui Garcia. Jacqui looked a lot like Melissa Downey, and listed her hobbies as 'Horseback riding, yoga and hanging out with my awesome bf'. Rachel stared, breathing deeply, before moving on to the next favourite. Laine Zabreski had a charming Victorian conversion in Charleston, South Carolina and if you squinted slightly could have been the girl in the Lovely Locks commercial. Then there was Amy Burns, a former high-school track star in Duluth, Minnesota and Kristin Coley, who had a beachside condo in Long Beach, California and was 'a self-confessed surf freak'. All conforming to the favoured personality profile. Rachel felt sick. There was still no reply from Rob's number. She took screengrabs of all the saved favourites, plus Linda's profile, then clicked the message inbox icon.

Four messages from the CasaMia customer service department. They all contained identical wording.

Your booking request for apartment in Austin, Texas cannot be processed at this time. Reason code: Host account suspended.

Your booking request for apartment in Charleston, South Carolina cannot be processed at this time. Reason code: Host account suspended.

And so on. So the CasaMia security firewall on the potential targets was working, which was reassuring. Rachel used her phone to forward the screen grabs to Paulie anyway, under the subject 'Suspect still active', then returned to Harland's browser history.

The social media pages searched through belonged to the hosts on CasaMia: Jacqui Garcia, Laine Zabreski, Amy Burns and Kristin Coley. Rachel found what she expected to find; the curated evidence of happy, privileged lives. Parties, family occasions, handsome boyfriends, laughing friends. Her mind went back to the conversation she had had with Rob when they were in North Carolina.

What are the characteristics that define the targeted group? Pretty. Spoilt. Popular. Self-absorbed. Entitled.

And there it was: the abundant evidence of those qualities, displayed in their online lives for the world to see. Curated and edited to seem aspirational. These women had not done anything to Harland and her accomplice, they just *were* a certain way.

Rachel logged out and shut down the laptop. It was time to move. Now. She would drive straight to Rob's office and lay out the evidence for him. They had the brains of the operation in Harland Rowe, all they need was to crack the identity of whoever was assisting her. The lookalike who was entering the homes of the victims she selected and killing them for her. The occupant of bedroom number two.

Rachel went back in there now for one last look around and to take the P keyring as corroborating evidence. As she slipped it into her back pocket, her heart leapt against her sternum and she darted into the hallway and shut the bedroom door.

The sound was unmistakeable. A key turning in the apartment's front door.

FIFTY

'How did you get in here?'

Harland looked displeased to see Rachel, but not surprised.

'The advantages of having a warrant card,' Rachel bluffed. She could feel sweat beading on her back and in her armpits, and her face growing pink. Garnering all her focus, she forced herself to stay calm. 'The doorman let me in.'

Harland smiled sourly. 'No he did not. Wesley would have told me about that. He saw me just now, and didn't say a word.'

Rachel shrugged with a *Whaddya know?* expression. *Keep your cool*, she told herself, *and whatever you do, don't let her know it's her you're after. Make her think this is all about Kaydance.*

'So then you probably know I still have some questions about your sister. I came here to try and talk last night, but you wouldn't answer the door.'

'And that gives you the right to break into my home?' Harland put down the bag of groceries she was carrying and hung up her jacket on the hall stand.

'I explained,' said Rachel, keeping her tone as calm as she could, 'I'm following up an FBI investigation.'

'Well, let's see now.' Harland went into the living room with her odd shuffling gait. 'I'm sure I can find a number for the local office of the FBI. Why don't I ask them about it?'

Rachel followed her. 'Really, Harland, there's no need. A couple of questions and I'll leave you in peace, I promise. Five minutes.'

'Well. All right then.' Harland's shoulder's dropped a little, and she managed a wary smile. 'I guess you may as well sit down. Coffee?'

Rachel held up a hand. 'No, I'm fine, don't worry.'

'I'm going to make some for myself, so it's no problem.'

As soon as Harland had gone into the kitchen, Rachel grabbed her phone and checked it. Rob hadn't called her back. She started composing a text, but hadn't got past '*Code 3. You need to*', before Harland limped back with the tray. She pressed 'Send' anyway, and pushed her phone back into her trouser pocket with what she hoped was a casual movement.

Harland glanced in her direction, then poured coffee and offered carrot cake. Rachel refused the cake, adding as much milk as possible to her coffee to cool it down. She needed to drink it down quickly and get out of there as soon as she could, without raising Harland's suspicions further.

'So why did you tell me that Kaydance is in Florida when she's here, in Baltimore?'

Harland stirred her coffee, apparently quite unconcerned at being caught out lying to a police officer. But Rachel now knew exactly what this woman was capable of. 'She was only just out on parole; I didn't want to see her going straight back to prison. Just being a protective older sister.' Once again there was that chilly smile.

'So if you knew she was here in Baltimore, you could have saved us a lot of wasted time, effort and expense. You do realise wasting police time is an offence?'

'Guilty as charged.' Harland remained unruffled, pointing to Rachel's cup. 'Coffee okay?'

'Yes. Thanks.' Rachel swallowed down a large gulp, eager to finish it and be gone.

'So this investigation, this reason you needed to speak with Kaydance… is it about stuff she's gotten into with the House of

Spirits?' Harland pursed her lips in distaste. 'They're a very troubled bunch of people.'

'Yes, that is part of it,' Rachel said vaguely, draining her coffee. 'And of course we are looking into other people too, not just Kaydance.' This much was true at least. An idea occurred to her. 'Did you ever meet any of them? Ever get involved yourself?'

Harland gave a dry laugh. 'I work at the most prestigious medical centre in the world. How do you imagine that would sit with my employers?'

'And what is it you do there?'

'I'm a lab tech.' She smiled smugly and poured herself more coffee.

The damp patches of sweat on Rachel's back had started to go from cold to hot – too hot – and her fingertips were suddenly numb. She pressed her hand to her forehead, which had started to sweat profusely. Harland was looking at her face, the unsettling green eyes fish-like behind the bottle-top lenses.

'Are you sure you're all right?' she asked.

'It's a little warm in here,' admitted Rachel. As she inhaled, it felt as though the blood was rushing away from her head. She was dizzy. Another wave of heat swept over her. She tried to think back to what she had eaten for breakfast. She had only taken yoghurt and some fresh fruit from the motel's continental buffet...

'Let me cool you off a little.' Harland limped over to the window and opened it. 'May I fetch you some water?'

'Thank you.' Rachel slumped in her chair, trying to shake the sensation of travelling backwards, fast, on a funfair ride. She accepted the water and sipped it, then pressed her hand to her mouth, afraid she would vomit. If she could just get out of the apartment, get some fresh air, she would surely start to feel a little better.

'I think I should leave.' Rachel hauled herself out of the chair and stumbled towards the front door. Just beyond the ringing in her ears, she could hear Harland's uneven gait, following her. She reached for the door, but bile surged into her throat, forcing her to cover her nose and mouth with a snorting sound.

'I think you need to use the bathroom,' Harland said in a low, firm voice. Rachel felt a hand in the small of her back, propelling her to the opposite end of the hall. The light was switched on and the door closed behind her. She knelt on the floor and vomited in the direction of the toilet bowl, splashing the floor. As the nausea briefly receded, a flash of acuity rose in her and she heaved herself up using the rim of the hand basin, closed the lid of the toilet and managed to sit down. The coffee. Harland had to have put something in the bloody coffee. With what little energy she had left, she berated herself for being so stupid.

She pulled out her phone with a shaking hand and opened the call log, looking for Rob's name. Another wave of violent nausea surged up from her core, and her vision started to blur. She couldn't read the names but her thumb hit the touch pad and dialled anyway. A call rang out a few times, then somebody must have answered but she couldn't hear through the noise in her head. She tried to speak, but no sound came out, and she collapsed to the floor, her phone smashing on the tiles beside her.

The ringing in her ears reached a crescendo, then faded to silence.

PART FOUR

'I take pleasure in my transformations. I look quiet and consistent, but few know how many women there are in me.'

Anaïs Nin

FIFTY-ONE

It took her a while to realise that she was awake.

Her head pounded, her throat was arid and her vision swam in and out of focus. Gradually, second by second, consciousness set in.

Rachel's first instinct was to sit up. She couldn't. She was lying on her left side, and managed with great effort to roll over onto her back, realising as she did so that her left hand was tethered. She had no idea where she was, or why. She only knew that she felt sick, and thirsty, and that her bladder was full.

A door opened and a woman came in. Rachel stared at her, and her heart began to pound as recollection came crashing in. It was Harland Rowe. She was in Harland's apartment. She had felt ill and passed out.

Harland looked her up and down, but said nothing. She offered a glass of water with a straw in it and Rachel took it with her free right hand and sucked on it desperately. After only a couple of mouthfuls, Harland snatched the glass away.

'Not too much; you already wet yourself once.'

Rachel looked down at her legs. She was wearing a pair of checked flannel pyjama bottoms. 'Where are my clothes?'

'I had to put them in the laundry basket.'

'But my phone—'

'Broken. It smashed when you passed out.'

They were in the second bedroom. Her legs slithered helplessly across the crimson satin of the bedspread; her left wrist was attached to the metal frame with a stout plastic cable tie. It was fastened tightly, and there were already red wheals on her wrist.

'Please let me up – I need to use the toilet.'

Harland looked at her steadily, then left the room and reappeared with a disposable cardboard bed pan. She put it into Rachel's free hand and stood there watching, arms folded, as Rachel awkwardly lowered the pyjamas and pushed it under her hips, silently willing away the sense of furious shame. Feelings like that would only cloud her judgement, and she needed all her focus. *Pretend you're in hospital*, she told herself. *And this is just a nurse.*

When she had finished, Harland removed the bed pan silently and took it away. She did not come back for what felt like a long time, during which Rachel tugged helplessly on her left wrist, searing the skin. If she shouted, perhaps someone would hear.

'Help!' Her throat was so dry and sore the sound was no more than a croak. But it did bring Harland back.

'Nobody's going to hear you, so don't waste your energy.'

'What time is it?' The watch normally on Rachel's left wrist had been removed.

'Nine thirty-five.'

'In the evening?' Rachel turned to the window. It was light outside.

'Morning. It's Saturday.'

'I need to get to the airport. I'm supposed to be catching a flight to London this evening. I have to get back by Tuesday.'

Harland shook her head, pouting with mock sadness. 'I'm afraid you're going to miss your flight.'

Rachel pushed herself backwards with her free right hand, sliding her buttocks towards the head of the bed so that she was more or less sitting.

'Look, Harland… I'm not going to report you for wasting police time. It's not such a big deal, and it's Kaydance we were really interested in.' She hoped she could still lie convincingly, despite her throbbing head and racing pulse. 'Just let me go, and I'll drive away and we'll forget this ever happened.'

Harland sat down on the end of the bed. Her calm – nonchalance even – was more disturbing than any aggression. 'You know why I can't do that. You know exactly why.'

Rachel shook her head. 'No. I don't know what you're talking about.'

'Then let me show you.' Harland reached into a wicker laundry bin in the corner of the room and pulled out Rachel's damp jeans. From the left pocket she pulled out a metal P.

Phoebe's keyring.

She held it up between finger and thumb so that Rachel could see clearly.

'You see? I know that you know.'

At some point Rachel must have slept, because when she opened her eyes, light was fading behind the slatted blind. She was lying awkwardly on her right side, and burning pain shot up and down her manacled left arm. Harland limped in with a tray laid with a pot of fruit yoghurt, a spoon and the water and straw. 'Nothing too heavy for now, your stomach's probably still sore.' With brisk efficiency, she spooned the yoghurt into Rachel's mouth, then let her drink more water. After the tray was removed, the bed pan routine was repeated.

'Harland, you know this isn't going to work. You can't keep me here like this, someone's going to come looking for me eventually.'

The green eyes stared back. 'Really? Are you sure of that?'

She held up something shiny, which Rachel realised was her phone. Then she started hitting buttons and brought up the text messages page, and held it near to Rachel's face so that she could read it. The most recent message was to Rob – not the '*Code 3*' that she had sent before being drugged (via the coffee, presumably) but another one. Sent by Harland.

Ignore my last, sent in error. All fine.

'You said it was broken!' Rachel twisted her body and tried to grab it with her right hand, but Harland was too quick.

'It is now. Oops.'

She held the phone aloft, then brought it smashing down against the metal rail of the bedstead, shattering the screen. For good measure, she dropped it on to the floor, then stamped on it.

'You can't hold me here for ever.' Despite her rising panic, Rachel kept her tone neutral. 'Someone will work it out and come here.'

'Oh, I know I can't.' There was that cold smile again. 'But first we need to talk. You want to know how I did this, and I want to tell you.'

'It's obvious you can't have done this alone. So who else was part of it? That's what I want to know: whose room is this?'

Harland gave her a disdainful look. 'It's mine. Who else's would it be?'

'But who helped you? There was someone – we have photographic images to prove it. Someone who looked like –' Rachel decided against using the word 'victims' – 'the girls.'

'You're a very good cop. Smart. You must be to have gotten this far. But you're just not quite smart enough.' She held up a hand to indicate that Rachel should not speak. 'It's okay, we're going to have a little show and tell.'

She walked to the end of the bed, and waited a couple of seconds to ensure she had Rachel's full attention. She took off her shoes, then the baggy trousers and shapeless roll neck sweater.

Rachel stared, wordless.

Harland was wearing a padded rubber garment that shrouded her body. It extended down from the neck, over shapeless drooping breasts and rotund belly, to the tops of chubby thighs and flabby arms. Nothing too grotesquely large; just enough bulk to give her a shapeless form. To make her a woman unlikely to turn heads in the street.

'A prosthetic fat suit,' she explained needlessly. 'Pretty commonplace in the movie industry, when characters need to grow smaller or larger as part of their story, or actresses are too vain to gain weight for a heavy role. Or to fake pregnancy, of course.'

She reached behind her head and released a Velcro fastening before lifting off the whole contraption. 'Always good to get out of it, the damn thing's heavy.' She held it up for Rachel to look at more closely before leaning it against the wall. Without the fat suit, Harland was slender and toned, her stomach flat and her naked breasts unnaturally perky. Harland cupped them with pride. 'Great, aren't they? The work of a top surgeon.'

She took off her glasses and reached into her mouth, pulling out a dental plate that had been giving her a mild overbite. She smiled broadly at Rachel, showing straight, perfect white teeth. Rachel's mind raced back to Phoebe's expensive veneers, bearing witness to her vanity amid her sad skeletal remains. She closed her eyes, unable to utter a word.

'Open your eyes!' Harland barked. 'I'm not done yet.'

Rachel obeyed.

'Wait there.' Harland flashed her now pretty teeth in a grin. 'Like you have a choice.'

Harland went into the walk-in closet and came out wearing black lace lingerie and carrying a box. She placed the box on the bed next to Rachel and indicated she should use her free hand to open it. Rachel jumped out of her skin; her adrenaline-loaded brain seeing a human head.

It was a long blonde wig. Harland was already pushing her short brown hair into a nylon skullcap, then she reverently lifted the wig and stood in front of the dresser mirror, positioning it with the expertise of long practice.

'This is a custom wig modelled on my own skull measurements and natural hairline. Real hair of course, chosen to be the same texture as my own.' She picked up a brush and ran it through the honey-coloured locks. 'Cost six thousand dollars, but worth it, don't you think? It's no good wearing a wig that looks like a wig.'

'Very clever. But I can see what you did,' Rachel said. 'So you can stop now.'

The hair looked entirely natural but the face below it somehow did not. It had an odd, foetal appearance; the forehead stretched, cheeks a little too pronounced, lips a little too full. The result of an aesthetician going to work with injectable fillers and toxin, Rachel guessed.

'Not quite done yet.' Harland reached into the dresser drawer and took out a long flat box, holding it up so that Rachel could see the contents. Contact lenses in various shades of blue, grey and brown. Of course. Those jade-green eyes of Harland's were far too distinctive.

'Brown eyes, that's what your little English actress had. That's what brought you over here, wasn't it? Phoebe?' She lifted out a pair and with swift, delicate movements inserted them in her eyes. 'Almost done.'

The next stage was to sit herself at the dressing table and get to work with her make-up, applying it with the zest and proficiency of an expert. Light-reflecting primer, foundation skilfully blended with a brush and set with powder. Then shimmering highlighter, three different shadows to create a smoky eye, eyebrow pencil to create perfect arches, eyeliner and false lashes, peachy blusher and finally the Tangier Nights lipstick.

'Harland!' Rachel's voice emerged as a croak.

She held a finger to her lips. 'Wait. Almost done.' She went back into the closet for a few minutes. When she emerged, she was wearing a short red dress and high-heeled sandals. It was, definitively, the girl in the shampoo commercial.

'What do you think?' Harland asked rhetorically.

That you're beautiful, Rachel decided. It was an artificial, contrived beauty; a beauty that worked on camera but would always look slightly strange in the flesh. And then it came to her. She knew who she had been reminded of at their first meeting: Bette Davis as the plain Charlotte Vale in *Now, Voyager*. The reveal of the formerly frumpy Charlotte as a poised swan of a woman with a lush mouth and huge eyes was a moment of immense cinematic power, yet it was the image of Davis's downtrodden spinster with her dowdy bun and thick spectacles that had triggered something at the back of Rachel's mind when she first saw Harland.

The swan incarnation twisted and turned in front of the mirror, her movements graceful. Rachel remembered something.

'What about your limp?'

'Oh, that's simple.' Harland sashayed over to her orthopaedic shoes and held one out to Rachel. On the inside a nail was just visible sticking out of the inner sole. 'Having that stuck in your foot all day long will make you limp, no problem at all.'

Harland put the shoe down again and struck a pose, waiting. She clearly wanted endorsement, praise.

Rachel reached her free hand over to the pinioned one and clapped slowly. 'Quite something,' Rachel told her. 'A real piece of work. Literally.'

Harland couldn't keep herself from smiling.

'But at what cost, Harland, for Christ's sake? What fucking cost?'

'Well, let's see now…' she started to count on her fingers. 'Rhinoplasty: six thousand dollars. Breast augmentation: ten thousand dollars. Liposculpting: five thousand dollars. The wig: six thousand dollars—'

'I meant what about the human cost of what you've done, you deluded woman! The suffering. The unbearable grief.'

Harland's eyes narrowed, and Rachel wondered if she had pushed her too far. But all she said was: 'I have to go out.'

Rachel was forced to watch as Harland took off the dress, heels and underwear, tossed the wig onto the bed and climbed back into her fat suit, fat clothes and ugly shoes. It was impossible not to be appalled, but also fascinated. The lenses and eyelashes were removed, the make-up wiped off and the glasses and dental flipper replaced.

'All righty then,' said plain Harland, more amiably. 'I won't be long. You try and get some rest.'

Rachel fought sleep as hard as she could, desperately trying to free her left arm, but the residual drugs in her system and the after-effects of shock overcame her once more and she fell asleep, the blonde wig lying on her right foot.

When Harland returned, it was dark again.

'I guess your flight will be taking off right about now,' she observed.

To react would be a waste of what little energy Rachel had left, so she pretended not to hear. Harland seemed cheerful, buoyed up by the earlier enactment of butterfly emerging from the prosthetic chrysalis.

'I've brought you some English muffins,' she said, after positioning and then removing another cardboard bedpan. 'I thought you might like those. And I've made tea. I know you British love your tea.'

She held out a plate of buttered muffins, and Rachel managed to take one with her free hand and make a decent job of feeding herself.

'I'm not going to let you hold the tea cup in case you spill it; the angle you're at.' She said this as though it were Rachel's fault she was in a semi-reclining position. Tied to a serial killer's bed.

The cup was lifted to her lips but was too scaldingly hot to sip. 'Can you let it cool down a little?' she pleaded.

'Well, all right.' Harland placed the cup on the bedside table and sat down on the edge of the bed. 'Now that you're comfortable, we can have a proper talk. I'm going to tell you a little bit more about me.'

FIFTY-TWO

'Raymond Rowe was a grifter.'

Harland settled herself comfortably as she began to talk. 'Shiftless. Feckless. Unreliable. All of that. There were no jobs in rural Oregon unless you were a farmer, so he moved here to get employment at the docks. There was always plenty of casual work in cargo handling. It paid okay and there was no responsibility or commitment involved. So it suited my father perfectly.

'My mom was not the sort of girl you would expect him to go for. Her father was a minister and her mother was a teacher. I guess they were comfortably off, and quite strict as parents. She grew up in Guilford, which is one of the nicer neighbourhoods here. It's toney, conservative. I suppose he had something of the wild west about him, which made him different to other men my mom met. Actually, when you think about it, she probably didn't meet many men. And he was handsome. Very handsome.

'He went back west for a family gathering when I was about three or four, got involved with Kathleen Starling and stayed out there. They had a son, Ethan. Then he left her and took up with Debra and they ended up coming out here again. For the work, I guess. He'd been working as a mechanic in Oregon, but was barely scraping by.

'I saw him a little when he was back here; that was when I got to know my sister Kaydance. But my mom didn't encourage it. She had a job as a librarian, a nice enough home thanks to help from her parents, some friends. She didn't want to be reminded of her failure. She didn't really want to have to raise Raymond Rowe's daughter either, especially a homely one who had his eyes. I guess looking at me was all part of being reminded.'

Harland stared into the middle distance for a few seconds, as if stirred by a particular memory, then continued.

'In many ways she was a good mom. She fed and clothed me well, she took care of me if I was sick, she made sure I always got to school on time and encouraged me to study hard. But we were never close, you know? She wouldn't let me get close to her. For her it was all about the duty and obligation. Zero about emotion and affection.

'And I knew deep down that I wasn't the daughter she really wanted. I got good grades and my report cards always said how smart I was, but I was heavy and had buck teeth and needed glasses. I sucked at sport. If I'd been pretty like Kaydance, maybe she'd have been different towards me; I don't know.

'I liked school at first. I mean, I liked the lessons and the learning and the teachers. If you were smart, there were teachers who took an interest in you, no matter what you looked like. They enjoyed encouraging you. So that was good for me. But I didn't have friends. The other kids teased me. At middle school they called me Walt. I don't know why. My mom kept my hair cut short so perhaps it amused them to give me a boy's name. I just learned to ignore it. To not look round when they shouted "Walt! Walt!" I really loved drama; I was desperate to act in school productions. But I never got picked. The female roles always went to the pretty girls, even though I could have delivered the lines a hell of a lot better.

'At high school things got a lot worse. A hell of a lot worse. As the hormones kicked in, there were deep divides between the jocks and the non-jocks. The popular kids and the non-popular kids. I was seen as a dweeb. I had things chucked at me when I walked down the hall. The boys would do this thing where one of them snatched my bag and ran off with it and when I tried to run after them, another boy would stick out his leg and trip me up. I did talk to my mom about it but it just ended up confirming to her that her daughter was a disappointment. She'd tell me the best policy was to ignore them. But how? It's impossible to ignore someone who's tormenting you: that's the whole point. They're in your space.

'The leader of the popular girls was called Christie Becker. I think you can imagine what she looked like…' Harland gave an ironic smile. 'Tall and tanned with great legs and breasts. Long blonde swishy hair, dazzling smile. She planned to become a model. Of course. That kind of girl never does anything original. If she'd joined the Peace Corps or tried to find a cure for cancer, then maybe the world would have owed her something. But girls like that don't think that way. They're not capable. They're happy just to rest on pretty.

'Anyhow, Christie made it her personal mission to taunt me and humiliate me every chance she got. Boy, how it made her laugh! It got worse and worse, and by our senior year she wasn't happy with putting glue in my hair, sticking my sanitary pads to the back of my sweater or making the boys smear boogers on the pages of my books. No, she wanted to go big, do something that would really make everyone say how hilarious she was. How cool.

'She was dating one of the jocks. Big surprise, right? He was called Josh Anstead, and he was good-looking but pretty stupid. He did great on the football field but his grades always sucked. So one day, when we were studying for final exams, he asked me to help him with calculus. He didn't get it at all, and I found it pretty easy. So I spent some time helping him. And he was nice to me. Told me I had pretty eyes, and he liked hanging out with me. Then one day after we'd finished studying, he kissed me. I said: "What about Christie?" He said, "Me and Christie are breaking up."

'I enjoyed the kiss, it felt pretty nice. I was surprised, of course I was. But so excited. I remember almost running home afterwards and going straight to my room to write in my diary. I wrote something like "I think I love Josh Anstead" and a load of hearts. Practised writing "Harland Anstead", which I thought had a lovely ring to it. You know, the hokey stuff teenage girls do.

'The next time, he told me to meet him outside behind the bleachers. I wanted to do more kissing, but he pushed me away from his face – quite roughly – and told me he wanted a blow job. I said I didn't really want to. He told me that Christie used to give him head, and if I wanted to be his girl then I needed to do it too. So I did the only thing I thought I could do. I got down on my knees and started... you know, sucking him off. I hated how it felt. It was taking him ages to get hard and he was getting mad at me; telling me I was doing it wrong and I was dumb. And then I heard laughing and I looked over my shoulder and there was Christie and some of Josh's friends, and Christie was filming me. This was thirteen years ago and people didn't have video on their phones, but a bunch of the kids at school had those little hand-held camcorders. And Josh pushed me away, and he was laughing too. "You didn't really think I'd be interested in you did you? You moose!" That was what he said.'

Harland looked down at her hands and shuddered.

'I was crying so damn hard my throat closed right up. I couldn't even see. I made it home somehow. Cried for about fifteen hours straight, till my eyes were like golf balls. But it wasn't over, oh no. Christie put the footage of me on tape, and invited everyone over to watch it one night when her parents were out. They gave it some dumb porno title like *Ugly virgin's first time*. No wait: *Gonzo gobbles*. That was it. Gonzo gobbles. When I walked down the halls the boys would be making turkey gobbling noises. Some of the girls started calling me Harlot instead of Harland. Christie thought that was pretty funny. Of course she did.

'And from then... all I can say is that I was completely broken. For years I'd done my best to do what Mom said and just ignore stuff. I had gotten quite good at putting up a front. I had a thick skin. And during senior year I'd made a couple of friends amongst the other uncool kids. I was just about okay until this happened. But afterwards I was frozen. That's the only way I can describe it to you. I walked around like a zombie. There were tears in my eyes all the time. *All the freaking time.* I was constantly swallowing or holding my breath to stop the tears coming. These days I'd be diagnosed with an anxiety disorder – I think that's what they call it now, right? I'd probably be put into therapy. But back then nobody cared. I didn't dare speak to anyone, didn't interact with anyone. I ate lunch on my own. Then I stopped eating lunch. I couldn't even eat. The few friends I'd had stopped talking to me because they were afraid to be seen near me. Except for one guy, called Marty Pogrow. But he'd been accused of touching some nine-year-old boy, and was such a pariah that being seen with him was worse than being alone. So I avoided him too. There are probably prisoners in Guantanamo who are less wretched than I was then.'

Harland gathered herself, forced a little smile.

'But... it was the last year, so high school ended. That's the only good thing I can say about it. I got a place at college to study biochemistry, then started working in the labs at Johns Hopkins. My mom died and I inherited money from her and from my grandparents and was able to buy this place. I worked hard, and I saved. I didn't go out and spend money, I had no hobbies, so aside from what I spent on food and bills I saved. I'd started losing weight during that last semester at school when I was too miserable to eat, and I kept it going. I went to the gym at work.

'I met a guy there and we dated for a few months, but it didn't work out. He didn't get it. He didn't get me. I had this rage inside me, but it had gone from that burning white-hot pain I felt at school to something cold. It was a cold kind of anger that I carried like a piece of rock inside my heart. What is it they say? Revenge is a dish best served cold? I get that totally. The anger turns cold in you, it turns hard. You know you're going to act, but you also know you can wait.

'And in the meantime I had stuff to do. I worked hard in the gym, and I augmented my efforts with lipo. I saved to get my boobs done. I got my nose done; it used to be big and hooked. Like a witch's. I had my teeth fixed and a cosmetologist worked on refining the shape of my face. I practised with make-up and I bought the wig. And size 6 clothes for my real shape.'

She waved at the wardrobe. 'I try them on in here. I like to experiment with different looks. I wonder what Josh Anstead would think of me if he saw me now. You know, I looked for him online, and he's lost almost all his hair. Not so cute now.

'I stopped using the gym at work and started wearing loose, bulky clothes. Colleagues thought I was gaining weight. Eventually I had the fat suit specially made by a theatrical effects business in New York. I told them I worked for a theatre company and we needed it for a production of *Hairspray*. I was going to be Tracy Turnblad. So to the world out there, to my co-workers, I was just plain, dumpy old Harland, with her lab coat and her protective goggles and her limp.'

Harland looked directly at Rachel. 'You're probably wondering why I didn't just go after Christie Becker, right? She still lives in Maryland, so I could have gotten my own back on her quite easily. Surprise, surprise: she never really made it as a model. She got married a couple of years after high school. He's a car salesman, and by all accounts a bit of an asshole. By the time she was twenty-five she already had a couple of kids and another on the way, and her pig of a husband was playing around with someone else. She gained thirty pounds and had some kind of a breakdown. Doesn't work; just stays home with the kids and chows down on Cymbalta and

Xanax. Probably washed down with some chardonnay or vodka. She's a mess.

'So, you see, going after her wouldn't have worked. I don't want revenge on someone like that. She's already messed up her perfect little life all on her own. Karma has come her way and done the job for me. Which is great.'

'So why not leave it there?' Rachel asked. 'Walk away? The best revenge is living well.'

Harland frowned as though she was a simpleton. 'Because there are so many more Christies out there. So many mean girls who still have their perfect little lives, who poke fun at girls who are overweight or plain. And I can be like them. I can have their homes. I can have their lives. And I can make them pay.'

FIFTY-THREE

Rachel was silent, her mind whirring. For a while she had even managed to forget about her throbbing wrist and the burning pain in her left shoulder.

'I expect you have questions.' Harland was still on the edge of the bed, her expression almost shy.

Rachel nodded, drawing on her experience of interviewing criminals and trying to remain as detached as possible. 'If you to managed to make such an incredible change to your appearance – all that work and money – why not be proud of it? Why not just live permanently as…?' She twitched her left shoulder in the direction of the wig and the make-up on the dresser. 'Why not just do that? Be that person. Get out there with your size 6 body and your pretty face and knock 'em dead. That would give the likes of Christie Becker something to think about.'

Rachel found it impossible not to forget her fear for a few seconds and inject a note of empathy into her words.

Harland was nodding slowly. 'I hear you. That's a tough one to answer.' She thought for a minute. 'Only way I can explain it is that you need a heck of a lot of confidence to pull that off, and I just don't have it. Not after I was broken down the way I was. I lack the confidence to carry off being that –' she pointed at the wig – '24/7. I like to be able to hide, I guess. Being able to switch in and out of it.'

Rachel remembered Brickall's treatise on bullying at school. Fifty–fifty. 'An awful lot of kids go through bullying,' she observed.

It doesn't make them killers.

Harland shrugged. 'We all react differently to different situations I guess,' she responded dispassionately, as though they were discussing taste in interior décor.

'So, how about your work as a lab technician? Didn't your employers think it odd when you…' Her voice trailed off as once more she tried to work out how to phrase the question. She couldn't bring herself to say *when you disappeared to kill people*. She was on the brink of gaining Harland's trust, and she couldn't risk blowing it now. Pussyfooting – flattery even – was essential. 'Why did they think you kept taking absences? Didn't they mind?'

'Oh, I'm self-employed,' said Harland airily. 'After I'd been there a few years I was given the chance to go onto a freelance contract. I set my own hours: work a few weeks on, a few weeks off.'

'I see. Okay, something else that I'd like to know.'

'Shoot.' said Harland, smiling now.

She craves attention, thought Rachel. *It's been that way all her life. Rejected, ignored, overlooked.* Something that can push you one of two ways: self-destruction or destruction of others.

'Why go through a home-sharing app to find people? It seems like… how can I put this?'

'Too much work?'

Rachel nodded. 'Exactly. It's another layer of detail and organisation, and that just adds massive risk, surely?' The investigator in her was genuinely interested in the answers to her questions. *Treat her as if you're in the interview room*, she repeated over and over in her head. *Don't lose it and lash out at her.*

'Well, first up, I enjoy the detail and the organisation. You could say that floats my boat. And remember, when you meet someone in that way, the interface confers a huge logistical advantage.' Harland spoke as though describing a marketing campaign rather than a psychopathic murder. 'Think about it: when you host on CasaMia you're electing to open yourself up to complete strangers.

You are inviting them right into your life. You're not suspicious or afraid, your guard is right down. Quite the opposite really; you're saying, "Here's my home, come on in!" That's why it was ridiculously easy to do what I did. Because they welcomed me in. They literally didn't see it coming.'

She glanced at Rachel for a reaction, but there was none, so she went on. 'But mostly it's what you get in exchange for that extra preparation. It's a trade-off, where the effort is matched by the reward. If you just, say, pick out a girl in the crowd and go after her, what are you left with? Nothing. I wanted to get inside the lives of these girls. I wanted to understand how it felt to truly be popular and entitled. I wanted to *be* them, just like I wanted to when I was at high school. When you create a home-sharing profile, you're giving people a little window into your life. I built on that basic information by researching my hosts thoroughly in advance. And if they then handed me the key to their home, I was rewarded with access-all-areas.'

'Temporarily. Each time, you knew it couldn't last.'

'Sure. But there are always more. There are a lot of entitled little homecoming queens out there.'

Rachel thought of Phoebe and Tiffany, and their callous treatment of the Harlands of this world. She thought about Melissa Downey, who by all accounts was a decent girl, but who couldn't resist a bit of body-shaming of her own. She made her next observation as delicately as she could, but there was no way of whitewashing it completely.

'So the pleasure was in inhabiting someone else's life,' she offered. 'It wasn't about ending it.'

Harland stared straight ahead, green eyes glittering. 'Exactly right, Detective. The God's honest truth is; I didn't like the killing part at all. I find it distasteful. It was something that had to be gotten out of the way.' She gave her odd smile. 'And believe me, a dead body is a massive inconvenience.'

'So, with Phoebe Stiles?'

'That was pretty straightforward.' Harland was matter of fact, and Rachel knew she must go along with this approach. Ensure things were unemotional, free of recrimination. Because keeping Harland on side was just about her only hope of getting out of that room alive. 'It was a nice clean blow; trust me, she didn't suffer at all.'

'And once you'd done it, you could go along to her modelling assignment in her place.'

Harland glowed. 'Exactly right. And I did enjoy that. I even had a go at a British accent. I had to wear the brown contacts – which gets uncomfortable pretty quickly – and the stylist was trying to mess with my wig. The shoes were the wrong size too, which nearly derailed the whole thing. But I thought it went pretty well, all things told.'

'I guess you could say that,' Rachel conceded, thinking back to the video, trying not to let her mind stray to Phoebe's flower-laden casket. 'And after that, impersonating her in phone messages wasn't too much of a stretch.'

'Exactly. And the boyfriend's texts let me know he was going to Reno, so all I had to do was use the spare key he gave her and make a gift of the weapon.'

'Your lab experience must have helped you when it came to cleaning up?'

'Sure,' Harland preened.

'But of course Tiffany Kovak was first,' said Rachel. 'I almost forgot.'

Harland pulled a face. 'Let's be honest; she was quite forgettable. Easy enough to get her out of the way, but her life wasn't exciting enough. She had a nice car, but that was about all. After I'd driven around in it a bit, I got bored. The school gym staging was probably the best part. I thought that was quite a stroke on my part. Took me right back to Christie and Josh.'

'But you made a mistake when you cleaned up. You left a lipstick.'

Harland laughed. 'No! No, that was deliberate! Out of boredom I guess. Just a little clue to keep things exciting. I knew nobody would figure out who it belonged to.'

Rachel gestured with her free hand. 'And yet, here we are.'

The silence that followed was tense. 'Tell me about Melissa,' Rachel prompted.

'Well that didn't go so well. To start with, anyhow. I had to, you know –' she mimed strangling – 'which I did not like at *all*. I hated it.' Harland shuddered, as though it were she who was the victim. 'But the boyfriend kind of made up for things. He reminded me a lot of Josh Anstead.'

'You killed him too?'

'I had sex with him, and *then* I killed him.' Harland's tone was boastful. 'Shows how much he must have loved her, right? But first I got him to help me with the body. He didn't know that it was his girlfriend he was lifting, of course. And he was very easy to finish off, which evened things up after the –' she pointed to her neck – 'business.' She spoke with genuine satisfaction.

'And Talia Schull? In Boston?'

Harland sighed. 'Mixed success there. But, you know, in some ways it was good that she stayed out of my way. There was no body to get rid of, and I had fun being her. I did her job in a lawyer's office, and that was a great experience. I put my latent acting talent to good use again. And I was actually pretty good at it anyway. I like to think I would have made a good lawyer.' She looked almost wistful. 'Plus, she had awesome clothes.'

'So overall, Boston was good?'

'Yes, I'd say so.'

Rachel felt a tsunami of exhaustion and delayed shock wash over her. The room was warm and stuffy and filled with the pervasive smell of cloying perfume. A dull pain pulsed at her temples. She wanted desperately to get up and move her legs. To run.

Sensing her mood, Harland stood up. 'You look beat. Tell you what, why don't I make you a little more comfortable?' She left the room and came back with kitchen scissors and a fresh cable tie, proceeding to cut Rachel's left arm free, but only once she had fastened her right arm to the bed frame in its place. The relief from the spasms in her left shoulder was immense, but it was only a matter of time before the right side took up the burden. The sores on her left wrist were open and weeping. After offering a bedpan, Harland wished her a good night and left, exactly as though she was a regular guest.

Rachel was desperate for sleep, but forced herself to stay awake. She could hear Harland in the other bedroom, moving around without her manufactured limp. There was some clattering in the kitchen, then taps running, a toilet flushing, the faint sound of a TV or radio. Eventually, with an effort that took every ounce of her strength, Rachel lasted out until she heard the click of a light being turned out. Silence. How long would it take Harland to fall asleep, Rachel wondered?

She did not have to wait too long. After what must have been less than twenty minutes, she was rewarded by the sound of long, loud snores from the other bedroom.

Adrenaline kicked in. The cup of tea had been left cooling on the bedside table next to what had been her free hand at that point: her right. Harland had been so engrossed in her tale, she had forgotten to clear it away.

Now it was Rachel's right hand that was tied and her left that was free. She performed a manoeuvre that was the bastard offspring of basic military training and hatha yoga, flipping her newly freed left wrist over her right shoulder and twisting, until she had rotated far enough to pick up the tea cup. She lifted it to her lips and drained the cold tea. She would pay for that later with the need to pee, but so be it. Then she took the china cup and smashed it hard against the iron bed frame. It cracked cleanly into two pieces which she managed, with great difficulty, to shove out of sight but within grasping distance, under the mattress.

Panting slightly, she fell back on the bed and drifted off to the sound of her captor's snores.

FIFTY-FOUR

It was light outside, thin fingers of sunlight penetrating the slatted blind and dappling the carpet. Since there was no clock in the room and Rachel no longer had a watch, she was unable to check the time. All she knew was that her bladder was so full that it was giving off sharp stabbing pains, and the headache that was a mere tapping the evening before was now a jackhammer. She attempted to exercise her sore, weak legs with a cycling motion and ankle rotations.

This was the second morning she had woken up to find herself lying here on this bed, almost immobile. Nearly forty-eight hours of thinking that surely, soon, someone would come. But nobody had. Where were they? Where was Rob? And what about Joe? Would he be worrying about his messages going unanswered? A wave of despair washed over her, bringing tears in its wake. She brushed them away with her left hand and wiped her nose on her sleeve, which was all she had.

Harland noticed her reddened eyes when she came in, but instead of mollifying her they seemed to cause fury. Mean Harland was back with a vengeance, jabbing the bed pan against Rachel's buttocks, forcing her to drink scaldingly hot coffee, refusing to let her feed herself cereal in case she spilled the milk. Harland didn't need to feed her at all – what purpose did it serve? And yet she didn't seem to be able to stop herself, as though propelled by some dormant nurturing instinct. Would she have been different,

Rachel wondered, if her family had been a functional one, if she'd been happy and accepted at school? Would that have put paid to the powerlessness that flipped itself inside out, becoming a need to overpower.

As she went to the door with the breakfast tray, Rachel asked. 'Could I have some painkillers? Please.'

There it was again: the tight-lipped, mean look. But Harland returned a few minutes later with two Tylenol and some water, waiting silently while Rachel swallowed the tablets. Then she left Rachel alone for what felt like hours. There was the noise of sweeping, then vacuuming in the background. Rachel continued her feeble attempts at exercise, waiting. It was Sunday. The next morning, Rob would be back at his desk. Back in London, in only a matter of hours, she would be a no-show at the NCA, and not answering her mobile either. Would someone there check on her, or would they think she was extending her paid leave into an unauthorised absence? Surely, given her potential promotion, they wouldn't think she'd stayed away of her own volition?

Harland eventually reappeared, looking serious. She sat on the edge of the bed. 'I want to ask you something.' She wasn't wearing the glasses or the dental plate or the fat suit, but her body was shrouded in loose clothes, as though she needed to keep it in check.

'Go on.'

'Do you think I'm crazy?'

Rachel did not reply.

'You do!' said Harland shrilly. 'You think the only explanation for this is that I'm crazy.'

Rachel shook her head. 'No, I was just thinking how to answer the question, that's all.' She drew in a deep breath. 'I think you suffered trauma in the past, and that's acted as a trigger for you acting in a way that many people would consider to be... abnormal. I understand that you were driven to your actions by some very powerful feelings. Not all of which seem crazy to me, no.'

Harland had stood up and picked up her wig, grooming it as though it was a pet. 'I don't believe you. You were probably one of the popular girls at school yourself. I expect you had things pretty easy.'

Keep her sweet, thought Rachel. Keep her talking, and someone might come. *Please let someone come.*

'Actually, Harland, you're wrong.' Rachel pulled herself up with her free elbow so that she was sitting. 'I was definitely not one of the cool kids.'

Harland gave her a wary look, but Rachel could tell that she really wanted this to be true. Which indeed it was.

'I was a bit of a heifer, and shy. Not a huge fat blimp, but tubby. In a kind of shapeless way.' She held up a strand of blonde hair. 'And before I could afford to spend a fortune on highlights, this was just plain mouse-coloured. I wore braces on my teeth for years. I wasn't academically gifted, or musical, and – like you – I never got picked for acting roles. I was okay at athletics, but way too clumsy to do well in team sports. I was just a bit of a nothing, really. And I was picked on.'

'For real?' She had Harland's full attention now.

'Yep. Nothing as extreme as you went through, just name-calling, having my bag snatched, my games kit nicked. That kind of thing. But it affected my confidence, even so.'

Harland sat on the bed again. 'So what did you do about it?'

'Worked as hard as I could and got a place at police college. I got into fitness and running, and shed the puppy fat. Lost the braces, dyed my hair blonde. But it was finding something that I was good at that made the real difference.' She tried not to let her voice shake when she spoke the next words. 'I'm a good police officer, and that gives me confidence. And that's what defines me now, not what happened in my past.'

It was impossible not to make this last bit sound like a criticism, but Harland disregarded it, instead latching onto the tale of Rachel's transformation. 'So in a way you're just like me.' This seemed to please her inordinately.

It was an uncomfortable idea, but Rachel was starting to see the truth in it. There were undoubtedly similarities between them, however minimal. Harland was a bloodless killer who disliked violence and gore and focused on details to make her crimes clean and tidy. Rachel had had her style of policing described as 'bloodless'. She didn't bear grudges or become angry with the criminals she pursued, preferring not to involve her emotions where at all possible. Her romantic partners complained of her self-containment, her detachment, her emotional unavailability. And some of that control stemmed from having been being bullied; she had learned to disassociate herself at will.

'I think we are alike in some ways, yes,' Rachel agreed, unwilling to voice the obvious fact that her own mild misanthropy was a long way from Harland's malignant narcissism.

Harland disappeared and came back with a peace offering in the shape of a bowl of Jello. She watched Rachel eating it; her eyes never leaving her face. 'Do you promise you didn't make that stuff up about when you were at school?'

'It's God's honest truth,' said Rachel. 'But come on Harland, you're highly intelligent, and you're observant. I think you know.'

Harland nodded. 'Yes. I believe you.' Her voice was soft. 'And I'm really, really glad you told me. You get it; I can see that now. And you've no idea how much that means.'

She removed the empty Jello bowl and gave Rachel a paper towel to wipe her face. 'If I were to let you go, what would you do?'

Rachel stared. She was so floored by this possibility that she didn't know how to answer.

'What would you do?' Harland persisted.

'I suppose I'd go straight to the airport and get on the next flight back to London.'

'Because I'm thinking that I should let you go. I think you deserve it.'

'When?' Rachel's insides curdled with adrenaline. Was there a real possibility that she was going to get out of that room?

'This evening, maybe. Yes, probably. I don't know. I've got some stuff to do now, but I'll think about.'

With that, she disappeared.

It was almost dark by the time Harland came back, by which time Rachel's whole body was one jangling nerve. She looked in dismay at the supper tray that was offered: cheese sandwiches and another yoghurt.

'I thought you were going to let me go?'

'Ah, yes.' Harland sounded sad. 'I thought about it, and I've decided I can't. Not just now.'

'What do you mean?' Rachel struggled to quell her rising panic. *Stay calm*, she told herself. *Stay on her side.*

'I need to keep you here just a tiny bit longer, just while I work some things out.'

'What kind of things?'

Harland picked up the tray and headed to the door.

'Harland, what did you mean, what kind of things?'

She turned back. 'It's like this: I can't use a CasaMia account any more. They've figured out what I've been doing, so any compatible home listings are being suspended. I need to find another way of getting into people's homes.'

Rachel stared, unable to prevent her mouth dropping open. 'But Harland, I thought…'

That you'd stopped. She couldn't say it, it sounded completely absurd now she tried to articulate it. *I thought now we'd had a good heart to heart and bonded over our mutual victimhood that you'd stop being a sociopathic killer.*

'I'm working on an idea right now, but I just need to progress it a little further before you can go.'

'What kind of idea? Can you tell me about it?' *Keep her engaged*, Rachel told herself, despite being on the edge of losing control.

'I'm going to offer health coaching.' Harland couldn't hide her delight at her own resourcefulness. 'All those super-healthy, look-at-me girls can't get enough of their juicing and their clean eating and their Instagrammed smoothie bowls. I'll offer home tuition, and they'll happily let me into their perfect lives.'

'I see.' Through a clenched jaw, Rachel pushed up the corners of her mouth into a rictus smile.

'Wait, let me show you…' Harland went out of the room and came back with her laptop. She pulled up a half-built web page. 'Look, this is what I have so far.'

Meet Your Health Angel!

Our health and wellbeing are about so much more than diet. It's all about a holistic approach to life, and being the best person we can be. Being our authentic selves!

We all know what we should be doing, but so often we're just not doing it. And it can be tough to do it alone. When you book a one-on-one consultation with Your Health Angel, we will discuss your goals and create a plan that works with your busy lifestyle.

This could be anything from clean eating, to fitness, to managing stress. After your initial consultation you will get regular follow-up support online, for as long as you need it.

Behind the text, there was a stock image of a fit-looking young woman doing yoga in front of a sunset, and another of a vibrantly green smoothie.

Rachel was at a loss. This was horrific: an online conduit to deceiving and killing innocent women. If she endorsed it, Harland would know she was faking it. But she couldn't risk flipping the switch marked 'Psycho Harland'. She might end up having all four of her limbs tied up. Or worse.

'The page looks impressive,' she said truthfully. 'I can see you've put a lot of thought into it.'

'Thanks,' Harland looked happy again. 'Maybe we can talk it through together when I've worked on it a bit more. You can give me some ideas.'

This is it, Rachel thought, when the door was closed and she was alone again. *I can't lie here waiting for someone to find me while she's cooking up a new plan to prey on women she sees as the mean girls of this world. There's only one option: I have to escape. Now.*

FIFTY-FIVE

It had been dark for hours, and for a few minutes the silence was absolute. Then, at last, came the faint sound of snoring.

Rachel had waited what seemed an interminable time for Harland to go to bed, listening to her tapping furiously on the keys of her computer. Her new 'health coaching' initiative was clearly keeping her engrossed. Eventually Rachel heard the noise of the toilet and basin being used and the tiny crack of light from under the door was eventually extinguished.

Meanwhile, she had put her waiting time to good use. Bracing her feet as hard as she could against the mattress, she had fumbled under its edge with her fingertips and strained to pull out the piece of broken cup she had hidden there. The satin coverlet made her feet slip and slide, and it took her several attempts, but eventually she pressed two fingers around the china in a pincer movement and edged it out. It had been severed cleanly, but with a slight bevel to the crack that had left the edge as sharp as a knife. She tested it gingerly with the pad of a finger. She could tell that if she were to run her finger over it with a quick movement, it would slice through the skin and draw blood. Good. This meant it was sharp enough for her needs.

Bracing her manacled right arm as firmly as she could, she rolled up onto her side and reached the piece of china to the thick plastic tie around her wrist. She attempted a sawing motion, but her porcelain blade just slid off the plastic. It didn't help that she couldn't really see what she was doing. Grunting and sweating with the effort, she tried again, but could not get enough downward purchase on the plastic binding with her makeshift tool. Instead, she was going to have to insert the sharp point of the china inside the loop of the cable tie and saw upwards, using a pulling rather than a downwards pushing movement. The risk was that if the china slipped she would sever the inside of her wrist, but it seemed a risk worth taking.

Saw. Rest. Saw. Rest.

Progress was painfully slow, but after around twenty minutes she could see that she was creating a furrow in the cable tie, shedding powdery plastic dust. The deeper into the plastic she penetrated, the quicker the progress, and after the best part of an hour of sawing at it, a sharp tug made the plastic tie snap. Her arm was free.

Rachel sat up and massaged her sore left shoulder and wrist. She did not dare get off the bed, not until she was sure Harland was asleep, but she did some silent leg exercises and some yoga stretches while she waited. She also weighed up how things would play out if it came to a physical confrontation. At five feet nine inches she was taller and heavier than Harland, and she had been trained in self-defence and combat techniques. And she was no stranger to running. On the other hand, she had been handcuffed motionless for nearly three days, which had left her weak and light-headed. The physical advantage she had before had probably been lost. All the more reason to proceed with infinite care, and get out of the building without being detected.

Once the snoring had started, Rachel inched herself carefully off the bed. Her soiled jeans were still in the laundry basket where Harland had left them, but the rental car keys were no longer in the pocket. She put on the jeans, thrust the piece of broken china – her only weapon – into her back pocket and searched around the room for her trainers, groping blindly underneath the bed. They were nowhere to be found. With slow, careful steps she went into the walk-in closet and closed the door behind her, feeling along the wall for the light switch.

The shoes belonging to glamorous size-6 Harland were all high-heeled and decorative, their un-scuffed soles confirming that they had never been worn outside this room. Rachel pictured Harland's presence at the homes of her victims. She may have been in heels when she arrived, but she couldn't possibly have disposed of their corpses, done a professional clean-up job and then fled wearing such impractical shoes. There had to be others, Rachel reasoned, but every second she spent searching put her at increased risk of discovery.

Forcing her pounding heart to slow, she scanned the shelves in a logical order, left to right, top to bottom. Eventually she reached a plastic storage crate on a lower shelf, containing a few pairs of flat ballet pumps and some canvas sneakers. They were in a slightly smaller size than Rachel's own, but they would have to do. She put on a pair of the sneakers and switched off the light before emerging from the closet. Bending over to lace up the shoes had left her dizzy, and her legs felt as wobbly as a newborn foal's, but she could not afford to waste any more time. She had to get out of the apartment immediately.

Out in the hallway, she paused and listened. The snoring had stopped, but there was no other sound. The front door was locked from the inside, but ever-organised Harland had left the keys on a hook on her hall stand. Breathing with such focused intent that she thought she would pass out, Rachel inserted the two keys in the locks, one after the other, and turned them. The second one made a heavy click. There was a faint movement from the bedroom. Rachel froze, but after a couple of seconds it stopped again. She eased the door open inch by inch, crept out into the communal hallway then pulled the door to behind her, afraid to close it completely unless the sound of the latch woke Harland.

Then she lunged towards the stairwell and stumbled her way down flight after flight until she reached the ground floor.

*

Rachel's rental car – a pale metallic-blue Mazda – was still in the parking lot where she left it, only now she had no key. She knew that it was nigh-on impossible to hotwire a modern car, but her bag, containing her trusty Swiss Army knife and her passport, was locked in the boot. She should have taken the knife with her: that had proved to be a costly oversight.

Using the point of her all-purpose piece of broken china, she tried to flip open the boot catch. No dice. She made a split-second risk–reward assessment in her head, scooped up a rock from the landscaping around the parking lot, and smashed the rear window.

The noise from the alarm was so deafening it was like a form of torture. Unable to endure it a second longer, and fearful of the attention it would attract, she reached into the boot, grabbed her bag and ran out of the parking lot, heading for the main road. Behind her, the car wailed indignantly.

The motel she had stayed in was only around a mile away. If she could reach it on foot as quickly as possible, the twenty-four-hour reception would be open and someone would help her to raise the alarm. She would be safe. But running was much more difficult than she had anticipated. The sort of speed she normally achieved – between ten and twelve kilometres an hour – was completely beyond her reach now that her legs were so weak. She staggered and swayed like a marathon runner with heat stroke, the too-small sneakers chafing her feet raw. After a few hundred yards she was forced to slow to a trot, then a walk.

The occasional car flashed past her on the road, their headlights dipping then blazing. Then came one that wasn't passing her. This car was slowing right down and crawling behind her, so close she could feel the heat from its engine on the back of her legs. She willed herself to look straight ahead, not to turn back. But she had to turn, and the light from the headlights illuminated the half-familiar number plate. She recognised her rented Mazda. And there was only one person who had the key.

Harland stepped from the vehicle without cutting the engine. She held out what looked like a gun and pointed it directly at Rachel's body. *Not a gun*, Rachel's muddled brain told her, *Harland wouldn't use a gun. Too messy.* Far too messy. And when the shattering pain surged through her body, felling her instantly, she knew she was right. It wasn't a gun; it was a taser. Available cheaply on the internet; easy enough for someone of Harland's resourcefulness to get their hands on.

Like a predator with its kill, Harland was on her, yanking her hands behind her body and snapping plastic cable ties onto her wrists. More ties on her ankles, so that she was trussed like an animal, and a fabric gag in her mouth. Then, with a surprising show of strength, Harland dragged her towards the car and manhandled her onto the rear seat. Her bag was tossed into the foot well next to her and the engine put into gear. Rachel closed her eyes, terrified and tachycardic from the taser.

'Wanna know where we're going?' Harland called over her shoulder as she drove. Rachel could not see her face, but could tell she was mightily pleased with herself. Rachel did not want to know, and did not ask. The car stopped after a few minutes, and when she was dragged from the car Rachel could see that they were back at the apartment block. But instead of going into the main entrance, Harland took her to a side door, and into what looked like a service elevator. The door clanged shut and it descended before bumping to a stop. They were in the basement.

'My storage unit,' Harland told her cheerily. 'There aren't enough for all the residents to have one; your name has to go on a waiting list.' She removed a padlock from a large metal sliding door. The space inside had a concrete floor and was about five feet across and six feet deep. It contained just one thing: a large wire cage. It looked like the puppy crate Rachel's sister had used for her Labrador when it was young.

'Dog crate,' Harland confirmed. 'Largest one you can get. It's supposed to take a hound up to one hundred twenty pounds. You're probably a little heavier than that – one fifty maybe? – but it should do just fine.'

Once she had manoeuvred Rachel into the cage, she removed the ankle ties and the gag, but left the handcuffs in place. Then she filled a plastic dog bowl with water and padlocked the cage shut.

'There you go.' Her voice was hard. 'Nighty night.'

The metal door of the unit was banged shut and the padlock clicked back into place with a rasping sound. Then all Rachel could hear was the sound of Harland's shoes as she walked away.

FIFTY-SIX

The dog crate was such a neat idea.

It worked like a dream: poor little Rachel didn't see it coming. And why the hell did she waste time trying to take the car, when she didn't have the key? She's supposed to be a top detective, but really, how dumb can you be? She left herself with only one option: to take off on foot. And I had the car, so it was not going to be hard to catch her. She should have knocked on a neighbour's door, raised the alarm that way. Still, it's too late for her now.

She can stay in the dog crate for a little bit while I figure out what to do with her. I haven't decided which option I'm going to go with yet. I could unlock the crate and let her go.

I could take off and just leave her there.

Or I could just get rid of her.

FIFTY-SEVEN

There was no light in the storage unit, so Rachel couldn't be sure how much of Monday had been and gone. Surely someone in London would have missed her by now? The searing pain from the taser barbs and the spasms in her limbs had subsided, but she felt like the living dead. The floor of the crate was hard chipboard and she could only lie down with her legs curled up tight to her chest. Having her arms restrained behind her back had set up a burning pain between her shoulder blades. Her thirst was so severe it made her shake.

She shuffled onto her knees, bent her head down and lapped water from the plastic dog bowl. Then she collapsed onto her side again and gave way to sobs. Rachel was not a crier, but now she cried so hard her whole body ached. No point trying to work out an escape route: there was none. At least in Harland's apartment there had been the possibility someone would find her, but not here. She was done for.

After some time like this – it could have minutes or hours; she couldn't tell – Harland unlocked the storage unit door.

'Oh dear,' she observed, 'you are in a sorry state.'

'How else would I be?' Rachel croaked.

'It's your own fault you know. I was planning on letting you go. Eventually. You just needed to be patient a little longer.'

'You have to let me go. *Now.*' Rachel shouted the last word, although it came out as a strange rasping sound.

'I can't, not now. It's too late for that.'

Harland refilled the water bowl with a plastic jug, then disappeared again. When she returned, she had her laptop with her.

'It's finished now – see?' She held up the screen against the bars of the crate, but Rachel's eyes were so sore and so unaccustomed to the light that all she could see was a blur of dancing colour.

'All I have to do is press this button and *Your Health Angel* goes live.'

She waited, but Rachel was no longer listening. She was sweating, and her body felt first icy cold, then hot and damp with sweat.

'One… Two… Three…' Harland clicked a button on screen. 'Go! I'm live. Let's see how long it is before I get my first client.'

'Harland, I'm ill. I need medical attention.'

'Drink some water, and get some rest.'

'I. Can't. Rest. I'm in a fucking cage.'

Harland ignored this. 'Maybe I'll bring you some Tylenol later.'

The door of the unit slid shut and Rachel was enveloped in darkness again.

Rachel must have slept, fitfully and feverishly, but woke feeling exhausted. Was it still the same day, she wondered? If it was Tuesday, then she had now been missing for three days. She forced her brain to use logic, when all she wanted to do was howl with misery and self-pity.

Someone must surely be looking for her, right now. Apart from anything else, she had failed to attend her promotion board. Patten would know she'd never do that willingly. So someone would eventually start searching for her. All she had to do was hang on somehow until help arrived. She had to keep going. She drank the rest of the water and managed to roll over, awkwardly, so that she was lying on her other side. She recited the colours of the rainbow, the words of the police phonetic alphabet – *Alpha,*

Bravo, Charlie, Delta, Echo, Foxtrot – and her times tables. Anything to keep herself focused. Anything to stop herself from screaming.

She needed Harland to return, because the alternative was being abandoned without food or water. And yet she dreaded her return too, unsure what form of torment she would dream up next.

'I have good news,' Harland announced triumphantly when she eventually pulled back the metal door. She had shed the fat suit and was dressed in wig, full make-up and a size-6 Harland outfit of tight white jeans and fitted striped T-shirt. In one hand she held a small blue plastic box, which she placed on the floor next to the cage.

Rachel's heart leapt. Harland was clearly heading out into the world, so had probably decided it was time to release her prisoner. She was tired of tormenting Rachel like this, wanted to move on to a new victim.

'I've got my first client. Already! Isn't that amazing?'

Rachel stared at her with blank eyes.

'She's very anxious for me to begin coaching her on her wellness journey. That's what she told me. So I'm heading up there to meet with her at her house. She says she can't wait to have her first session.' She laughed happily.

'What about me?' croaked Rachel.

'Well now, that's the thing.' She checked that the padlock on the cage was secure. Rachel saw that she was also wearing latex gloves. Her heart started hammering.

'I can't just go off on a trip out of state and leave you here. I could be gone days. Weeks maybe, if things go well. So I'm afraid it's time for you and I to part ways, Detective.'

'You're letting me go?' Rachel knew as she said this that it made no sense. Why would she be released now, just as Harland embarked on a new spree?

'I guess, in a way, I am.'

She opened the blue plastic case and took out a syringe, a glass vial and a needle sealed in a clear plastic wrapper. With deft movements she attached the needle to the syringe and inserted it into the vial, pulling up a measured dose and holding it towards the light to check it.

'Jesus Christ! What's that?' Rachel was trembling so fiercely she could barely speak. Her tongue felt huge and thick in her mouth.

'Potassium Chloride. It's what they use in voluntary euthanasia. Also execution by lethal injection. After administering anaesthesia first, of course. They keep it in a locked box in the labs, but as a senior tech I can access the key, no problem.'

Rachel had never heard three sentences that were more measured, or more reasonable. Or more terrifying.

'Harland, you don't have to do this. Please. Don't do this. Just talk to me, please.' Rachel edged back against the back wall of the crate but it made no difference where she positioned her body: she could not get away this time.

'It's *me* that gets to make the decisions,' Harland said in a low voice. 'Me. It's not me that's at the mercy of others any more, it's the other way around. I get to decide things.'

There was a bang and a scuffling noise. Someone else was in the basement. Harland darted round the side of the cage, thrust the needle through the wire and held it up ready to plunge it into the back of Rachel's exposed upper arm.

'Joe,' whimpered Rachel, her only thought now for her son. 'Joe!'

As Harland brought the tip of the needle to her skin, the door of the unit slammed open. From where she huddled, Rachel could see an oddly familiar pair of shoes. Their owner lunged at Harland, grappled with her and dragged her backwards, away from the bars of the cage.

'Christ, Prince, look at the fucking state of you.'

FIFTY-EIGHT

Brickall dropped to his knees beside the dog crate. He pulled frantically, ineffectually, at its padlocked door with one hand, groping through his pockets with the other to find something to open it with.

'Fuck!' he yelled. 'Fuck, what's she done to you?'

It took Harland no time at all to capitalise on Brickall's concern for Rachel. She clambered over him, bolted for the door of the unit and sprinted away.

'Go!' Rachel urged through cracked lips. 'I'm okay. Go after her!'

But Brickall ignored her and picked up the syringe. 'What is this? Do you know?'

'Potassium chloride.'

'Jesus fucking Christ! Did any of it get into you?' He held up the syringe to check the level of the fluid inside.

'I don't think so.'

'Thank fuck for that. Help's on the way, we'll have you out of here in a second.'

'Mark –' it would have been wrong to call him anything else, but still it sounded strange – 'you need to go after Rowe. You've got to stop her. Seriously, leave me and go.'

'I'm not leaving you, Prince. Tough.' He squatted beside the cage.

A few seconds later they heard the faint drone of a siren and two burly Baltimore County police officers appeared, weapons drawn.

'Suspect's gone,' Brickall told them. 'Few seconds ago, so she can't have got far.'

One of the policemen disappeared again, while his partner radioed for an ambulance and fetched a bolt cutter from his squad car.

'Go after her!' Rachel urged Brickall again as she was loaded onto a stretcher with a saline drip attached to her arm. 'Go up and check her apartment, at least. 714.'

Brickall hesitated, his face still taut with shock.

'Go on, Detective Sergeant, that's an order! I can't exactly go, so you need to do it for me.'

He reluctantly handed the syringe to one of the paramedics and followed them out of the basement, leaving the second policeman to wait for crime scene officers. 'All right, if it will shut you up.'

He hovered, watchful, as a grey-faced and sweaty Rachel was loaded into the back of the ambulance, then turned and headed back into the apartment building.

Several hours later, Rachel lay admiring a sunset streaked with rose and amber from the window of her room in the University of Maryland Medical Center. The sky had never in her life looked more beautiful. It probably never would.

Brickall appeared in the doorway and stood watching her silently for a few seconds. She was wearing a hospital gown and attached to two drips: one giving fluid and the second an antibiotic. There were dressings on the pressure sores on her wrists. Her hair was still lank and greasy, her lips blistered and her skin waxy, but she had never felt more alive.

'I've got a bladder infection,' she told him, when he pointed to the second drip.

'You really know how to turn a guy on, Prince.'

Rachel patted the edge of the bed, but he pretended not to see this and lowered himself into the blue vinyl visitor's chair at the side of the bed, wary, as though he might catch something from her.

'I'm not great with ill people,' he said unnecessarily.

'And you didn't bring any bloody grapes. You're as much use as an outside toilet in a submarine, Brickall.'

He reached in his pocket and slapped a half-eaten chocolate bar on the bed. 'There, you ungrateful cow.'

She reached for his hand, but after the briefest touch he pulled it away.

'I am grateful. You will never know how grateful. Really.' There were tears in her eyes. She made no effort to wipe them away.

'Pack it in, Prince.'

'So do they know where Rowe is?'

Brickall shook his head. 'Not a scooby. She wasn't in the apartment, or anywhere in the vicinity of the building. But half the FBI are out there looking. They'll nab her eventually.'

'And how on earth did you find me? Who told you to come?'

'You did.'

Rachel gave him a shrug of incomprehension, rattling the drip stands that connected to the tubes in her forearms.

'You called me from your phone. At about 3 p.m. on Friday, UK time. You didn't really speak, just made horrible noises like you were being strangled. Then it sounded like you'd dropped the phone, and after that the line went dead.'

Rachel thought back. That was mid-morning, east-coast time. She had just drunk the poisoned coffee, after Harland came back to the apartment and caught her snooping.

'But…' She thought she had phoned Rob, but didn't want to say so out loud, with all the implied slight that would carry. She must have hit Brickall's number instead. 'I don't remember doing that.'

'There was clearly something going on, and I tried to call you back about a hundred times, but your phone rang out every time, and then eventually started going straight to voicemail.'

She nodded. 'Rowe broke it.'

'So then I got hold of details for your hunky Interpol contact in Washington. Old Jason Bourne.'

'Rob.'

'That's the one. He said he'd had an emergency message from you, but soon afterwards another one saying you were fine. So he'd left it.'

Rachel looked down at her blackened fingernails. So much for being there at the end of the phone. *Nice one, Agent McConnell.*

'Sunday evening I still couldn't get hold of you. Then Monday morning you didn't show up at back at HQ. Patten said he'd heard nothing from you, so did Joe when I texted him. I phoned your mum—'

Rachel groaned and stared at the ceiling. 'Oh God. Poor Mum!'

'It's okay, I phoned her a few minutes ago and said you're fine, without going into detail. And I phoned Joe. But you can break the news about the bladder infection yourself.' He grinned. 'Patten reckoned you'd probably just missed your flight and got a later one, and were planning to go straight to your interview. But by first thing this morning when there was still no reply to my texts and calls – this morning UK time, which I suppose was Monday night for you – I went to Heathrow and flashed the badge to get a look at incoming flight manifests. You hadn't checked in, but you hadn't changed or cancelled the original flight either. They said you were a no-show.'

Rachel grimaced. 'That's one way of putting it.'

'So then I knew for sure that something had happened. Meanwhile, your mate Rob had at least been able to supply Harland Rowe's address, so I sweet-talked a check-in girl into finding me a seat on the next flight out to Baltimore. Got here lunchtime, went straight to the address. You weren't at the apartment. She opened the door, Rowe, let me look around. Nothing.'

Rachel grimaced. 'I was locked in the storage unit by then.'

'There was something about her, something in her manner that didn't sit right. Call it my gut, if you like. I pretended to go away satisfied, but really I just hung around until she came out of the apartment and headed down to the basement.'

Rachel shuddered visibly. 'So it might have been because you came looking for me that she decided to give me the lethal injection? Or maybe she'd already planned on it before you arrived.' She broke off a piece of chocolate and popped it in her mouth. 'Maybe we'll never know.'

'We won't know anything unless we catch her.' Brickall helped himself to the chocolate. 'And if they don't grab her before she has the chance to go out of state, I'm guessing things are going to get a fuck of a lot more complicated.'

'Wait,' Rachel sat upright in the bed. 'I bet I know where she's headed. She told me she'd lined up a fresh victim. Someone who contacted her via her new website.'

'She didn't say where?'

'No, but if we can get into the website we'll be able to get their details. 'It's www.yourhealthangel – all one word – dot org: I told myself I'd memorise that web address if it was the last thing I ever did. When I was locked in the crate.'

'So all we need is someone who can hack into the site.'

Rachel smiled. 'And I know just the person.'

Mike Perez's delight at receiving a Skype call from Rachel had been matched by his dismay at seeing her in a hospital bed, wired up to drips.

'Prince-ess! What the hell happened to you?'

'Long story. Listen Mike, I need a really big favour, and I need it in a hurry.'

He sighed. 'Same old, same old. What is this, like, favour number six?'

She summarised the events of the past few days as efficiently as she could.

'Wow!' Perez rubbed his stubbled jaw. 'You sure you're okay? Sounds like we nearly lost you.'

'I'm fine,' Rachel assured him. 'But I'll be even better if you can get into Rowe's website and go through messages. Sent and received. Identify the person who's set up a meet with her.'

'He seems like a good bloke.' Brickall observed as Rachel ended the call.

'He's the best. Would never have cracked the case without him.'

He raised an eyebrow. 'And yet you decided to fall for the other one. Always the bad boys, Prince.'

Rachel flushed slightly, but did not rise to the bait. 'Go and find me nurse or a doctor who can get these tubes out. I want to get out of here.'

Rachel was insistent on discharging herself, against medical advice. Once she and Brickall had checked into the first budget hotel they could find, she was equally insistent that they share one room.

'Don't be stupid; I'm not doing that. That would just be fucking weird,' Brickall protested.

'I honestly don't think I could lie there alone in the dark. Not after being locked up in that crate.'

'Should have stayed in the hospital then. Lights would have stayed on all night long. Plus loads of machines making nice bleeping noises. Lots of lovely nurses coming and checking your vitals.'

In the end they compromised on two adjoining rooms with an interconnecting door, which Brickall agreed to leave ajar. 'And don't you be creeping in for a sneaky fumble!' he shouted through the door after they had checked in.

Rachel shampooed her filthy hair under a scalding shower, which felt blissful. She put on a hotel bathrobe, threw her stinking clothes into a plastic laundry bag and lay spreadeagled on the clean sheets. This also felt blissful. All her limbs were free. She could move them into any position she liked, light as a feather.

Crippling exhaustion swamped her as soon as this novelty had worn off. She switched out her light and fell asleep curled up on top of the covers.

Three hours later, waking to darkness and an unfamiliar room, she experienced what she guessed was a panic attack. Her brain jolted her back to the cramped, humiliating space of the dog crate. She heard Harland's voice, felt the raging thirst and cramping muscles. Felt the tip of the hypodermic needle sting as it probed her skin.

Heart hammering, lungs clamouring for air, she sat up and screamed, louder than she had ever screamed in her life.

'Christ on a bike, Prince!'

The interconnecting door was flung wide open, letting in light from the other room, along with the comforting low murmur of a TV. 'People will think we're having sex. Only even at my best I don't think I've ever made anyone scream like that.'

He pushed her across from the centre of the bed to make room. 'Don't go getting any ideas,' he said, as he lay down next to her. 'And don't think I'm staying, either.'

But when Rachel woke after six hours of the deepest sleep of her life, Brickall was still lying beside her. The phone on the bedside table was ringing.

'You stayed.'

'Answer the bloody phone, Prince,' muttered Brickall. 'Jesus.'

It was the front desk, saying that a Baltimore City Police officer had just dropped off her suitcase, found in the rear of the Mazda. Her bag, found in Harland's apartment, would be kept as evidence, but they had agreed to return her passport. A grumbling Brickall went downstairs to reception to fetch them.

'At least you'll be able to put some clean clothes on,' he told her, as he handed over the suitcase ten minutes later. 'You smelt pretty rank yesterday.'

'Sod off, Brickall.'

Rachel flicked him on the back of the legs with a towel, using as much strength as her still-aching arms could muster, then went in the bathroom and put on clean underwear, jeans and a white T-shirt. Then she followed Brickall down to the restaurant, where they devoured bacon and eggs, a huge stack of pancakes dripping with maple syrup and several mugs of coffee. Brickall glanced up from his, nodding in the direction of the doorway, where two strapping men in blue nylon FBI coach jackets hovered awkwardly.

'Oh look – your date's arrived. And it looks like it's going to be a threesome.'

They introduced themselves as agents Flores and Henderson, and after waiting politely for her to finish eating, they drove her five miles to their regional office in Windsor Mill, shut her in an interview room and debriefed her relentlessly for four hours. They were very kind, offering frequent cups of coffee and pastries, but the sustained recounting of the past month's events left Rachel bone-weary.

She was asked to begin with the phone call she had received at the NCA in February, and work her way through her time in Los Angeles, the side trips to San Francisco and San Diego, her return to Washington, then to North Carolina and San Francisco again (with Rob), and on to Madras and Portland, Baltimore, Florida and Baltimore again.

'Hope you were collecting the air miles,' joked Henderson. 'You've visited more states than I have.'

'With the greatest respect to your wonderful country –' Rachel smiled at them wearily – 'I don't plan on seeing any more of it for the foreseeable future.'

Brickall was lying on his bed watching *CSI: Miami* when she returned to the hotel. Rachel flung the interconnecting door wide, unable to hide her excitement.

'Guess what?'

'You love it so much here; you've decided to emigrate.'

She shook her head.

'You're pregnant again.'

'Don't be a dick, Brickall.'

He grunted and turned up the volume on the TV.

'They've arrested Harland Rowe.'

He muted the TV. 'No shit!'

'A call came in just as I was leaving the FBI building. Good old Perez found an address in Asheville, North Carolina on her website. She'd arranged to go there to meet a girl called Leila Griffin.'

Brickall sat up and switched off the TV altogether. 'Please tell me they got to her in time.'

'Not exactly. Rowe attacked her. Tried to strangle her. But Leila managed to fight her off and lock herself in the basement. Incredibly, when the FBI got there, Rowe was still in the house, trying on her clothes.'

Brickall gave a shudder. 'Fucking psycho. Thank God, though. Now it's well and truly over, we can piss off back to London.' He stood up and stretched. 'Start packing.'

'Hold on.' Rachel took her laptop to the desk and, from force of habit as much as anything, started a search for Leila Griffin. And there she was, displaying her toned abs and tiny waist on

Instagram; all honey-coloured hair and caramel limbs. Posting selfies with 'my gorgeous fiancé' and 'my adorable little pooch'. In some pictures dog and owner wore matching outfits. Rachel couldn't help smiling slightly. Knowing Harland Rowe as she now did, she was sure the pictures with the dog would have enraged her. Oh yes, Leila had definitely been true to type.

And lucky. Lucky, lucky Leila. The case was closing with a perfect girl who survived, and that felt like a good thing.

'Shall I ask for a cab to take us to the airport?' Brickall asked, as she put her laptop back in her case and closed it.

Rachel shook her head. 'Not yet. There's just one more thing I need to do.'

FIFTY-NINE

It was hours since breakfast, but when she arrived at the Slipstream coffee shop Rachel ordered the toast and home-made jam anyway. It seemed like the right thing to do.

'So, here we are,' said Rob five minutes later, kissing her swiftly on the cheek before taking the seat opposite her. 'Right back where we started.'

It was a warm spring day, and he was wearing an open-necked white shirt and a lightweight grey jacket. And there were the familiar tan lines in the corners of his eyes, where the sun had hit his face when he was smiling.

'Exactly,' observed Rachel. 'I thought you'd appreciate the symmetry.'

'I certainly appreciate seeing you alive and well.' Rob's face became grim when he caught sight of her bandaged wrists. 'I heard about what happened. Jesus, Rachel.'

'I'm okay.'

'Are you really? You sure? You look a little washed out.'

Rachel raised an eyebrow. 'Thanks.'

'No, you still look great. Of course. But you know what I mean.' He covered her hand with his. 'Seriously, it's me that feels terrible. I should have known something like this could have happened to you. I should have stopped you.'

'I wouldn't have stopped, though.' Rachel waited for the waitress to put coffees in front of them. 'Not just because you'd told me to. I was

like a train on a track. I couldn't have stopped, even if I wanted to.'
She pulled her hand from under his and picked up her mug of coffee.

'But Rachel, you nearly—'

'If you pursue dangerous criminals, you risk being a target. I know that. It's part of the job.'

'Except you weren't officially on the job.'

She shrugged. 'Details.'

'So when are you going back to London.'

'This evening. There's something I wanted to ask you first, though.'
He smiled. 'Of course. Name it.'

'It's going to take the FBI a while to process Harland Rowe's case and piece all the evidence together. Meanwhile, I doubt she's going to make a neat little confession. That's not her style.'

'I guess not.' Rob took a piece of her toast and bit into it.

'So I want you to make sure that Matt Wyburgh is off the hook for Phoebe's murder. Rowe's already told me she used Phoebe's keys to plant the doorstop in his garage. It forms part of the statement I gave to the FBI. Make sure the LAPD know that. Make sure they drop the charges.'

'I will do my very best. If I can't get out there myself, I'll speak to our liaison at the LA County Sheriff's Office and get him to pursue it.'

'Thanks, Agent McConnell.' She bestowed a beaming smile on him.

'Rachel, about the other stuff…'

'What other stuff?'

'You know – the personal stuff. Between you and me.'

'Ah. But there wasn't any. Not really.'

He coloured slightly, glancing around the café to make sure no one was listening to them. 'But I did come on to you. And I shouldn't have done.'

Rachel gave a little shrug. 'Yes, you did, and not just the once. I managed to resist you though… so no harm done.'

'I know. But I still feel bad.'

'There's really no need. And it's not like I wasn't tempted. I almost gave in.'

'Really?'

'Really. But professionalism prevailed.' *For once*, she thought. She reached across the table, touched his fingers lightly. 'Maybe if things had been different.'

'Another time, another place?' Rob's ironic smile acknowledged the cliché. 'But we did good.' He became wistful. 'In fact we did great. We pretty much cracked the case.'

'I think you'll find *I* cracked the case. It was me that tracked down Harland Rowe.'

'But it was me that put you onto Ethan Rowe's DNA profile.'

'True.'

'We were a team.'

'Like Bonnie and Clyde,' Rachel reminded him.

'And we had fun, didn't we?'

She nodded, smiling broadly now. 'Until you hung me out to dry.'

'Ouch.' Rob examined his fingernails. 'I'm really sorry I wasn't there. I don't know what else I can say, except sorry.'

'You can stop apologising. It's water under the bridge. That's why I came here today. To make peace.'

Rob waved a crust. 'To eat the toast of peace.'

The waitress cleared the table and brought the bill. Rob held up a hand and reached for his wallet. 'I'm really glad we did this—'

Rachel put a finger to her lips, to indicate that he had said enough. They went outside onto 14th Street and Rob wrapped his arms round her, kissing her gently but firmly on the mouth, before walking away. He turned briefly, and held up a hand in a salute, then strode off towards P Street, his tall figure gradually being absorbed into the moving diorama of passing pedestrians. She watched until he was gone.

EPILOGUE

TRAGIC PHOEBE STILES IN SERIAL KILLER SHOCK.

Rachel smoothed out the newspaper on the table in front of her and read the article. The facts were more or less correct. There were large, flattering photos of Tiffany Kovak and Melissa Downey, and a smaller one of Clayton Hill. Harland Rowe had been dubbed 'The CasaMia Killer'. That was inevitable, however much Paulie Greenaway would hate it.

The prosecution in Phoebe and Tiffany's murders would be brought by the State of California, which had abandoned use of the death penalty in recent years. So had North Carolina, where Melissa Downey and Clayton hill died. Rachel couldn't help thinking of the syringe full of potassium chloride that almost ended her own life. And yet she would not have wanted Harland to be put to death. She pictured her locked up in prison with hundreds of other female inmates. Would she still be trying to plot revenge on that community's mean girls? Possibly. Or maybe, just maybe, there was some hope for her rehabilitation. But in the meantime Rachel wanted her safely locked away where she could no longer harm other people.

She checked her phone. She had texted Brickall and asked him to join her in the Pin and Needle, but he had not replied. There had been plenty of non-replies from him since their return from the USA three weeks ago. Her two weeks of mandatory medical leave were over, and she had been offered a date on the next round of DCI boards. Easter had been and gone, along with Lindsay's chicken versus lamb debate and all the attendant family reproaches. Joe had joined them for the family meal this year, along with Sophie. And all the while her attempts to communicate with Brickall had met with a wall of silence, just as they had when she had taken the leave she was owed and returned to the States. But enough was enough. Now that she was set to return to normal duties, they needed to have it out. Whether his behavior was to do with the release of Shaun Rawlings, or something else, she needed to find out what was going on.

She had finished reading the 'CasaMia Murders' article and was skim-reading the rest of the paper while making inroads into a bottle of Zinfandel when the door was slammed open and Brickall walked in. He slapped his phone and wallet on the table before plonking himself into the seat opposite her.

'All right?' He glowered.

'Hello stranger.' Rachel's smile was more benign than she felt. 'Can I get you a drink?'

'I'm not stopping.'

'Look, Detective Sergeant—'

Brickall glanced at the newspaper. 'Still obsessing about that fucking case?'

Rachel folded it up and put it in her bag.

'I know you're annoyed with me. I've been away from the office a long time. A lot longer than I would like. But I'm back on Monday—'

'If you can even remember where the place is.'

'Look, I know you've had a difficult couple of months. I'm also aware my actions have had consequences for you, and I'm sorry. Your workload must have been hellish for the last month or so, and I promise as soon as I'm back, I'm going to work all the hours God gives to take over my share again and get things back to normal.'

'Normal!' he scoffed. 'Are you sure you even know what that is, Prince?'

'Detective Inspector to you.'

'Fuck's sake.'

'Mark, give me a break. I've had a bollocking for acting without authorisation, and been made to take enforced sick leave. I've still probably got to go back to the States to give evidence in both of Harland's trials, unless she decides to cave and plead guilty. I've said I'm going to pull my weight in the meantime. What more do you want from me? Blood?'

Brickall was staring at her, and his expression was still hostile.

'You really don't get it, do you?'

'Get what? Explain it to me.'

'You nearly died. I know – I was there. If it weren't for me being there, you would have done.'

'I told you. I told you over and over. I'm grateful.'

'It's not that. It's not about gratitude. I was scared. So scared. After being in the force for ten years there isn't much that frightens me, but I really thought I'd lost you.' His face coloured as he spoke, and his hand went reflexively to his phone, tapping it on the table.

Rachel waited.

'That's why I'm so angry with you. Because every second I was on that fucking plane to Baltimore, I thought you were going to show up in a body bag.'

He's like a parent whose child takes off without permission, thought Rachel. The minute they're found, the relief makes them furious. It was her turn to feel her face going pink.

'I'm sorry.' She looked down at her hands. 'I'm really sorry I put you through that.' Rachel stood up and went to the bar, coming back with a second wine glass, which she filled for him.

'I just don't get it, Prince,' Brickall's tone was stern, but she could tell that the storm of his anger was blowing over. 'Can't you see how you were acting? You just became obsessed. It wasn't normal. It wasn't professional.'

Rachel sighed. 'I can see now that I was a little... taken over by Phoebe's case.'

'You think?' His voice dripped with sarcasm.

'But I did try to get you involved. I took you up to Birmingham with me. And if you'd been able to join me in the States, that would have been brilliant. There was hardly a day out there that I didn't wish you were there too. Swear to God.'

Brickall swallowed several mouthfuls of wine, so as not to have to appear mollified. 'I doubt that, Prince. Would have cramped your style while you were shagging your hunky Interpol agent.'

'Nothing happened between us. Scout's honour.'

She held up her middle three fingers in the Scout salute, and they both laughed. 'You must be losing your touch, Prince.' Brickall said, but she could tell that he was pleased. 'So is that completely over, then?'

'It never even started.' She scrutinised his face, running a mental check. 'How about you? What's the latest on Rawlings?'

Brickall grimaced. 'Still enjoying his freedom.'

'He'll slip up again; his type always do.'

'Oh, for sure. And don't worry, when he does, I'll make sure I'm there to see the bastard banged up again.'

Rachel nodded her approval. 'So...' she said, after taking a large gulp of wine. 'Am I forgiven?'

Brickall curled his lip. 'Possibly. Depends how you behave.'

Again, the once-frightened-now-gruff parent speaking. His face became serious. 'But I want you to promise me something.'

'Of course.'

'Don't ever do anything like that again. Don't ever get a bee in your bonnet about a bloody case and go rogue. Not without taking me along too.'

Rachel grinned. 'I think I can manage that. If you think you're man enough.'

'Cut the crap, Prince, and go and get us another bottle of wine.'

Rachel's left leg became stuck under the table and she knocked her glass over, splashing the dregs over Brickall's wallet in a crimson stain.

'Some things will never change, Prince,' he laughed. 'Strike One.'

A LETTER FROM ALISON

Thank you so much for choosing to read *Perfect Girls*. If you enjoyed reading it and would like to keep up to date with all my latest releases, then please sign up using the link below. Your email address will never be shared, and you can unsubscribe at any time.

www.bookouture.co.uk/alison-james

This third case has taken Rachel Prince a long way from home and a long way from her comfort zone, and it was as rewarding to write as it was for Rachel to solve. I hope you will continue to follow her personal and professional journey in books to come.

If you loved *Perfect Girls*, I would be very grateful if you could write a review. I love hearing what readers like most about the characters and story, and it really helps new readers discover my books for the first time.

I also love hearing from readers – so do get in touch via my Facebook page, Twitter, Goodreads or my website.

 @AlisonJbooks

Alison-James-books

Made in the USA
Las Vegas, NV
20 November 2020

11200841R00177